AFTERGLOW

PROLOGUE

CHRIS

"Dave, we can't keep doing this."

But Davey had too much of Chris's ass in his hands. Chris knew he wasn't going to stop now—not that he ever did unless Chris shoved him away.

Instead, Chris leaned back against the wall, and Davey took it as an invitation to shove his hand down his pants.

Chris's cock was hardening under Davey's hand, his friend's lips pressed against his ear.

Well, *friend* might be too strong a word for what they were. Exes didn't quite work, either. One of those on-again-off-again things that never seemed to stop. Sometimes they were drunk. Actually, usually they were drunk.

Mostly because Chris was too damn weak to say no. Two months of dating every guy to come along, trying out everyone from twinks to bears, and he still hadn't found anyone who hit his buttons like Davey. He smashed those buttons and ground Chris's nerves in the process, but hey, at least he hit them.

So whenever Davey knocked, Chris opened the door. Every damn time.

And it didn't help that he had a lot to forget tonight.

"The stunt you pulled with the water bucket and our new member of the team... I understand it's a way of bonding around here, but that was a little too far."

"Okay." Chris didn't talk back to his commanding officer, but it was hard hearing it from Chief Williams.

Especially when the next words were, "So, considering your request for a promotion..."

Davey's lips were on his ear, his lithe body pressing up against Chris's as he fisted his hand around Chris's cock, managing a slight stroke despite the tight space.

"Fine," Chris hissed, turning his face away as he bucked his hips forward and unbuttoned his jeans. His arms tangled with Davey's and he shoved them away, but the moment his jeans and underwear were around his knees, Davey pressed so close Chris lost his breath.

Chris's toes curled into the floor as Davey stroked him good and slow, pressing just hard enough—the way he liked it.

Think what I want about him, he knows how to get me off better than a random guy from Grindr or Tinder or wherever. And I do owe him a lot.

"You like that?" Davey whispered, his breath warm against Chris's ear as he tightened his grip until Chris whimpered. "You miss me?"

"Yeah," Chris breathed out, then realized the little trick and clarified, "I like that, Dave."

"I know you miss me. I'm the only one who knows how to do this." Davey bit his shoulder, and Chris made a sharp sound. "And you owe me this." Davey's interactions with him were always threaded with that strangely aggressive note. Like he was still resentful or angry at Chris for something.

Well, duh. Maybe for refusing to confront the closet he lived in and dumping Davey a couple years ago.

Or more likely for dumping him the second time... what, a few months ago?

Chris couldn't remember a thing while Davey was grinding their cocks together like this. His knees were buckling, so Davey pressed up against his body to pin him in place.

"You want a piece of my sweet little ass?"

His heart thumped as he dug his nails into Davey's back, his cock twitching against Davey's. "Fuck, *yes*." They were so good together, even if he felt like shit the next day. Every damn time.

As he sank into Davey, Chris closed his eyes.

I'm a sucker for him, but I can't say no.

1

ASH

"One more for the garbage."

Ash hooked a finger through the neck of Benny's t-shirt and tossed it into the *trash* pile, then turned to survey his work.

"And his t-shirt, too," Ash muttered under his breath. "Fucking men."

Ash was done with them this time, he swore to God. He hadn't even had the energy to clean the place since kicking Benny out three weeks ago. He barely kept on top of the dishes, and that was it.

He had an excuse: working at the carwash, buffing rich young trust fund babies' Beemers, had kept him busy every day, until yesterday.

He was only seasonal, and summer was over, so his boss had let him go. Back to the job market, and resumes, and putting up with shitty tips in dingy restaurants. He had an interview in two days for an admin position in an office, and he was praying to anyone listening that he got it.

And then, even when he was working, there were Ash's days off—days he spent barely getting out of bed.

Why would he bother? He didn't have friends to see, and now he didn't have a boyfriend to get up for. Now and then, maybe once a week, he opened Grindr up and found the closest hunk looking for *right now*—and preferably one who could host.

Not that he wouldn't bring a guy back to this little house in the Santa Barbara hills, but... well, *he* wouldn't. Benny would, though. A bunch of them, apparently.

The landlord hadn't lifted a damn finger in months, so the maintenance problems were stacking up. He had to hip-check the front door open or closed. One cupboard door in the kitchen had broken off when he opened it too fast. The shower seal leaked if he took a long shower. The front porch wobbled if more than two people stood on it at once.

And there was still a hole in the living room drywall where his ex's bony ass had been shoved into the wall by one of the drugged-up meatheads Ash had walked in on him fucking. Apparently, Benny forgot his promise not to bring that shit home at the first prospect of a good chemsex party.

Gritting his teeth at the memory of Benny trying to focus on his face long enough for an apology, Ash pushed it aside. He grabbed a black garbage bag to shove Benny's leftover crap into.

He'd sucked it up long enough to text Benny once, last week, telling him to pick things up within a week, or he'd throw them out. Benny had texted back that he didn't care and he was in Wisconsin.

How the fuck had he ended up there? Oh, well. Not Ash's problem anymore.

Ash yanked open the last drawer in Benny's bedside table— his secondary bedside table, now—and made a face at the Ziploc he found in it.

Of course. This was where he'd kept his stash, apparently. He recognized the poppers, bright tabs, and the baggie of weed, but there were other pills he couldn't identify. He'd Google the marks on them later.

Ash tossed the Ziploc on top of the bedside table and headed for the bedroom door, pulling the black garbage bag along after him.

He really should tell Benny what he'd left behind—that shit was expensive. But Ash couldn't summon up enough will to care about that asshole's bank account. Besides, Wisconsin had no doubt had a warm welcome for the prick.

He'd already been through the bathroom, living room, and kitchen for any trace of Benny, and this was the last room. Gross body wash, even grosser curry noodles Benny had been inexplicably obsessed with, and the ratty blanket Benny passed out under every time he came home high—all gone.

"Done."

Ash tied the bag shut and hauled it out to the porch, stepping around the warped board he least trusted to toss the bag to the ground. He'd put the cans out soon.

The one good thing about living up in the scorched scrubland hills—aside from the minimal tourists who made it up this far—was the view. He took a moment to appreciate it. It was a million-dollar view. The only reason he'd gotten to rent this place so cheap was because of the state of the house.

It had been half-burnt out in the fires a few summers back, and the landlord apparently hadn't been able to rebuild with the insurance payout. Ash figured he was trying to turn enough of a profit off renting it out as cheap as he could that, after Ash left, he could afford to rebuild an actual nice place.

In the meantime, there was a distinctly toasty smell from the floorboards under the cheap laminate, and the scorch marks on the back of the house were easy to identify.

Whatever. It was a place to sleep, and one of the cheaper ones out there.

God, if Ash could afford to live in Santa Barbara proper, he'd put up with the crowds of unreasonably happy tourists and get a cheap apartment closer to the town center.

For now, this was all he could afford, so even if it violated a few building codes, he couldn't report it—and his landlord knew it, too.

But if he could get that job... That was the ticket to a brighter future. Maybe. Until he ran out of money again, made some bad choice or had his car break down and got fired. But he had to try. He *had* to.

Ash bypassed the kitchen and headed straight to his room at the back of the house again to crawl under the sheets. His few ounces of energy had been used up on caring about purging every sign of Benny from the house he'd shared with him for, what, six weeks? Eight?

Benny was just the latest in a string of assholes who'd tried to use him for the little he had. It never lasted long, and it never surprised him, ultimately.

Good luck to the next jerkwad who wanted to try it. Ash was pretty sure he had no energy left to care about himself, let alone anyone else.

The apathy was the worst part. He couldn't remember a time *before* it, when he'd cared about life. Logically, he remembered when he'd had hobbies, a promising college career, and parents who were alive and happy.

But that thought made the Ziploc in front of him dangerously tempting. Ash didn't do drugs, so he had no idea how much of these things it would take to feel something—or nothing at all.

He wasn't sure which he'd prefer.

2

CHRIS

"Nope... nope. Definitely not. Too old. Too young. Too much beard..."

Chris dragged his thumb along his phone screen as he scrolled down his messages.

Considering the sheer volume of incoming Grindr messages, it was frustrating that he'd only had a handful of good dates come from them, and none had turned into a relationship. He always went on one, maybe two dates with a guy, and then they drifted apart. Guys he met in real life first—at the store, the bar, or on the beach—had a similar track record.

It was way easier to find a hookup and way harder to find a real spark with another guy than he'd expected when he'd decided a few months ago to broaden his horizons.

Not that Chris hadn't known he was bi. He and Davey had always had that *thing* between him, ever since they'd met at firefighters' academy. Davey had dropped out after the first week, but their relationship had continued until Chris had refused to come out for him.

He hadn't known it back then, but it had turned out to be a good call. By now, they might be engaged.

Bullet dodged. Chris managed to contain a shiver. The only time that sounded like a good idea was at two in the morning, after another hookup with the guy.

His closest coworker at the fire station, Liam, had helped him come out as bi and navigate his first gay bar. Now it was down to him to find himself dates who *weren't* his ex, Davey, trying for a third chance with him.

Chris had been through the mill already in these last couple months—he'd lost track of his first dates, and even of his one-night stands.

Liam had told him that it was a good thing to figure out what he liked before he started committing to guys. Yeah, Chris knew now that he liked a twinky guy with a brain and an attitude, but that didn't make it easier to find them.

"Look at me," Chris muttered, closing the app and pocketing his phone as he looked around his house. His neighbors were having a barbecue tonight, but he had very little interest in hanging out with all the happy middle-aged couples who lived around him.

His work buddies were his closest friends; firefighting shifts were two-on, four-off, and it made it hard to keep schedules with other friends.

Still, a bit boring though it might be, Chris was happy with his life. He only felt lonely now and then, which seemed normal for any human, not just a bachelor in a big, empty house. Someday, he'd get a dog or a cat, but he wasn't in a rush for that, or a relationship, or even a bigger friendship circle.

Chris hummed under his breath as he slid the skillet back and forth to keep the chicken browning evenly. He was cooking a casserole so he'd have leftovers ready when he got off work in couple days' time.

When his phone went off with Liam's ringtone, Chris wiped his hands on the tea towel, then answered on speakerphone so he could keep cooking.

"Hey, man. What's up?" Chris greeted his good friend. At least, he assumed it was Liam and not his boyfriend, Dylan, who sometimes called from his phone.

It was indeed Liam. "Not much. You?"

"Cooking a casserole."

"Save me some."

Chris snorted. "Dude, you have a boyfriend to cook for you."

"Awww. I keep telling you, that last guy would have cooked for you. Dumb as a brick, but he was sweet."

Chris laughed. "You can't just say that!" he protested, but he couldn't disagree. Kev had been totally sweet, but an airhead who couldn't hold a conversation for more than a minute. No chemistry.

"I can." Liam's voice rose like that when he was smirking. "I shouldn't, but I will. So, stop beating around the bush. The promotion?"

Chris winced. He thumped his head against the side of the kitchen cabinet, then sighed. "Chief Williams passed me up."

"Again? Why?" Liam exclaimed.

"Because I'm unprofessional... and stuff." Chris winced at the memory of the conversation. He'd blotted it out with Davey, but fuck, that had been a bad idea too. "Same as usual."

Davey always was. He always took him back anyway, if only for the night.

Liam snorted. "That's bullshit. You joke around at the station, yeah, but not when we're out. Not when it matters. We should, like, talk to him about it."

"Nah. I'm not that invested in it. If it doesn't happen, it

doesn't happen. But thanks, man," Chris said. He wasn't about to mope, so he let it drop.

Liam hesitated but followed his lead. "Anyway, you picking me up tomorrow?"

"Is that a come-on?" Chris grinned, sprinkling salt and pepper across the chicken pieces. Since they'd come out to each other, pretty much nothing about their banter had changed. "I should be so lucky. Yeah, at seven."

"Perfect. I'll put my best heels on."

Chris laughed at the memory of tottering down State Street a month ago beside Liam. They'd walked a mile to represent the fire department at a charity event, and Liam had turned out to be surprisingly good at it. Chris was pretty sure Dylan had coached Liam ahead of time. Talk about unfair advantages.

"Well! I'll get my car washed for the occasion," Chris promised, grinning. "See you tomorrow, man."

Once he hung up, Chris smiled to himself and stirred the chicken around once more before turning off the heat.

Yeah, promotion or not, Chris's life was pretty good.

3

ASH

Wanna get Benny out of your system?

Ash stared at the message, then thumbed back to the profile. He wanted to tell the guy to fuck off—that he had no right to even type his ex's name. Catching him with his pants down in his living room, balls-deep in his ex, and then getting hit on by him? Hey, his life was fucked-up already.

The one-night-stand of his ex didn't seem like *that* bad of an idea right now. Not just because it was two in the morning, but yeah, that probably had something to do with it.

RJ's profile said he came to town every month for work. That explained why he was suddenly getting in touch now, almost a month after his tryst with Benny and the other three naked guys Ash had found lounging on his couch.

Then, RJ sent another string of messages.

Benny leave anything good?

Bring it along. We can share. I've got the booze.

I'll do it off your sexy little stomach.

I bet you're better than him.

"Fuck," Ash whispered as his dick slowly hardened.

RJ sent a photo—a dick pic. Not that Ash didn't remember seeing it spearing Benny's tight little ass up against the wall.

That's for you if you come over now.

It was a visceral reminder of how long it had been since someone had gotten hard for him. When was the last time he'd had someone else's hands on him? A week? Two?

Fuck, without a job, Ash had no reason to look at a calendar. He barely ate and slept too much. Time was compressing into one long, indistinguishable blur of day and night.

Ash had to get out of the house before he just swallowed all the pills he'd put back in the bedside table drawer, and there was a guy waiting for him and those pills. No better reason to get out, even if it was, apparently, half past two in the morning.

He hauled himself out of bed and sent back a quick message.

On my way. Where?

A second later, he had his answer: a hotel downtown. Parking would be a pain in the ass overnight, but whatever. He could park on a side street and move it before the parking cops even woke up for the morning.

Ash's hands shook as he grabbed the baggie. The guy couldn't be a cop, or he would have busted Benny's ass already.

And, frankly, he'd swallow anything that made the dawn come a little earlier.

The guy's hotel room was on the second floor. Keeping one hand on the Ziploc stuffed into his jacket pocket, Ash took the stairs instead of the elevator. That way, he didn't have to walk past the reception where a bored clerk leaned back, eyes fixed on his computer screen.

Ash barely knocked on the door before it was yanked open,

and the dark-eyed man pulled him inside. He had his underwear on again, his bulge visible.

RJ's pupils were large, and he swayed where he stood. He was already on something—booze, his nose told him a second later. The burn was unmistakable.

And from this angle, Ash's brain spun into action, trying to place him. He was familiar in a different way. Shit.

"You brought anything? What's your name?"

Ash nodded. He didn't always get asked that question. "Ash."

RJ's hands ran down his sides to his ass, squeezing. As the jolt of pleasure ran through him, the familiar tingle of a bad decision he didn't care about making ran through Ash's nerves. "Ash..." he hummed. "You work tomorrow?"

"No. Interview the next day though. I'm up for anything tonight," Ash said quietly, closing his eyes.

"Funny. I'm giving 'em that day," RJ snorted. "Probably not to men like you, though."

Ash ignored it for the sake of the way RJ was rubbing his dick through his jeans already. God, that felt good. "Brought everything he left. You can have it." He let RJ push him up against the wall and pull the bag out of his pocket, then rub his cock through his jeans in thanks. His mind was spinning over that comment, though. "RJ? You're not... Ray-John, are you?"

RJ went still. "Who's asking?" Then, his eyes narrowed as he swayed again, bracing himself against the wall. "You're one of my inter...viewees. Ash. I know the name now."

Ash had already shrugged off his jacket and unzipped his jeans, but he paused with his hand on the button. His heart pounded.

Shit. He'd never seen the recruiter face-to-face before. He'd never known that this guy worked in HR. Of course he hadn't put two and two together.

"Should I...?" Ash breathed out.

"Way too late for that, you filthy little slut." RJ pushed his shoulder with one hand, that rough palm cupping his cheek with the other hand. Ash sank to his knees, sliding down the wall and resisting the urge to slump. "You won't get the job, but I'll give you something else. Open up."

Two fingers, not a cock—yet—met his lips. Ash didn't ask; he just clumsily dry-swallowed whatever RJ put on his tongue. It was a small world, but just one more thing he really, *really* needed to forget right now.

Then, Ash took a messy gulp of the cup RJ pressed to his lips. Vodka, he thought, since it was almost tasteless. RJ was still tipping it back, so he swallowed and swallowed until the cup was empty.

Anything could be in there, and some tiny part of Ash was surprised at how little he cared.

The next thing against Ash's lips was hot, thick, and velvety-soft. He knew what to do with *that*.

In ten minutes—maybe five, if the tingles shooting through his fingertips were any indication—he'd feel something brand new. Maybe that would wake him up. Variety was the spice of life, after all.

Ash swallowed RJ's cock until his nose pressed into coarse hair and moaned around it, rubbing himself through his jeans as he bobbed his head.

Oh, there it was. He was floating out of his skin, his dick hardening and throbbing. No wonder guys took this shit.

Ash found himself smiling as RJ pressed his head against the wall and thrust into his mouth. It didn't feel like his own throat clenching around the head of RJ's cock, or his dick he was clumsily palming.

No more me. Good.

Ash's muscles were weak, and he couldn't stop himself from shaking. When he stilled himself, he only started again a second later.

His head was killing him. Someone had his temples in an invisible vice-clamp and was tightening it one screw at a time.

He was only halfway back in his body, but he already felt the burn in him that meant RJ had been busy with him.

Is there anything left? He needed more. Booze, drugs, sex, anything. He was coming down, and the world was closing in around him again.

No. Wait. Fuck.

He caught his breath, his mouth cotton-dry as his temples pounded.

Shit. Fuck.

He was becoming Benny.

Ash pushed himself up, looking around. The room still spun around him, but his dick was soft. He could vaguely remember coming so many times last night. Or had he never been able to come? Maybe he'd plateaued all night.

Either way, the ecstasy had taken him soaring so far beyond his shitty life over the last few weeks... years, really... and the downswing was just as harsh.

Ash was in a dead end. No job, no money, no boyfriend. Nothing left for him.

Not that he had anything to lose. He hadn't had anything for years now. Since his parents died, it had been a slow, one-way slide into this fucking... pit of despair.

And don't even think about trying to escape. Even the cult movie reference didn't make him smile.

"Get your ass up, loser." That was RJ's voice, harsh, as something slammed. It was the bathroom door—Ash registered that much before RJ raised his voice. "*Now*. I have to go to work and interview real men."

Rage filled the space where Ash's numbness had been at a speed that almost scared Ash. "Excuse me?" Ash mumbled, pushing himself to sit upright even if his world spun. "Fucking dick."

"You heard me. Fucking sluts in this goddamn town," RJ snapped and stepped back into the bathroom.

Ash's body shook from head to toe. Rudeness? A little cold shoulder to make sure there were no strings? He could take that.

This was more. RJ was trying to piss him off.

"Did you hate me interrupting you and Benny?" Ash fired back, pushing himself to his feet. Oh, fuck, he wasn't sure he could even walk to his car, let alone sleep off the rest of this high in it. "Couldn't last long enough last night to make up for it?"

He didn't know what was making him say this shit. Was he still high? That would explain the room spinning.

He couldn't hold onto that thought long enough to ground himself. It was gone, drowned by a sea of rage he couldn't even put into words.

RJ was leaning in the bathroom doorway again, buttoning up a white collared shirt. "I was wrong. Benny was better."

"Yeah? That's not what you said two hours ago," Ash mumbled, pulling his clothes back on. It took almost every ounce of concentration to do it, so he missed most of RJ's response until the very end.

"...come crawling back tomorrow night."

"What?"

"You." RJ pointed, speaking loudly and slowly, like he was a child. "Druggie. You'll. Call. Me. Tonight." He smirked. "Won't you? You want that job or not?"

The *fuck* he would. And he wasn't born yesterday. RJ wasn't gonna give him the damn job no matter how many times he sucked his dick.

Then, Ash's heart sank. For the first time in weeks, he felt *something*. Not joy and light, but something darker—self-knowledge. Realization.

I will call him tonight.

His gaze strayed to the window as he pushed his shoes on, one foot at a time. It was a Juliet balcony, and the doors were open. That explained the smell of rain and the breeze.

God. How the fuck had he gotten here? He wasn't the kind of guy who got drunk and high in a stranger's room off god-knows-what and let him talk to him like that, but...

That had been true when he felt like he had a future. Now...

"Or you can stay." RJ's voice dropped to a hoarse whisper as he shrugged a suit jacket on and grabbed a briefcase from near the door. "There's nothing of value in the room. Steal my clothes or get room service and I will *fuck you up*. I know where you live. I even know your work references now."

Words were floating back from last night, in snippets he wasn't sure if he was imagining or remembering. *Nobody cares about you.* That was probably his own brain. RJ couldn't know about his parents. *Good-for-nothing druggie slut.* No, that wasn't self-loathing. He remembered RJ saying that one, maybe. It was true either way.

Ash's mind spun again as he leaned on the bed—just for a moment, just to rest. When he managed to turn to the door and open his mouth, RJ was gone. And it was slightly lighter outside.

And he was alone. Again. As always.

Like he always would be.

Unless...

Ash's gaze wandered to the window again. Slowly, step by step, Ash pushed himself to his feet and stumbled in that direction, following the cool breeze.

Just for a breath of fresh air, he managed to lie to himself until he was one step away from the balcony railing, which stretched up to just below his chest.

Ash was shaking again, but the numbness was fading. A wave of adrenaline hit him, pushing the crushing despair, the loathing, the nothingness away.

Yes. This. This was feeling something. He wanted to ride the wave as long as it would take him.

He wanted to go out feeling *something*.

Ash didn't stop to think twice about it. He wrapped his hands around the railing and pushed himself up, clutching the edge of the doorframe as he swayed, looking out over rooftops ahead of him.

Santa Barbara's main street stretched out, blanketed by the thick fog that rolled in until noon. It smelled clean and fresh, and for a moment—just a moment—a smile touched his lips.

It's pretty.

The strangest calmness settled through Ash's body, his shaking subsiding.

The future yawning in front of him was gone. Without it pressing in on him, squeezing every bit of life from him, his heart lifted and the world stopped being so *big* and *loud* and *painful*.

It was going to be okay.

Ash let go.

4

CHRIS

The morning was Chris's favorite part of the day. Once he was awake, dressed, and out of the house, he loved the hour before he had to show up at work.

The fog was a welcome relief from the heat of midday in this town, especially in the summer. Not that it was stiflingly hot like inland, but Chris wasn't a big fan of the summer.

The rest of the year was vastly preferable. Cooler and fresher in the morning and evening, and better working conditions.

He parked a few streets away from the cute little craft shop above which Liam and Dylan lived. As always, Chris smiled and shook his head at the thought: Liam and Dylan were regulars there.

Chris wasn't going to make fun of it, though. Liam had found the PTSD support knitting circle invaluable in his recovery, and anything that helped his best friend feel better was okay in his book.

Crunch.

It wasn't a simple noise like a stick breaking, or even two

cars colliding. The noise was a crackling, thudding crunch, and the kind of unconscious scream that tore out of someone's throat from the depths of their body.

Then, bystander noises—two or three voices shouting as he saw someone bolt out of a cafe, across the street, to the sidewalk below the hotel. Someone else screamed and ran into the hotel lobby.

Chris's brain was halfway to work mode already, so he responded almost solely on instinct as he broke into a run. He knew without a shred of doubt that that was a body on the sidewalk.

No, the body moved slightly, and then another inhuman noise of pain rended from his throat. He was still alive.

Chris was at his side in seconds, the words falling from his mouth in a well-trained drill.

"I'm Chris. I know first aid. Can I help?"

"Please. Please, God."

The man lay awkwardly on his side, half-curled, noises of pain spilling from his throat as he mumbled senselessly. Blood streaked down his cheeks and stained his jeans, the sidewalk, his shirt.

Airway, breathing, circulation.

Chris looked up and around. The guy who'd come running from the cafe was standing in the street, going pale as he stared at the sight. The only other bystander this time of morning was the one who'd run into the hotel, and he couldn't count on them calling the hospital.

"You. Call 911 and tell me when you've done that, and how long they'll be. Got it?"

It took the guy a second to respond to Chris's authoritative tone, but then he did. "Y-Yes. Yes. Of course."

Chris waited to make sure he was taking out his phone before he looked back down at his patient.

Fingers dug into Chris's arm and Chris caught his breath, meeting the guy's eyes. If his face hadn't been twisted in anguish, Chris would have said he was pretty—high cheekbones, dark hair, deep brown eyes that were glazed over in pain.

He looked up and spotted a balcony on the second floor, its window open.

Chris was certain of it: this wasn't a slip-and-fall accident.

"It's okay," Chris breathed out, covering the guy's hand with his own. Adrenaline rushed through him and he made note of it, pushing it to the side to remember his training.

Stabilize the patient.

"What hurts?"

Finally, the man on the sidewalk closed his eyes, his whimpers ceasing for a second as he tried to catch his breath, then resuming again. "E-Everything. My leg. Oh, fuck, my leg. It's... help."

"I'm here," Chris soothed, lowering his voice and speaking calmly and slowly.

"Ambulance is on their way."

Chris acknowledged his helper with a quick jerk of his head.

"Don't move," Chris told his patient. "You could have head or spinal injuries. Okay? Stay just as you are."

There were more bystanders gathering now, and the guy's eyes flickered open, then around at the others. The intense pain on his face was outweighed by just one emotion: shame.

Chris's teeth gritted in anger at the rubberneckers all around. He looked at his helper and jerked his chin around. "Keep people away. We've got this."

He didn't want this guy going through a second of suffering he didn't have to.

Even as his helper shooed people away, they tried to look. It was a grim sight: the guy's leg was bent at an angle it shouldn't have, and Chris was pretty sure he saw bone fragment.

That reminded him of the next step: the blood loss could turn critical within a minute.

"I'm going to give you a tourniquet," Chris told him, still speaking slowly. He saw the dilated pupils, the way he moved jerkily. His patient wasn't sober. Maybe if he had been, he wouldn't have tried to jump from a second-floor window. Or, worse, he would have jumped and succeeded.

Chris felt a chill run down his spine as the guy slowly let go and nodded. He'd said something, but too quietly for Chris to hear over his intermittent moans.

"I'm Chris." Since he could have forgotten in these few minutes. "What's your name?" Chris asked, keeping his voice low.

He heard a siren. Thank God.

It took Chris all his concentration to hear and see it on his lips: "Ash. Harvey."

"Ash," Chris repeated quietly to make sure he got it right. Then, he hastily added, "Don't nod. Hey, you."

He got his helper to kneel and hold the guy's head steady between his palms, but that left them without a defense against the crowd.

"Don't go."

"I won't," Chris promised. He ripped his overshirt off and open without hesitation, easing it as gently as he could under the broken leg to tie it tightly. His shirt lifted as he did so, and it took him a minute to tug it back down.

"Oh. You have abs. M'jealous."

Thank God. He was joking... or flirting. There was life in him yet, and Chris grinned with relief. "Firefighter, baby."

"Ah," Ash whispered, his face flushing with another wave of pain. "Don't... Don't go."

"I'm not. I'm here. You're gonna be okay," Chris said, keeping him talking. Better chance of keeping him awake that way.

Jesus. How many fucking people were downtown in Santa Barbara at this time of the morning? The streets had been empty, but now there were too many, all of a sudden. Chris couldn't waste time worrying about Ash's privacy, though.

"I wanted to die." Ash's voice was so quiet, Chris barely picked up on it. His moans had ceased and his skin looked pale and clammy.

He was about to pass out—blood loss, no doubt, and maybe from the drugs.

"I know, darling," Chris whispered, then touched his arm. "I'm glad you didn't."

Ash watched him with hazy eyes that flickered shut, his lips parted, but didn't answer.

"Hey. Hey, stay with me," Chris told him firmly, patting his shoulder and pinching his shoulder lightly. "Hey. Ash."

Ash was limp on the pavement, his fingers still outstretched toward Chris's leg like he was about to grab hold of Chris for dear, sweet, precious life.

The rumble of an engine, the clunking of opening doors: the EMTs were there.

Chris relayed what he knew as he eased himself away, giving them room to lift him onto the stretcher.

Paul, the EMT, was checking him for shock. "Do you have someone to bring you to the hospital if need be?"

"Yes. I'll be fine," Chris assured Paul, pointing to his t-shirt. Without his overshirt, used as a temporary bandage, it was a little chilly in his t-shirt this time of day. But it made his affiliation obvious. "I'm a trained first responder, man. Don't waste time on me. He's going to Cottage, yeah?"

"Okay," Paul nodded, his eyes flitting to the fire station logo. "Yeah. Are you two...?"

"Oh. Oh, no." Chris's cheeks flushed as he looked at the back of the ambulance, then nodded at Paul. "You take off." Surely Ash had someone else to look in on him.

When the ambulance was gone and the crowd dispersed, Chris slowly walked down the street toward Liam's apartment.

Chris's stomach sank with inexplicable regret that he'd said *no*. He couldn't get Ash's desperate grip out of his mind. He'd look in on him when he'd finished his shift... just to make sure someone was with him.

He deserves that much. Everyone does.

"Of course there'd be a fucking brush fire after all that. Hey, man, you sure you're fine?"

The last day had been a blur of action as they provided backup to the fire near the edge of their turf. Now that they were back at the firehouse, thanks to Liam's questioning, Chris's mind was back on yesterday morning.

With injuries that bad, Ash would definitely still be in the hospital. He had to have made it. The blood loss hadn't been fatal—not yet, anyway.

"Yes," Chris told him as they stepped out of their turnout gear to hit the showers, keeping his tone sharp to shut down Liam's questions.

Liam didn't say anything, probably too exhausted to push it. They'd needed all hands on deck today.

It was only a minor fire, but there was no such thing as a minor fire now. With the drought as bad as it had been in recent years, something like this could spark the kind of fire that would level a city. They had to treat every damn fire like it could explode out of control, because it could.

Fighting any kind of fire bigger than a single pot on a stove left a guy exhausted. No matter how much he trained to carry his own gear and hoses, the weight of it bore down on him by the end of a shift.

And it was only four o'clock in the afternoon. They still had until eight AM tomorrow before the next shift was in to relieve them. They had to shower, eat, and sleep, in that order, to stay fresh for anything else in their district.

Kevin was already in the showers, trying to scrub the soot and sweat away.

None of them said much until they got to the kitchen. Hans, one of the fresh new faces they'd been sent, was at the stove.

"Food's just about ready."

Chris could have kissed him. "We can keep this one," he managed and crashed on the couch. He wanted to make the kid feel better about not coming out on this one. Not that it was *that* exciting, but to a newbie, it felt like a sting sometimes to be left to housesit.

Hans turned a little red and smiled, passing out Coke cans.

"Oh, I love you," Liam groaned, crashing at the table as Hans brought over plates of chicken breasts, rice, and broccoli. A simple meal, but God, Chris was ready to inhale it.

What was Ash eating? He'd been talking okay—no dental injuries that he could tell, but the blood across his face had made it hard to tell where it was coming from. Hopefully just abrasions.

At least Liam waited until after they ate and they were alone on the couch before he nudged Chris. "Go check on him."

"What?"

Chris had told him just about everything except the distressing parts—the sound Ash had made when he hit the pavement, and the way Ash had held onto him.

Liam had intuited it, though. His expression was gentle. "We have Hans here, and Greg in the engine room. We can handle an hour. Go grab donuts or something, and visit him. It's bothering you."

"Yeah." Chris didn't even have the energy to banter with Liam or deny it. "Just wanna make sure—"

"He made it. I know." Liam slung his arm around his shoulders and squeezed. "Go on. You need to see him once."

It was all the encouragement Chris needed to follow his gut instinct. It sounded insane, but he just *felt* like Ash needed someone there.

Chris was gonna feel like a dumb lump if he got there and Ash had his friends and family surrounding him, but he could sneak away again.

"Thanks."

"Pick up a card for him or something."

"You think he'd like that?"

Liam smiled and punched his shoulder lightly. "Of course. Everyone likes cards. And there's that dollar store next to the bakery..."

"I get your hint," Chris laughed, but the smile faded rapidly as he headed out to his car.

He was in his station t-shirt. That should get him in the door. He just had no idea what he'd say when he got there.

Hey, I'm the guy who found you. I hope you don't want to die now.

That was it—the thing that most bothered him. He'd never gotten an answer when he told Ash he was glad he hadn't died.

He couldn't imagine being in a place where it ever seemed like the best idea, let alone... something not to regret. Chris's hands tightened on the wheel as he pulled out of the fire station driveway.

It was stupid how much he'd thought of Ash over the last day and a half. Ash probably didn't even remember him.

What the hell am I doing?

But Liam was right: he needed to see Ash once, just to make sure that... he'd made it. A chill ran down Chris's thought at the possibility he hadn't.

He turned up the music and bobbed his head, but his heart wasn't in it.

"Just down the hall, to the left."

"Thanks, darling." Chris flashed the nurse a big smile. His fire station t-shirt had indeed gotten him in the door, along with a well-placed flirtatious smile.

And maybe a half-truth about knowing Ash, but whatever it took.

He clutched the chocolate box close as he knocked on the door and gently pushed it open.

Ash was unmistakable even in a hospital gown, still pale but cleaned up, no longer bloody and writhing in pain. He was asleep, long lashes not even fluttering as his heart monitor rhythmically beeped.

Shit. He *was* gorgeous.

Chris stopped in the doorway for a second, then realized how fucking massively creepy this would be if the guy woke up.

A blush swept through Chris's cheeks as he looked down at his card and chocolate. It was the dumbest thing, but maybe it would make him smile. He tiptoed over to the table next to Ash and set them down, opening the card and grabbing a pen from his pocket to scribble a little addition to his message.

There. He'd seen that he was okay, but he didn't want to wake Ash up if he was asleep. Chris closed the envelope and set it on top of the parcel. He ran his finger across the table and chair by the bed, looking for something to nervously fidget with.

Ash looked so goddamn fragile, light bandages on his face—definitely abrasions, then—and arms. The blankets bulged where he probably had a cast or bandages.

Then, it hit Chris: there was nothing on his bedside table, and when he raised his finger, there was dust on the chair next to the bed.

It took him a minute to find a nurse, but when he did, his suspicion was confirmed.

"Ash, the man in that room? No, he hasn't had any visitors."

Chris felt almost sick as he looked back toward the room.

"If he wakes up..." he trailed off. *Does he even want to see me?* It was awfully presumptuous to think so, but on the off-chance that maybe he did, he had to say it. "Never mind. I'll be back myself."

He thanked the nurse for her work before heading out, his head still spinning.

Oh, Ash. What the hell is your story?

5

ASH

There was no way for Ash to lie comfortably, so sleep came in fits and starts only when the numbness of painkillers settled into his bones.

He didn't know the full extent of his injuries. He knew about the open fracture in his left leg, because he'd had surgery yesterday for it. His other leg ached, too, but apparently those were just acute soft tissue injuries.

The laundry list of pain was too extensive for Ash to keep going through. Long story short: all of this agony, the frustration, being trapped in the hospital, having that nurse with the brown hair look at him like some homeless junkie... almost worth it for that brief second of utter peace.

Ash didn't remember a lot of what had come before, but that last second?

Balancing on his toes on the steel railing, his arms outspread: he couldn't forget that.

"Mm?" His voice sounded hoarse even to his own ear as he shifted under the thin hospital blanket, trying not to move his legs.

All he had to occupy him was the tiny TV near the ceiling —his insurance was paying for the cheapest room they had—or his phone, but the screen had smashed in the fall. Doing anything on the spiderweb screen was annoying, to say the least.

Something was on his bedside table.

It looked like a card and a package. Who the hell could have sent those?

He wasn't used to getting gifts—not since the crash that had killed his parents. His dad's side of the family was either dead or distant, and his mom's side had ditched them when she married his dad. Since he'd been over eighteen, he didn't get any foster family or real support. He was just, suddenly and overnight, alone.

And he'd been alone for a very long time.

He told himself he liked it.

Even reaching for the card made him ache. He was just glad he hadn't fractured his arms or ribs, even if he'd bruised the crap out of everything.

Apparently, the human body wasn't made to hit concrete.

He tore open the card and blinked at the front. It was a generic picture of a lake with reeds, like he'd send to his neighbor if he'd heard they broke their arm or something. Assuming he had neighbors he cared about.

Ash flipped it open, his eyes landing on the signature first, then the rest of the message.

> *Hey Ash,*
>
> *I dropped in to see where they put you and how you're doing. (Update: Glad it's the ground floor :))*
>
> *Hope you're feeling better. I brought you chocolates. I hope they let you eat them. Fuck hospital food.*
>
> *Chris (the guy with abs)*

And there was a phone number next to Chris's name.

Ash snorted with laughter. The nurses had all tiptoed around the suicide attempt once they'd established that Ash didn't need to be sectioned.

Thank God for that, too. The only thing worse than lying here unable to do anything interesting would be being shut in a padded room.

Of course Ash remembered him, though. Not just because of his abs, but because of his sweet bedside manner. Well, sidewalk-side manner.

How long ago had that been? Two days now? Time was blurry for him now, not that he'd had a grip on it before his attempt.

His attempt. Ash was a guy who had an *attempt* to talk about now.

Fuck.

His heart sank, and the distraction of a nurse walking in was welcome—especially since it was Julie. She was the nice blond one, not the brunette who gave him smaller pain medication doses.

"Hey, nurse," he greeted hoarsely, offering a little smile.

She offered a smile as she came to his bedside. "Hi, Ash. Glad to see you awake. How are you feeling?"

"Crappy," he admitted. "Pain's getting better, though."

"Good. I see you found your note."

Ash smiled again as he eased the tape away from the packaging to peek at the chocolates. "Oh, See's chocolates. Wow."

"Someone was glad to see you. He asked about your condition. He seemed sweet," Julie said and smiled.

What the hell? Ash's heart fluttered at the mention of Chris. He'd never even properly met the guy, but he told himself it was only natural to idolize him.

He'd been right there for him, compassionate and not judgmental, sheltering him from the folks around, waiting with him for the ambulance. And then he'd come back to see him again.

Ash didn't have those hippie-dippie ideas about all people being good, but maybe some of them were all right.

"He seems like it," Ash admitted softly.

"Is he your... brother?" She carefully chose her words.

"No," Ash chuckled, even though it made his ribs hurt. That was never the real question. "Nor my boyfriend, sadly."

"Oh, he caused quite a stir at the nurse's station." Julie winked at him. She fussed with his blankets.

There was something else on her mind. "I hate to ask, but... do you have anyone else you'd like contacted?" Ah. There it was.

"No." Ash pressed his lips together for a moment. "Why?"

"Ah, the doctor's likely to want to release you into someone's care. But we can hold onto you for an extra day or two," she told him, clearly trying to smooth the thought away.

It hit Ash right then that this random stranger was the only person who'd come to see him. Well, duh. He didn't have friends or family. Who else would?

"Okay."

Julie was looking over at the doorway, smiling. "I'll be around in a bit."

Ash followed her retreat to the door and then froze.

It was him. Chris.

He'd only seen him that one time, kneeling over him, one firm hand on him to help him stay grounded in his own body. But that was enough to sear the man's face in his mind.

Chris filled the doorframe with a faint whiff of wood smoke, the light gleaming off his white t-shirt and blond hair. He looked like a goddamn guardian angel, but the smoke was disorienting.

For half a second, Ash wondered if he'd died. Then the thought made him smile. *What the fuck? Get it together.*

They were alone now, and Chris's eyes never left his as he hovered in the doorway as if waiting to be invited in.

Finally, Ash managed a quiet, "H-Hi." His throat was dry.

"Hey." Chris was wearing a fire station t-shirt just like the one he'd ripped off to make a tourniquet.

Ash's eyes fell to it, and he looked up again. "Sorry about your t-shirt."

Chris blinked, then laughed. "It's all right. Any excuse to get my shirt off. Can I... Do you mind me visiting?"

"Yes—no—I mean, yes, please visit. And come in." Ash suddenly felt self-conscious as he adjusted the thin blanket around his waist and eased himself up. He got halfway up before his ribs started aching and he winced. "Ouch..."

Chris was there, a hand on the small of his back and his shoulder, helping him sit up.

The spark that crackled through Ash made his heart thump. He suddenly smelled him—the wood smoke stronger now, the fresh cleanliness of soap, and something else. It was exactly what he'd smelled, aside from the iron tang, a day or two ago, and he was back on the sidewalk, helpless under his hands.

When he was leaning back against the pillows, Chris froze, then pulled his hands back. He stayed right there, in his personal space. "Sorry," he breathed out, a line furrowed between his brows.

"It's okay," Ash whispered back, acutely aware of how close Chris was until he took a step back and sank onto the chair by the bed.

Finally, he could breathe again.

What the fuck was that about?

6

CHRIS

What the hell was he doing here? He didn't know anything about suicidal people, or what to say.

I'm sorry you tried to jump out a window?

Well, he'd successfully jumped. Hadn't been so successful at the end goal.

"Were you high? Oh my God, no. That's probably the last thing you wanna talk about..." Chris quickly interjected, barely finishing the question.

To his relief, Ash cracked another smile, then a breathy chuckle. The way his lips curved gave him the sweetest smile. "I don't mind. The nurses don't want to talk about it now they've decided I'm not a risk and I don't need to be carted off to crazy town."

"Oh, good," Chris murmured. "I mean... sort of good."

Ash nodded slightly, folding his hands on the covers. He was pushing his fingers together, lacing them nervously and twiddling them. "Yeah. I don't—I'm not a druggie."

"I didn't say you were," Chris quickly answered, holding up his hands. "I'm not judging anyway."

"I don't... I don't know. It was a bad night. I was hooking up with some guy..." Ash trailed off, his cheeks stained pink as he quickly looked over at Chris, clearly about to backtrack.

"We've all been there." It was the best way Chris could think of to come out without, like, *saying* it and interrupting the moment.

Relief drew Ash's features into a softer smile again, and he nodded in appreciation. "Yeah. Bad night after a bad month, and... I just wanted to stop existing."

"Ouch," Chris murmured, folding his hands between his knees as he leaned forward. "Do you have friends or family around?"

Ash shook his head, gazing across the room for a moment before meeting his eyes again. He looked Chris carefully up and down. "Let me guess. You're one of the popular guys."

Chris smiled sheepishly, shifting in his seat. "I am at work, yeah. Not so much outside work. I kinda get it. I don't talk to my family often, but not because we don't like each other. Just... yeah."

"You're a firefighter, right? In the city?"

"Yeah. Up in the foothills."

Ash frowned. "You had an... incident today?"

"God. I smell like smoke, don't I?" Chris groaned with a quiet laugh. "Sorry. I showered the best I could. Sometimes it clings."

"No, it's okay." Ash was suddenly stroking his hair, a teasing smile on his lips. "Your hair gets fluffy after you shower." Oh, man. If it weren't for the circumstances, he'd hit on Ash so fast.

"It goes all over. If I don't keep it short, it's a crazy professor look," Chris grinned as Ash pulled his hand back.

"I don't think that'd suit you," Ash agreed, smiling. "Were you just on your way to work when you... um... found me?"

"Yeah. Picking up my best friend. Liam. He lives with his boyfriend above this little craft store," Chris told Ash, happy to settle on the safer conversational topic. "We're on the same shift, in the same house. Fire station."

"I'm sorry if I got in the way of your work." Ash looked worried now, his brows pushing together.

That wasn't just worry, it was shame.

Chris reached out for Ash's hand before he even realized what he was doing, his fingers sliding around the frailer, thinner ones in his palm. "No need to apologize. I'm just glad you made it."

Ash caught his breath as their eyes met, and a moment later, Chris felt a light squeeze in return before Ash pulled his hand away and looked away, clearly wanting to change the subject.

"What was the fire today?"

Chris's heart sank as Ash let go of him. The brief contact... was nice. Really nice. "Wildfire. It was a hard shift. Not as bad as some I've had—no people involved, you know? But hard."

"That must be worrisome."

Chris nodded. "Yeah. Don't want to let anything get out of control. These days, fire season isn't over this late in the year."

He should know—he'd been working here for nearly a decade. Certainly for long enough to get a promotion if people took him seriously once in a while. Pushing that thought away, he refocused on Ash.

"What do you do?" he asked, hoping this wasn't another tricky subject. "Do you work?"

Ash shook his head. "Nothing right now. Just got laid off at the end of the season at a carwash. I wait tables sometimes or do yard work. Lots of under-the-table stuff. I was..." he trailed off.

Chris stayed quiet and nodded, encouraging him to talk.

"I'm dumb. I don't have any degrees. I'm good with people, sometimes, and manual labor... but I had an in for a stupid entry-level office job."

He doesn't think much of himself. Chris shifted uncomfortably, but he wasn't about to interrupt him now.

"I..." There was the shame again, coloring Ash's cheeks. "The guy I slept with, got high with, was the recruiter."

"Oh, *fuck*." Chris covered his mouth and looked at the room door for nurses. When he looked back, Ash was laughing softly. "I mean, wow."

"You can swear. We're not in the pediatric ward."

Chris laughed. "So you're... gay? Or you were just hooking up with a dude because?"

"Yeah." For a moment, Ash looked nervous, like he was going through all the interactions they'd just had. "I am. Are you—I mean, that's cool?"

Chris rushed to reassure him. "Yes! Oh, yeah, it's fine, man. Me too. Only for like, two months—well, no, I'm bi, and I've been with a guy before that, but I never—I mean, I only came out then."

Ash's lips twitched into a smile, and he said nothing to stop Chris's slide into embarrassment.

Oh, God. Shoot me now. "But I spent so long feeling like I *had* to be into women that I'm, like, catching up on lost time. Not that I'm sleeping around, if that's a bad thing. Not that much. Okay, I kind of am. But..." Chris looked around for something else to focus on. "That's a nice card. Oh, that was my card."

Ash's laugh was a warm hit of pleasure. It spilled from his lips until it filled the room, and Chris had no choice but to laugh along. "I don't mind. It's nice to talk... or listen."

"Okay." Chris laughed sheepishly, playing with the card and opening and closing it to give his hands something to do.

"I'm not sure the nurse approved the message," Ash told him. Was he teasing him? Definitely; his eyes gleamed. The spark of playful mischief on Ash's face suited him.

Chris blushed and set the card down again, but he laughed. "I really hoped you had a good sense of humor when I wrote that."

"The guy with the abs. I didn't imagine that part, then."

"The part where you caressed my abs?" Chris deadpanned. When Ash's jaw dropped and he started to sit up straighter, his hands spreading, Chris laughed. "No, joking. You just complimented me."

"Oh my *God*," Ash laughed, and he was bright red now. His heart monitor beeped faster. "You had me going. I'm so gullible."

Chris winked and cracked his knuckles. "My work is done." Despite how pleasant it was to hang out with Ash, sleep was dragging at the corners of his eyes. They'd had another early-morning medical call and he hadn't had a chance to get back to sleep after that. He wasn't running on a full tank.

"Thank you for seeing me." Ash looked hesitant. "Are you gonna... I mean, you don't have to keep seeing me. I'll be okay."

Take the risk. Chris cleared his throat. "Would you like me to? Or would you rather I fuck off now?"

Ash hesitated and chewed on his lip for a moment. "I could use a friend."

Chris nodded. "Me, too. I'll be back tomorrow, then, after I've slept. If that's cool."

"That'd be great. The doctor might even let me go home."

"Great." Chris smiled and rose to his feet, already looking forward to tomorrow. He squeezed Ash's shoulder again. "Need help getting back down?"

"I think my abs will do the trick, but thanks," Ash smiled at him.

Chris was tempted to lean in for a hug, but he reminded himself that they didn't know each other *that* well yet. Instead, he patted Ash's shoulder and forced himself to let go. "Cool. See you tomorrow, then? And finish those," he pointed at the See's chocolate box with a grin. "Medicinal purposes."

"Yes, sir," Ash winked. "See you. Thanks, Chris."

Chris waved, and as he drifted out of the hospital, a smile kept hovering on his lips.

He'd only meant for a short visit to make sure that Ash was okay, but now he had a friend. A new, tentative friendship, but definitely one. It was easy to talk to Ash, and coaxing smiles out of him was a pleasure.

Even when he hit the shower at home, Chris hadn't stopped daydreaming about his new friend. Yeah, not just because he was gorgeous despite the sadness that tugged at his eyes and lips sometimes.

Ash was broken, physically, and his spirit was scarred. Chris had no doubt there was a story he hadn't yet heard. But, at the same time, there was that sparkle of life underneath.

Chris wanted to help it shine.

7

ASH

"I can't get the hang of this. I'm such a dumbass."

Ash slumped against the wall, holding himself up with one crutch. His good knee—relatively, anyway—twinged with pain from the soft tissue injuries all around his kneecap and leg.

The other leg ached from thigh to shin. Fucking surgery. At least he wasn't in a full-body cast, but he resented being so damn slow.

He could *see* the end of the hall. He could envision himself walking down to the end in his usual quick, purposeful stride, like he had no time for anything else. But his damn legs weren't going to be able to do that, maybe ever again.

He'd gotten the news a couple hours after Chris left. The surgery was considered successful, the pins were in place, but he'd tuned out the majority of what they'd said about it. It made him dizzy to think about.

He'd listened to the important part: he might never walk normally. They couldn't tell until he healed and they saw how he progressed.

Well, the most important part was that his insurance was

covering pretty much everything, and Ash wasn't asking too many questions about why. Maybe they hadn't counted it as a suicide attempt since he'd been high. Plenty of people got high and did dumb shit. But wasn't that excluded, too?

Maybe his plan was good. It was government-funded, after all. He was too broke to pay his own bills, let alone health insurance. He wasn't supposed to be here—in any sense of the phrase.

"Do you want another demonstration? Have patience with yourself. It's a skill that takes time to learn."

Bless Julie for everything. She was kind and sympathetic and hadn't made fun of him even once.

Ash slowly pushed himself away from the wall, wobbling between his crutches. He heaved a sigh and nodded. "At least so I can go short distances and they'll let me out today."

"Good man," Julie praised, squeezing his arm and staying right by him, ready to catch him again.

His knuckles ached as his grip tightened with his frustration. He tried to loosen his grip on the handles to let them drop into his fingers like she'd taught him.

"One step at a time."

Ash clunked with his crutches, then his leg as he mentally rehearsed the instructions: injured leg first downstairs, uninjured first upstairs. But avoid stairs when possible.

His gut clenched with nerves. How the fuck was he going to get another job? All the unskilled jobs he worked relied on having mobility. Even retail—cushy compared to most of his gigs—would want someone who could stand up all day and kneel to stock shelves.

Don't think about that yet. But he couldn't help but stress. There was nobody else to think about those details for him, and nobody to carry the bills. He wasn't sure exactly how much was in his bank account, but there was the deductible that he'd put onto his credit card to worry about, and rent, and food...

He made it back down the hall to his room with Julie's help, and she clapped for him when he did.

Slumping with relief against the padded torture bars of the damn things, Ash smiled lightly at her. "Thank you." He slowly headed toward the bed. He needed to sit down and rest.

"You're welcome, doll. I'll go tell the doctor the news."

"Great." Ash drew a breath and made his way through the room, one damn step at a time.

Despite his grumpiness about the whole shitty situation, Ash wasn't even close to that place he'd been in *that* night. Even if he had to go bankrupt, or get disability, or find some sugar daddy... hell, he'd do what he had to. Eventually go to school, get some qualification for a real job.

This was a hell of a hole to land in, but fuck it, he gritted his teeth with determination, he *could* claw his way out somehow.

He was just starting to sit when he heard a voice from the doorway. "Hey. Who's up and moving? Wow."

That was Chris's voice. Thank God Ash could wear pants now. When Ash managed to turn on his crutches, he hurried in. "Oh, don't let me interrupt you. You need a hand?"

"I think I've got it. Maybe. Only slid off the bed, like, twice," Ash snorted with laughter as he managed to ease himself onto the edge of the bed and lean the crutches next to him. "See?"

Chris grinned back at him. "You're looking way better. Did you hear back from the doctor?"

"No, he might be in any time now," Ash told him. He was still out of breath from that short wander. "Just managed to get down the hall."

"That's great progress. Yesterday, you looked like I'd have to strap you to a skateboard to get you anywhere."

Ash laughed despite himself at the image. "You're one of those damn perpetual optimists, aren't you?" he accused Chris.

"Guilty." Chris beamed at him, plopping into the chair by the bed. "I get into trouble for it." Then, a brief frown flickered over his face.

"Really?"

"Got passed over for a promotion, actually. At work." Ash winced, and so did Chris. Chris hastily added, "Not that I should complain."

"Dude, whine if you want," Ash shook his head. "I'm pissed off at myself today. I'd rather be distracted."

"About the whole leg situation?"

"Everything," Ash sighed, waving it off. "You know, who the hell gets high and jumps out a window? I'm not trying *anything* a second time."

"Do you know what you were on?" Chris drummed his fingers against his knees, his arm draped along the back of the chair as he sat sideways.

Ash grimly shook his head. That was one of the worst parts; that RJ guy could have given him literally anything. At least he knew where the guy worked. If he'd tried anything too nasty, Ash could report him... somehow.

"Shit, man. Don't be angry at you. Be angry at whoever gave you that shit. Did they talk you into it?"

Ash half-smiled. "Got that covered. My ex bought the stuff, R—I mean, the guy I hooked up with—gave it to me... but I decided to let him... to take it. I wasn't thinking straight, but that doesn't mean..."

"He took advantage of you, then." Chris shook his head. "Yeah, I get you're trying to be responsible, but... fuck it, dude. Be pissed at that R guy, too."

Something in Ash's chest felt looser and relieved. Nobody had told him he could be angry at RJ. Now that Chris said it, yeah, it *had* been a dick move. Everything RJ had done and said to him—had he been *trying* to make him suicidal? At the very least, it was emotional abuse.

Before he could answer, there was a throat clearing in the doorway and he looked over quickly.

Dr. Green was there, his clipboard in his hand and white coat sweeping after him as he entered the room. "Hello again, Ash. And you are...?"

"Chris." His new friend rose to his feet to shake hands.

"I assume you're here to take him home?"

Ash's cheeks flushed. He couldn't impose so much on Chris without asking! He was just drawing a quick breath to say no when Chris looked at him, then nodded. "If he wants, if it'd be helpful, yeah."

"Certainly helpful. He won't be able to drive in this condition."

Ash's sigh of relief came first, but he hastened to ask, "Are you sure? You really aren't responsible."

"Dude, I don't mind." Chris looked earnest as he looked over at him, twisting his fingers together. "How else were you planning on getting home?"

Ash had to admit he had no idea. He couldn't get on a bus in this shape, not that any headed close enough to home. He couldn't drive, and his goddamn car was probably towed by now. He didn't know anyone else he could ask for a ride, and he couldn't even call a cab and bail on it without paying the fare—not hobbling at his speed.

You're stranded. Learn to take help when it's offered. Maybe you wouldn't be here if you'd done that.

Ash winced and nodded. "Yeah. Thanks."

"No problem." Chris's smile was gentle now before he looked back at the doctor. "So, what do we need to know?"

In a few sentences, the doctor filled him in on Ash's condition—the soft tissue injuries, the bruised rib, facial lacerations (and thank God he had those bandages off now so he didn't look like The Mummy), and worst of all, the open fracture and surgery. Open fractures were nasty—when bone jutted out through skin.

Chris took in everything, nodding a lot as he intently watched the doctor. "So basically, rest up a lot."

"That's the key. We gave him a prescription for some limited pain medication, but he's handling the pain well."

Chris shot Ash a look and Ash rolled his eyes. *Yeah, and they think I'm a junkie.*

"Well, what if the pain doesn't get better? You'll renew his prescription?"

"We'll evaluate his condition in our follow-ups," the doctor promised, but already, he was taking Chris more seriously than he'd taken Ash.

Typical. Whatever.

Chris had sensed that and was sitting up straighter, his jaw firm. "Right. How often are these evaluations? And how long is the prescription?"

"I want to see him in a week, and we've given him a week's worth of Vicodin."

Chris nodded. "Right. Next Friday? Okay." Chris looked back at Ash. "That's fine, right?"

Ash nodded, dumbfounded. It had been so long since anyone took over for him or spoke up for him that he didn't really know what to do.

"Now, I'm assuming he's going to be resting lots, right? How long in the cast?"

"Four weeks at least. I'll get the nurse to give you a care sheet with instructions. He can take a bath today as long as you're careful to keep that leg out of water, or sponge baths."

"When can he shower? Not until the cast is off, right?"

E. DAVIES

"Not yet. That'll be on the care sheet. And there's one important thing I've already discussed with him—he can't rest all the time, either," Dr. Green told Chris, like Ash wasn't even there. "There are risks associated with that. He has to work on strengthening the muscles in his legs as they recover from surgery and damage, respectively."

Chris nodded. "Makes sense. I won't let him loaf around," he promised with a cheeky smile at Ash.

I can't stop smiling. Ash was pretty sure he was blushing, too, as he nodded once at Chris.

Thank God Chris was buffering him this time. The first conversation with Dr. Green hadn't even been five minutes long, and Dr. Green had brushed off his questions about painkillers before leaving the room. He should have known better than to ask about them first.

But Chris was bulldozing through the important stuff. "So, he's free to go now?"

"Yes, you are." Dr. Green finally looked back at Ash. "It's been a pleasure. We'll see you on Friday—the receptionist will call you with your appointment time for the follow-up."

"Thank you, sir." Ash leaned forward to shake hands, and Dr. Green shook firmly before raising his hand in a slight wave and striding out of the room.

"Well. That was easy," Chris commented once he was gone, smiling at him. "You got anything to bring?"

Ash shook his head. He had his phone, wallet, and keys in one shallow pocket of his hospital clothing. The rest of his clothes were gone—bloody or cut off.

The hospital-issued thin cotton shirt and pants that he'd graduated to wearing the day after surgery and these hard plastic crutches were all he had. It was a weird thought to send an involuntary shudder of anxiety through him, but there it was —a tightness in his chest as he eased himself to his feet.

48

"Hey, no chocolates to carry around," Chris commented, picking up the card he'd left and pocketing it. "I see you followed my dosage instructions."

Ash managed a smile.

Chris punched his arm lightly enough that he didn't sway. "You're getting out of this place, at least. That's worth a smile."

"See? Incorrigible optimist," Ash said with a light smile. He did appreciate Chris's attempts to cheer him up, at least. "Let's go."

Chris strolled next to him, hands tucked in his pockets, as he slowly swung his way down the hallway.

Ash was a little disappointed not to catch sight of Julie on the way out. When he caught himself thinking that, he chuckled to himself. *What the hell? I don't like people. I just appreciate... what she did.* Apparently, Ash had to remember to be grumpy around Chris.

"Hm?"

"Nothing. Lead on."

As Chris held the door for him, warm air rushed over Ash, and he breathed out a sigh of relief.

Chris was right: at least he was getting out.

8

ASH

They made it to the pharmacy to fill the script and *almost* to Ash's house before Ash couldn't hold his tongue. He had to warn Chris now, before Chris thought he was bringing him to some shack to harvest his organs. "My place is kinda... run-down. Sorry."

"What? You don't gotta apologize," Chris told him simply, glancing over at him from the driver's side.

Getting him settled into the car had taken a few minutes and some fiddling with the seat position, but now he was so comfy he almost didn't want to move. Still, the anxiety rose into his chest from what Chris would think of it.

"But you don't have stairs, right?" Chris followed up, furrowing his brows.

"There's steps up to the porch. And a few boards to avoid. I'll point them out."

Chris eyed him, his lips quirking into a smile. "Right."

"And the driveway... fuck. That's right, my car." Ash thumped his head against the back of his seat. "Park wherever you like in the driveway, then."

"Don't worry about your car. I'll figure out a way to pick it up for you," Chris told him.

Gravity pushed Ash back in the seat as Chris's car climbed the hills.

"Fucking hell. I can see why you weren't walking home," Chris snorted. "You could have jumped down the hill, you know."

Ash wasn't sure whether to be mortified or amused, so his cheeks flushed scarlet as a laugh escaped. "Dude, you don't... you can't just say that."

"Why not?" Chris grinned at him, then cleared his throat. "Unless it bothers you, I mean..."

Ash had no idea how to wrap his brain around his new friend. Chris seemed so easygoing, like nothing was off-limits. It normally made him uneasy, but it wasn't coming from a place of malice with this guy.

Chris was honestly just... that open. That explained the detailed history of his sexuality he'd given before managing to shut himself up. That was the only time so far that Chris had really looked embarrassed.

"Not really. I just..." Ash trailed off, chuckling quietly. He changed the subject to a more pressing question: "Why are you doing all this? Left, around this corner."

Chris blew out a quiet sigh and flicked his signal on. "It sounds lame if I say I don't have any hobbies, right? And it just feels like the right thing to do."

"I'm a hobby now?" Ash laughed, scrunching his nose. He wasn't sure whether to feel objectified or flattered.

Before this week, he would have doubted anyone did the right thing just for the sake of it, but he could almost believe it from Chris.

Or maybe he just wanted his dick sucked, which Ash wouldn't complain about. Chris *was* pretty fucking hot.

"No!" Chris laughed. "I mean, not really. Um. I just... I don't know. It's not like I have anything else on the go... you know, boyfriends, friends outside work..."

"You're lonely, too," Ash surmised.

"Ouch. Don't hold back."

"You say to the guy who lives alone in the hills, growling at neighbors who get too close."

Chris eyed him to make sure that was a joke, then snorted. "Noted. I can put a leash on you if you like."

"Ooh, I'm not sure we know each other *that* well," Ash smirked.

Chris opened his mouth, then seemed to change his mind on what he was about to say. Instead, he laughed. "Around here somewhere, right?" His phone was telling him they were arriving at their destination.

"Two more houses, actually. The crappier one."

As they pulled up into Ash's driveway, Chris's eyes narrowed. He pulled the parking brake and shook his head. "I'm gonna say your landlord is straight outta some TV show."

"Yeah, he's... not great," Ash admitted, gazing up at his house. The scorch marks were mostly confined to the back of the building, but there was still plywood on the outside, and the roof was partly covered in a tarp. It worked well enough, and they didn't get enough rain that he'd seen it as a problem.

"We lost this place in the Jesusita fire."

We was a weird word to use, unless... A shiver ran down Ash's spine. "You were involved?"

"Of course. Pretty much everyone in the area was." Chris got out of the car and shut the door, heading around the other side.

It had been a massive fire, ripping down through the canyon. Dozens of homes lost, as far as Ash knew, though most had been rebuilt by now. Those not owned by shitty landlords.

"Wow." Ash waited for Chris to pull the door open and hand him his crutches, then carefully levered himself up to his feet with Chris's hand below his arm as extra support. He winced the whole time until he was more or less balanced.

"Dude. Okay, it's your choice, but I'm not going to leave you to recover in a place like this where you can't even get out of the house." Chris's voice was firm as he reached into the seat to grab his keys, which had fallen out of his pants pocket. "I have a guest suite on the ground floor of my house, my place is half-empty all the time, and... man, you need company."

Ash couldn't disagree with any of his points, but all he'd concede to before Chris actually saw the place was, "You might have a point."

He pretended not to see Chris's glare as he hobbled up to his front porch.

As his crutch hit the board he was trying to avoid and he heard a distinctive *snap*, all the energy Ash had left went into a sigh. He was on his ass before he knew it.

Damn it.

9

CHRIS

"Dude, you *broke* your porch."

Ash was clearly trying to pretend he was better-off than he really was, but Chris wasn't going to let it go.

"It was just from the pressure of my crutch, and whatever," Ash mumbled, leaning on the side of the house now as Chris stepped around the hole and took the keys from him. "You gotta hip-check the door open."

"Mmm." Chris gave him another pointed look, and Ash looked away and laughed.

"Okay, I do see your point," Ash admitted.

"Good." Chris jiggled the knob and pushed his shoulder into the door until it unstuck. "We'll get your stuff, though."

It wasn't *that* bad inside—he'd seen worse. Only in condemned houses, but still. There wasn't a thin layer of mold all over everything, and the place had intact floors and a ceiling. It looked like someone's temporary home while they were building a real house, but Chris didn't want to rub it in.

How the hell does someone live here and not *get depressed? Even if everything else is going well?*

Chris hung back to let Ash lead the way as he clunked his way into the house.

"My schedule's pretty weird," Chris spoke up. "Two on, four off, 'round the clock."

"Fine with me. You could give me your shed to live in and I'd be glad," Ash laughed quietly. "Um, can you help me pack? Sorry."

"Of course, man." Chris didn't stop to think how weird his life had gotten that he'd made a new friend, offered him a room, and was now gonna be touching his underwear. He just followed Ash into the bedroom in the corner of the cabin—er, house—and grabbed the duffel bag Ash pointed out.

He shoved as much stuff as he could fit in there—t-shirts, sweatpants and his loosest two pairs of jeans, socks and underwear, a sweater, some shorts, a bit of everything.

Then he took a look around the bathroom and grabbed everything that looked relevant from there, too.

"Anything else? No pets?"

"Nah," Ash chuckled from where he sat on the couch. "Thanks again. I mean, just... thanks."

Chris held up a hand. "Okay, no more thanks," he grinned at Ash. "You'll get my ego too big to fit through the doors." He really didn't want Ash thinking he pitied him or something. Even if he did, just a little bit.

They made it out to the car with much less incident than the way in, avoiding the hole in the porch. "You know, man, we could go after the landlord," Chris suggested.

Ash winced. "I can't afford anywhere else, so."

"Really?" Chris was determined now. "I guarantee my rent will be cheaper, as long as you cook sometimes."

As he settled Ash into the passenger seat, Ash grabbed his arm again. "You... You're sure about this?"

Chris leaned on the side of the car, fiddling with the crutches. "Why wouldn't I be?"

Ash's gaze flickered between his eyes, like he was choosing his words carefully. "You're... I'm not used to people being nice to me for no reason."

Ah. Chris nodded slowly. "Right."

"And I just... I don't want to promise you anything that I can't—" Ash started.

"No, no, man. This is not a sugar daddy thing." Chris held up his hands, then opened the back door to toss the crutches inside before leaning on it to shut it again. "This is... if my buddies were in a tight spot, I'd want someone to help them out, too. I promise."

Ash relaxed again and nodded. "I'm sorry. I don't want to accuse you, or anything..."

Who the fuck hurt him? If I ever find out... Chris pushed aside the protective instincts that were rising in him and just offered a gentle smile. "No, it's cool. I get it. We're good?"

"Just let me say it one more time," Ash started.

Chris groaned and leaned away, slowly closing the door while he scrunched his nose. "If you have to..."

"Thank you," Ash managed over his laughter before Chris shut the door.

Chris grinned through the windshield at him and headed to the driver's side. By the time he climbed in, Ash was looking... dare he think it, *excited.*

Damn straight he should be excited. Chris was gonna make his recovery as easy as he could.

And that conversation had made it clear: absolutely no hitting on Ash.

10

ASH

It was practically a mansion: a cute little square house in a cute little suburban neighborhood. "Damn, man," Ash murmured as they pulled up outside Chris's house. He'd never lived anywhere this nice.

Chris glanced over, and it was his turn to look nervous. "It's not a big place, I know, but the guest suite is pretty big—"

"No," Ash interrupted with a laugh. "It's big." Despite himself, the innuendo won over his momentary insecurity, and he snickered.

Chris broke out laughing, too, and swatted his arm. "You're terrible. Okay, stay there."

Ash didn't need to be told twice. He pushed open the car door and patiently waited for Chris to come bring him his crutches.

When Chris pulled the car door open, he mock-bowed and curtsied at the same time, nearly tripping against the car. "At your service, sir."

Ash snorted with laughter as he slowly peeled himself out of the car seat and draped himself on his crutches. "Dumbass."

"You say that like you're not laughing." Chris winked. He grabbed the duffel bag of Ash's stuff and shut the car door, then stuck by him as they made their way up the driveway.

Ash's face was taut with amusement, but also pain. The painkillers were wearing off.

Quieter this time, Chris said, "Hey, you doing all right?"

"I'll make it," Ash answered, trying to keep his voice even. He'd been aching all through even the brief rest in the car, but moving around made him feel like all his bones were going to jiggle out of place.

He still felt like he'd gotten hit by a truck... and to be fair, his injuries agreed. Even his "good" leg was still unable to bear weight for too long, making the steps up onto the porch awkward.

"We'll get you inside, get some painkillers into you," Chris promised.

Ash was too worn out by the pain to give the cheeky comment he normally might have. Instead, he waited as Chris unlocked the door and held it open for him.

Then, Chris even offered him a hand, guiding him down to sit on the stairs while he got his shoes off.

When Ash got his shoes off, he put them aside and drew a deep breath. He could finally focus on something other than the awkward complexity of his own half-usable limbs.

"Want to get settled in bed or on the couch? Or use the bathroom? I saw you have bathing instructions..." Chris trailed off at Ash's look.

Ash laughed and shook his head slightly. Chris was a bit like an overgrown puppy, all eager to please, but with his heart on his sleeve. It was hard for even Ash to suspect him of having ulterior motives. "Just painkillers, one way or another."

"Let's get you on the couch, then," Chris decided and leaned down. He had his arm halfway around Ash's shoulders, his broad chest filling up Ash's frame of vision, his fresh, cool scent tingling his nose, before he paused. "You don't mind this, do you?"

Ash laughed faintly, trying not to betray the way his heart skipped a beat. Totally skipped a beat.

Fuck.

He did *not* have a thing for the burly firefighter who was taking care of him every step of the way. And he wasn't going to get one now.

"Yeah, no," Ash murmured. "I mean, I don't mind. Thanks for not, like... ditching me and running."

Chris laughed shortly and slid his arm around Ash's back to help ease him to his feet while Ash grabbed his crutches. "Of course. I don't mind."

"I think the nurses thought you were crazy for taking me," Ash added, focusing on planting his crutches solidly and swinging his weight. One of these days, he'd get the trick of it.

"Nurses are crazy anyway, man," Chris grinned easily, distracting him from his moping. "You should hear my stories. Only people crazier are EMTs."

"Oh yeah?" Ash, despite himself, smiled again as Chris helped him settle into the corner of his comfy sectional couch. It was a cute living room, with an overstuffed armchair, a flat-screen TV, and a gorgeous open-plan layout into the spacious, sunlit kitchen.

It just felt peaceful here. Oddly like his parents' house once had. Or maybe that was because it was somewhere totally new to him, and he was desperately reaching out for the familiar.

"Mmm," Chris nodded emphatically. "They have the darkest sense of humor, though, Jesus. But they're solid." Satisfied with the way Ash was settled, he nodded once and strode for the kitchen. "Coffee? Tea? Juice? Milk? Water? Oh, and I have pop—"

"Water first, please," Ash laughed. He was getting more of a sense for Chris. He was probably the kind of guy who was buddy-buddy with everyone. "Then you can give me the full menu."

"Right. Good idea."

Within a minute, Chris was out with pills in his palm and a glass of water in the other. "Right. I have a timer set on my phone for your next dose, if you're not asleep by then."

Ash took the pills and swallowed them, then kept the glass of water cradled against his chest as he nodded. "Thank you."

"Oh, stop thanking me for any little thing," Chris laughed. "I was bored anyway. You know, little cookie-cutter suburb... everyone's married off, has kids and their own little cookie-cutter life..."

Ash raised his brow. "So I'm a project." He kept a straight face.

"Oh, God, no." Chris turned red as he dropped onto the couch next to Ash and waved his hands. "Not at all! I mean, it's no trouble helping out..."

Ash couldn't repress his laugh at the sight of Chris's face. He really *did* show it all. "No, I was teasing. I don't mind being a project anyway. God knows I *am* one."

"I don't think so," Chris frowned, rubbing his hand down his face and settling back. "We've all got our own issues, right? There's no such thing as being a project."

"I am, though. I'm... a project to myself," Ash said with a slight smile. "I'm working on it. I'm gonna get a job, whatever... I can get now... and start thinking about the future properly. I won't waste this chance."

Chris frowned slightly and nodded. "Okay. But you're not earning the right to be here or anything. You're enough as you are."

And he's sweet, too. Of course. The full package deal. It's gonna be really fucking hard to live with him.

Ash didn't really know how to answer, but he smiled and shifted to squeeze Chris's shoulder. "Thanks, man."

"Anytime, man." Chris flashed him a bright smile and nodded at the TV. "Want to watch something?"

"God, yes. I've seen fish-finder screens bigger than my hospital room TV."

Chris laughed as he turned on the TV. "Oh my God. You're not a sport fisher, are you?"

"No," Ash shuddered. "One of my exes was. The rich one. God, I dunno why I dumped him. I could be in a helicopter sipping martinis right now. Well, probably not both at once."

"Oh yeah?" Chris laughed. "Not the most recent one with the drugs and things? Coke or whatever seems like a terrible combination with helicopters."

Ash shook his head. "Nah. I've made a wide range of creative poor choices in my life."

"Noted." Chris grinned and kicked back, flipping through the channels. "Medical drama?"

That was a teasing grin on his face. Ash rolled his eyes. "Oh, fuck off. Game show."

"Ewww. You're a daytime TV fan." Chris tossed the remote to him like it had germs.

Ash managed to catch it, wincing as he laughed. "Not normally." The car commercial that started made him wince again, harder. "Oh, shit."

"Your car... you mentioned it," Chris said, sitting up straight again and intuiting what was bothering him.

Ash nodded slightly. "Um, I hate to ask..."

"I'll pick it up or whatever, sure." Chris looked as eager as a dog who'd just been told he was going for a walk. "Hopefully it's not towed. I'll sort that all out."

God, Ash was lucky. Ironically, it had taken hitting absolute rock-bottom before he landed this one good thing—a man who seemed determined to help him through this first stage of recovery. "If you wouldn't mind." He let out a breath of relief, then looked over at his jacket. "My keys are over there with my wallet."

"Of course." Chris was halfway to slapping Ash's knee before he jerked his hand back like he'd touched a hot stove. "Shit! Gotta remember that," he scolded himself and launched up to his feet.

Ash couldn't remember laughing so deeply in... forever. "If you slip up on my sliced-up knee, I *will* punch you," he warned. "It's only a slap for the other one."

"Noted." Chris winked and headed across the room to grab his keys. "These ones?"

"That's the one. When you drive... oh, you'll figure it out," Ash waved him off.

Chris laughed. "Is there a hole in the floor there, too?"

"Not yet. It just pulls to the right. But don't climb in too hard, just in case."

"Reassuring." Chris grinned, but it wasn't a tease at him for having a piece-of-shit car and house. It was the kind of light humor he seemed to treat everything in life with.

Ash relaxed again and smiled. Sleep tugged at the corners of his eyes as he felt the painkillers kicking in. "Thanks."

"No more thanking me, or I *will* go for the knees," Chris warned, and when he bent over to slide his shoes on, it took all Ash had *not* to sneak a glance.

Just because the man had a nice ass didn't mean he had to look to make sure it hadn't gone anywhere.

"You gotta give me some other way to thank you, then," Ash laughed. Shit. Had he just come on to him?

"We'll figure that out when you're not half-dead," Chris waved it off. "Casserole or something, I don't care."

"I can make a mean tuna noodle casserole."

Chris lit up. "See? I knew I chose right. Well, not that I make a habit of plucking men out of their hospital rooms and bringing them home..." He disappeared into the foyer.

Ash gravely shook his head. "The louder he talked of his honor, the faster I counted my silverware."

Chris's laugh echoed through the hallway, followed by the click and swish of the front door opening. "See you in a bit, man."

"See you," Ash answered.

Once the door was closed, he was fully aware of the comforting, tingling numbness setting into his bones again. It took no time at all before he was fast asleep.

11

CHRIS

"There it is."

Chris sagged against the half-wall next to him with relief at the sight of a beaten-up red station wagon. It matched Ash's description of his car.

After squeezing his own car behind Liam's on the side street next to the yarn store, Chris had walked up toward the hotel. He'd taken a side street to avoid the spot where he'd found Ash.

It was still too weird to think about that stretch of pavement, probably all bleached and with the crack mended. Wouldn't want the tourists scared off, after all.

Good god, the parking ticket had to be insane after a few days. He wished he'd thought of coming here to move the damn thing earlier. He'd take care of it.

He dialed, and to his relief, Ash answered his phone after one ring. "Hey, did you find it?"

"I did. It's the license plate with the little tree, isn't it?"

"Yep, that's mine. Oh, thank God." His voice sounded murky, probably with sleep. Cute.

Chris smiled. "Great. I'm just gonna talk to Liam first to leave my keys with him, and then I'll drive yours home. Need anything while I'm out?"

"Nah. The Vicodin's kicked in. I gotta sleep, man. Than—I mean, uh."

Chris laughed gently. "Okay, get some rest. See you soon." He hung up and strode back toward the craft store.

In the month since Dylan had moved in with Liam to share their cute little studio apartment, they'd been inseparable. Still, Dylan was cool.

Chris didn't begrudge Liam's decrease in spare time. He needed someone to be around, and at least he'd found someone cool.

Meanwhile, Chris had fumbled around dating everyone under the sun and he'd never clicked with any one of them... except his ex. And Davey was bad for him—he knew that.

He stopped by the craft store first to check if they were there. Dylan worked there, which was how they'd met in the first place—from what Liam would tell him, anyway.

"Morning," he greeted the proprietor, Velma. She was older and no-nonsense, but she had a wicked streak of humor that Chris liked. He hadn't spent much time around her directly, but he *had* visited the PTSD knitting circle just once on Liam's invitation. It had been an overwhelming one session in which he'd failed at knitting.

"Hi, darling. Here to see Liam, or are you picking me up?" Vee winked.

Chris grinned and winked. "Oh, not so loud, Vee. He can never find out about us."

"On my heart," Vee solemnly told him, then jerked her head toward the stairs. "Dylan's off today, so they might be upstairs... innocently knitting." She raised her eyebrows meaningfully. "I'm sure that's happened now and then."

"Not likely. I'll take my chances," Chris laughed. "Thanks."

"Any time, gorgeous."

Chris ducked into the narrow hallway through the side door in the shop and headed up the stairs toward the apartment door. He knocked and waited.

Liam opened the door to him. "Oh, hey!" He was in casual jeans and a t-shirt, at least, so it looked like Chris hadn't interrupted anything. Liam patted his pocket for his phone.

"I didn't text," Chris admitted with a smile. "Sorry. I was in the area."

"No worries. Wanna come in?"

"Just for a minute. I gotta get back to him."

Liam's brows rose, and Dylan made a sound of intrigue from somewhere behind him.

"You should definitely come in," Dylan called out.

Chris laughed and followed Liam inside, taking a moment to admire the gorgeous, flowing space. Somehow, in the few weeks since Dylan had moved in, the space had become so much less of a bachelor pad and more of a homey couples' place.

Maybe it was the hand-knitted coasters.

Chris stifled his snort as he dropped into a chair at the table and poked at it. Liam glared at him, and Chris raised his hands. "Sorry. Seeing you nest never gets old."

"Way to change the subject," Dylan smirked. He trotted over to the table and pulled up a chair. "So, I hear there's a guy."

Chris looked at Liam, who raised his shoulders in a sheepish shrug. "Fine, yeah. There's a guy. Sort of. Not that way," Chris scolded Dylan as he started to grin.

"Another guy?" Liam teased. "This is totally the guy in the hospital, isn't it? Uh... Ash?"

Chris drew a breath. "Yes. Actually... he's in my guest suite now."

Both Dylan and Liam stared at him for a second. Then, Liam stifled his laugh with a cough.

"Shut up," Chris groaned. "He needed a place to go."

"His own home wouldn't work?"

"No. He's in this slum... I shouldn't say that," Chris rolled his eyes. "But it's as good as."

Liam had stopped laughing. He was leaning forward, looking concerned. "Oh, shit. Really?"

"Yep. I was only gonna drive him home since his car was parked down here—which is why I'm here now—but then I saw where he lived. And you know I've got that guest room..."

Dylan and Liam both nodded. "Neat," Dylan smiled at him. "So, you decided to just take him in? Do you really know the guy?"

"Um..." Chris shook his head. "But I have a good feeling about him."

"Like you did the guy you went to coffee with last week?"

"Which o—" Chris winced. "Ah. Good point." He'd forgotten about both his most recent dates pretty much as fast as he'd gone on first dates with them. As far as he was concerned, it was always worth a first date, but the second one was the real test. "No, there's nothing going on between us."

And there it was: the word *yet* had almost slipped out.

It took him a second to wrap his brain around that fact. Liam was talking, and he quickly focused on him.

"—be careful, is all. You don't *have* to look after him just because you were the first responder."

"No, I know," Chris assured him. "It's not that kind of attachment. He's just cool to hang out with, and he needs a hand getting around. I have a spare room."

Liam and Dylan looked less worried with his reassurance,

relaxing back into their seats. "So, what's the damage?" Liam asked.

Chris winced. "Um... I think he had surgery on one leg a few days ago. Soft tissue injuries on the other. There's some rib bruising, and his face got torn up, and... I think that was about it? I have to go over his paperwork."

Liam looked amused. "And how long is he sticking around?"

"At least until he can drive. He lives up past the canyon, right in the burn zone. His neighbors aren't really friendly. If he can't drive..."

"He'd be stuck there," Dylan concluded with a nod. "Smart."

The way Liam watched Chris told him that he understood the other implication: with no neighbors to help him out, in case of another fire, he'd be helpless. Sure, it was a long shot, but to guys like Chris and Liam who saw fires break out every shift... it was a very real possibility.

"And, honestly, the company would be nice," Chris added after a moment.

That was as sappy as he was going to get, but of course Liam picked up on it. "Awww. Do I need to order you a singing telegram?"

"Fuck off," Chris laughed and rose to his feet. "He's probably passed out on the couch on Vicodin now. I should go make sure he's all right."

"Good luck. You're gonna let us know when the two of you are a thing, right?" Liam was smirking mischievously as he accompanied him to the door.

Despite himself, Chris's cheeks flushed red. He *never* blushed. What the hell?

"Aww. Remember what a dick he was when we were just

starting to date?" Dylan grinned. "He can dish it but he can't take it..."

Chris flipped Dylan off. "Bye, losers. Liam, my man, I need you to pick me up in my car for work on Tuesday." He tossed Liam the keys to his car. It was far from the first time they'd shared cars. They wound up in all kinds of weird situations swapping and sharing rides. "Don't scratch it up."

"Sure, I'll try not to. Bye, man." Liam caught the keys, still laughing as he pulled open the apartment door and clapped Chris's shoulder. "Good luck with the patient." His voice was warm, and it made Chris smile anyway.

"Thanks. See you Tuesday."

It was an awfully warm September day, which was definitely the only reason Chris's cheeks still felt hot as he stepped onto the street and briskly strode for Ash's car.

Whatever surprises that old rust bucket had in store, at least it wouldn't tease him as badly as those two did.

They were right, though. He'd earned every bit of it by embarrassing them both. Now, it was coming back to bite him, and he really should be grateful it was just teasing words and not a bucket of water or a fake spider on his back or something.

"Dicks," he mumbled under his breath. But Chris was still smiling even as he walked by the unremarkable patch of sidewalk where his life had changed just a few short days ago.

12

ASH

It took Ash three tries to wake up. Every time he stirred, the most comfortable bed he could imagine caressed him, and the rustling sheets whispered ideas to him about going back to sleep, so he did.

The third time, though, the bone-deep ache couldn't be ignored. Ash groaned as he rolled onto his back, then slowly pushed himself up against the headboard.

His ribs were feeling better, so breathing was no longer painful, but sitting up was such a damn chore. At least he hadn't seriously bruised or torn anything there.

It was funny—in a matter of days, he'd gone from wishing he'd finished the job to being glad he'd gotten off so lightly. What had changed?

He had no time to sit around navel-gazing, though. He had to get up and eat, and get medicine, and he wasn't even entirely sure whether Chris would be at work or not. He had to ask what his work schedule was like.

It took him a moment to realize that Chris was giving him a reason to get out of bed.

There was an en-suite bathroom attached to the guest room, a small mercy that he was endlessly thankful for.

Pain shot through his torso, down to his hip, then down his whole leg as he shifted the blankets off himself. God, he was a wreck. Thankfully, there was a dresser close enough to the bed that he could grab it, and then it was only one or two steps to the doorframe.

Ash glanced at himself in the mirror, and for once, he didn't have that moment where he stared at himself and tried to find *himself* behind his eyes. Instead, he was all action, focusing on what he had to do: get clean.

Bathing took some effort, since his dressings weren't supposed to come off for another few days. He had to sit on the edge of the tub, soap up, and scrub off his body one piece at a time, keeping his bad leg out of the tub. Well, worse leg.

Even once he'd finished that chore and hobbled back to the bedroom, clutching the counter, doorframe, and dresser the whole time, he still faced the prospect of getting dressed.

Ash was still too stiff to easily bend and he didn't want to move one leg more than necessary. He gave up and flopped onto his back when he was tired of trying to pull his jeans around his feet without bending his knees.

"Fucking jeeeeans."

He flipped them off for good measure.

There was a knock on the door, making him lurch and almost roll off the bed. "Hey. You up?" Chris's voice slipped under the door.

"Yes, just getting dressed. I'll be out whenever my jeans decide to, like, work."

Chris laughed in that same easy roll of his voice. "Need a hand?"

"Nah." Ash was blushing—he could feel his cheeks burning. And it wasn't just embarrassment because he was so damn helpless.

"Okay. Breakfast's ready." Chris's voice faded like he was walking away.

"Thanks." Ash thumped his forehead with his palm. He *really* wanted a hand.

No. Behave, he scolded himself. He wasn't going to hit on Chris and ruin the one good thing he had going.

Not that it seemed like Chris would object. He was totally the kind of guy who got hit on all the time. Not like Ash, in the *I bet he's desperate enough to say yes* way, but the *look at that hot firefighter, I wish he'd just look at me* way.

Fuck. He wasn't jealous, was he?

Ash mumbled under his breath as he rolled onto his side to pull his jeans on one foot at a time, wiggling them gradually up his shins until he got past his knees. It was easier than to pull them up and zip up.

He did a quick double-check before that final move, just in case. Last thing he needed to lose was that.

Nope, he could keep it in his pants.

Before he left the room, Ash stole one more glance around. Chris's place was so *nice.* So warm and comfy and middle-class. The living room was a bit bachelor pad-esque, but this room was cozy, at least. All he needed was a fluffy comforter, soft mattress, and a nice bright en-suite.

He balanced himself on his crutches, awkwardly tugging the comforter over the bed to make it before hobbling out to join Chris in the kitchen. At least his less-bad knee was hurting less today than it had for the last few days.

"Hey!" Chris greeted, beaming at him. He was wearing the kind of thin, silky cotton t-shirt that clung to every goddamn muscle and bone in his body. It was nigh-impossible for Ash to drag his gaze up from the curve of his bicep and pec to his face as Chris looked at him, but somehow, he managed.

"Hey," Ash answered weakly.

Thank God Chris mistook it for pain. Hell, that *was* probably part of the dizzying feeling that swept through him, so he'd take the excuse. "Oh man, sit down," Chris urged him. "I made scrambled eggs and toast and bacon. Are you vegetarian? I hope not. I mean, it's cool if you are. But."

"I'm not," Ash laughed quietly. No way could he afford that. "Th—I appreciate you thinking of me."

Oh, man. The scrambled eggs smelled *divine*. And bacon on top of that, and the crispiness of perfectly browned toast.

The hospital food hadn't been terrible, but it sure as hell hadn't been home cooked breakfast. When was the last time someone had cooked him breakfast, anyway?

"No problem." Chris helped him sink into a chair, and Ash steadfastly ignored the creeping disappointment that tingled through his body when Chris let go of his bicep. "And to drink? I assume you remember the menu."

"Whatever you're having."

"Orange juice it is." Chris balanced two plates and served them with a swish, then followed them up with glasses of juice. He looked like he was having the time of his life, so Ash didn't dare thank him any more.

Chris seemed to be telling the truth that he really *did* just want to help Ash out. It was harder and harder not to believe Chris when he seemed to take such joy in helping. He was definitely one of those guys who became a firefighter to save people.

Ash wished he were that good a man.

"Oops, and the Sunday paper. I love the comics." Chris was up and out of his chair before he even sat down, trotting to the front door.

Ash laughed under his breath. How much damn energy did he have? As he dug into the scrambled eggs, Chris's phone went off not once, but three times in a row.

He wouldn't have peeked ordinarily, but that was enough to draw his eyes to the phone. Just before the screen went black, he saw a few words he recognized even upside-down.

Text me baby.

He didn't see the other two messages—they were longer—but he didn't need to. Suddenly, Ash had the sneaking suspicion he was the distraction.

Oh, boy. Chris has his own issues, doesn't he?

He smiled up at Chris when he brought back the paper, letting him grab the comics section first. While Chris read through them, Ash ate his breakfast and skimmed the job ads section, just on impulse.

These days, there was nothing useful there. Sometimes there were odd job ads, but almost everything wanted applicants to apply online, and that always involved bizarre multiple-choice questionnaires and resumé-scanning software looking for keywords and stuff.

Chris shoved the comics at him and choked with laughter on his eggs. "Look at the dog cartoon."

It broke Ash out of his train of thought, and he reluctantly skimmed the page.

He had to admit the comic *was* funny.

Chris did that twice more before Ash laughed under his breath. He was doing it deliberately.

"If you want me mooching instead of job-hunting..."

Chris raised his hands. "Hey, by all means, job-hunt. But only if you'll be relaxed and stress-free while you do it, and that little eyebrow thing you keep doing..."

Ash was totally red. He resisted the urge to look around for his reflection to confirm that. "I do?"

"Yeah. Don't stress out, man. Nobody has ever, as long as I've lived in this place, stayed in my guest suite more than one night. And even that was just Liam a few times, but he has a *boyfriend* to get back to now." Chris rolled his eyes and laughed.

Ash's curiosity was truly piqued. "And you don't? Are you jealous?"

Chris shook his head. "Hell, no. I mean, boyfriends are nice. Just... I can't seem to find one, so I'm not deliberately looking."

"Smart," Ash murmured, smiling at him. "You'll find one."

"Oh, yeah. Sometime. I'll keep going on dates, and sooner or later it'll click," Chris said with the kind of brazen, confident air Ash could almost remember.

God, he'd been just seventeen when he first came out, and he'd been so optimistic then that he'd find someone to spend his life with within three years. It had all been part of his life plan.

To hell with that plan now.

"Don't do the eyebrow thing."

"I'm not!" Ash protested and laughed. "I just wish I had that kind of... confidence."

Chris nodded. "We'll work on it together if you want. Get you set up with a nice man."

"My God." Ash was still laughing, though. "Everything is a project for you. I... I miss that, too."

Chris shook his head. "Try living with me for a few weeks. You'll be ready to go take over the world to get away from me sooner or later."

"You're that bad a roommate? 'Cause dude, so far..." Ash gestured around as if to say *What's the problem?*

"That's 'cause I'm playing nice. So far."

Ash raised his brow.

"I'm kind of a... prankster."

Ash groaned as the understanding hit him. "Ahhh. Salt in my coffee..."

"...snakes in your bed..."

"*What?* Dude, if you put a snake in my bed—"

"Hypothetical!" Chris protested, looking innocent. "I dunno what you're like. I would never subject a snake to that."

"Oooh." The burn made Ash laugh, not feel bad about himself. *This* was the kind of humor that RJ had pretended he was using. "Fine, but man, if you're gonna do that, use a rubber snake. A boa is the last thing I need constricting *any* part of me. Rubber stretches. Safety first."

It took Chris a few long seconds to get it, and then he burst out laughing. "Dude!"

"What?" Ash grinned. He pushed his plate back and arranged his utensils. If he was going to reference cock rings, he was going to be completely unashamed.

"You can give as good as you get. Maybe we'll be good," Chris grinned.

It hit Ash just then: his painkillers had kicked in, his belly was full, and he was smiling.

Chris was a fucking *genius*. He should be a therapist or something, not a firefighter. Maybe a life coach.

"Okay, I'll stop saying it," Ash raised his hand to cut off Chris's protests, "but I really appreciate all of this."

"No problem." Chris gave him a warm smile. "It's great to see you coming around."

Ash drew a deep breath and let it out, then nodded. No way could he go into detail about how much his life had sucked —still did suck, aside from this nice little vacation from reality.

He wasn't gonna ruin the mood by bringing all that shit up. Chris really didn't need to hear it.

"So, the doctor wants you walking..." Chris rubbed his hands together with a wicked smile.

"Oh, I changed my mind." Ash groaned. "I don't like you at all."

"Just around the block once... or twice."

"How big is it?" The sentence had barely left Ash's lips before he grinned broadly, unable to resist the extra innuendo. "I could go by myself..."

Chris winked. "Guess you'll just have to find out. And nah, you could cheat that way. Besides, it's more fun with two."

"This isn't gonna be boring for you?"

"Nope! I'm off until Tuesday morning at eight. That gives me all day today and tomorrow to do absolutely nothing," Chris told him, waggling his brows. "No escaping this, mister."

Damn it. Ash was curious, too—in both ways. He grinned and grabbed his crutches to ease himself to his feet.

"Fine... lead on."

13

CHRIS

"Can you do sick stunts yet?"

Ash's laugh was as magical as ever, sharply cracking down the quiet suburban street like he was shattering their peace for a moment.

Good. They deserved a little shake-up.

"I'm lucky to be walking at all!" Ash protested.

They were walking slowly, heading down the sidewalk first before they looped back around the trail that ran behind Chris's backyard. Ash seemed to have the rhythm of swinging himself along now in a kind of one-two step. It was almost hypnotic to watch. Or maybe that was just because it was Ash.

"So no taking out robbers with your crutches yet... pole-vaulting over tall buildings in a single leap..." Chris frowned in disappointment.

"I'll work on it."

The weather was the perfect temperature, since it was mid-September—not too hot or cold. It wasn't even noon yet, so the heat still had time to creep in, but the sunshine and mild heat seemed to be improving Ash's spirits even further.

Chris bounced on his toes with every step, trying to keep them slow enough for Ash to easily keep up. *I really should get outside and walk more, just because.* He said just that a moment later.

"At least I'll save my pennies."

"What?"

"You say everything that comes to mind," Ash laughed, his eyes twinkling. And damn, did it feel good to be teased by him. "I like that."

"Yeah? It's a love it or hate it thing." Chris smiled. "And I don't mind. Keeps things easy. What you see is what you get."

"On all those personality tests, I always go for *still waters run deep*," Ash admitted, then smiled. "But I don't know. I don't think I'm that deep."

Chris hummed. He disagreed, and he couldn't work out in a short second or two how else to say for it, so as usual, he went for it. "No. You're smart as hell, and you're disappointed in yourself and how life's going. Felt like a dead end, didn't it?"

Ash stopped walking for a moment, his hands loosely curled around the bars of his crutches. He wasn't saying anything, but he watched Chris oddly.

It took a moment for Chris to realize that perhaps a psycho-analysis on the spot wasn't what Ash had been looking for. Before he could apologize, though, Ash nodded.

"Yeah. That's... fair."

Chris patted his back once, lightly, and nodded. "We all get those moods. But you're getting back on track now."

"Am I?" Ash frowned, but he started moving again, his eyes on the sidewalk to keep his balance.

"Well, you're up and moving around," Chris pointed out. "That's better than a few days ago."

"And here we go with the optimism again," Ash laughed,

giving him a quick, fond smile. "No, I appreciate the effort. It's just... depression doesn't just lift like that."

"No," Chris agreed quickly. He knew that much from watching Liam battle his own demons. He saw a lot more of it than he'd ever tell Liam—they weren't that kind of friends—but the turning point had only been when Liam had decided he was ready to change.

And now, after a lot of hard work and weekly therapy sessions and knitting circles Liam never talked about, he at least seemed a little more comfortable in his own skin.

Even so, sometimes Chris saw it in Liam's eyes—that weird look, like nostalgia or yearning or... something. Chris wasn't the kind of guy who could read the specifics, but he got it. Liam wasn't mended, and Ash wouldn't be, either. He knew that. But how to say it?

"It's like the plates in Japan. I saw an article on them," Chris burst out with, the moment the image came to mind.

"The broken ones they repair with golden metal to make them better than they were before?"

Chris gave a broad grin. "See? Smarter than you want to admit, huh."

Ash blushed and tried to shift his weight onto one crutch to poke the other at Chris's feet, making him laugh and dodge them. "Yeah, yeah."

"Down this path," Chris suggested. They'd already reached the trailhead.

Ash nodded obediently and turned the corner.

"Your other knee's holding in there?"

"Yeah. I think I'll graduate to a cane by my next doctor's appointment," Ash told him. And that was pride in his voice, just for a moment.

Chris wanted to encourage that. "Awesome, man. The doctor did say that walking would help."

"You did a better job listening to my marching orders than me."

"I'm good at those. In my job, you always listen to the boss."

"What's it like? At work?" Ash asked, his voice light and curious.

"Um... that's a big question," Chris laughed, but he was happy to distract Ash however he wanted him to. *Whoa, there, big boy. Not that way.* He dragged his mind back to the question. "It's great, though. I love it. I mean, there's fewer fires and more strokes than I anticipated when I started... but being there to help people is so... nice."

"Eloquent," Ash teased.

Chris laughed, ducking his head in embarrassment. "I haven't had a smart conversation with a guy who wasn't Liam or Dylan in... um..."

"We can just say *too long*," Ash offered with a sympathetic smile.

"Yeah. Too long."

And there it was. Chris's eyes met Ash's and caught and held his gaze. Ash kept walking slowly, his hands and body doing the work along the flat, smooth path, and Chris matched his pace at a leisurely amble.

Ash's lips were parted slightly, pink and wet and so ready to be kissed. His dark eyes flicked down to Chris's lips, like he was thinking the same thing.

The stubble on his jaw was almost all gone, so he'd shaved that morning. Chris's fingers itched to touch it, run his finger along that sharp cheekbone, and pull him in for a kiss.

Just one stolen kiss. What harm could that do?

Fuck. So much damage. This wasn't just another first date he was trying out and tossing aside.

This was the guy who was counting on him for help and

protection for the next week or two, or even more. Ash needed him, and he wasn't going to take advantage of him.

If Ash wanted anything, he'd have to make the first move.

"I like the birds around here." Oh, God, that was a dumb line. Chris's cheeks flushed and he quickly broke the gaze, looking up and around. Ash paused, stared at him, then laughed.

"Yeah. The birds are nice."

Don't mention it, Chris silently begged, and thank God, Ash didn't.

Chris's phone went off again, and he resisted the urge to roll his eyes as he pulled it out for a glance.

Davey was up to six unanswered texts, and he wasn't getting the hint.

Got plans this weekend?

He'd say anything to get the guy off his back, but yeah, if he had to know, he *did* have a date lined up. Guy probably wouldn't show—he *was* a Grindr find, after all—but it would do. Chris swiped to respond.

Yep.

Seconds later, there was a response.

LOL. Any of them working out for you?

Well, no, but that wasn't a fair question, Chris wanted to say. He wasn't gonna answer that, though.

Davey messaged again since he didn't answer.

I thought not. You know we can work, baby.

Chris resisted the urge to roll his eyes.

Still drunk? Must have been a hell of a night. Go back to bed.

The rhythmic clicking of the points of the crutches against the ground kept Chris grounded and reminded him that he had better things to do.

With you? Sure.

"What's that about?" Ash finally asked. "Liam?"

No. I'm busy.

"No," Chris said, echoing the word he'd just typed as he slid his phone back in his pocket. It took him a second to realize that he'd used the right word. "Uh, no, another friend. Teasing me about this date I've got coming up." His phone buzzed, but he ignored it. He could read the messages—or rather, delete them—later.

Ash smirked. "Ooh. You mean I could be getting some mileage here? Fill me in."

"Oh, God," Chris laughed. "It's a Grindr thing."

"You actually meet men from there?" Ash looked horrified.

"Well, not everyone who wants to meet," Chris shook his head. "But there's some normal guys there, if you look for them."

"Maybe we saw each other," Ash laughed. "Can't remember you..."

Chris gave him puppy eyes. "Maybe you blocked me."

Ash almost fell off his crutches. "Oh, no. Dude. I wouldn't have."

Well, that was a hell of a compliment. Chris's lips twitched into a smile, and then Ash seemed to realize what he said.

He went redder than a fucking tomato.

"I mean—not that—I mean..."

Chris spared him and winked. "Thanks. Compliment accepted. But it's a big city."

"Yeah. Probably haven't seen each other," Ash mumbled, half to himself. "That's your yard, isn't it?"

"Yeah! How'd you know?"

"The lemon tree helps."

Chris snorted. The top of the tree peeked over the tall wooden fence that separated them from the walking path. "Fair point," he admitted. "So, back to the firefighter thing... I like all the guys from the house. They're great. We're all drinking buddies and poker buddies and stuff."

Ash hummed.

"But, uh, most of them don't know I'm bi yet."

"Right," Ash nodded. "You want me to keep it hush-hush."

Chris winced. That sounded so fucking harsh. "No. I mean, don't, like, hire town criers to spread it to the four corners..." Ash laughed. "I'm just taking it slow. Our chief is gay anyway."

"Wow. Really?" Ash looked startled. "Didn't know that."

"Yeah. Dude, we're everywhere. Well, I say *we*, I mean, gay and bi and whatnot—" Chris explained.

"Good for kids today," Ash said simply. "If I'd seen more gay guys doing well..."

"Role model wise, huh?" Chris sympathetically nodded. "But it's not too late for you, either. Seems like a good time for a career switch, life shake-up kind of thing."

Ash glanced down again and nodded. Either his spirits were sinking or he was tired out, judging by his shorter responses.

Time to get him home and resting again.

Chris took him around the corner to their street, then up to the porch and in the house again. As he did, he checked his phone and his gut twisted. Davey was just lonely, but he really shouldn't engage with him. He was bad for him.

Once he ushered Ash off to the bedroom to take a nap, Chris went to clean up the breakfast dishes. It was his turn to frown with worry.

Nobody could cure or fix Ash, Chris knew that much. He just hoped these bits of companionship were enough to help him.

14

ASH

The first day and night without Chris around was weird, but by Wednesday, Ash was almost used to being home alone.

This was how he'd lived in the weeks since kicking out that asshole anyway. He'd always thought he preferred it, but now... he wasn't sure. It was just strange not having Chris be there.

The moment his phone went off, therefore, he nearly jumped on answering it. "Hey!"

"Hi, man. How's it going?" Chris was cheery as ever. Ash was glad he knew him well enough to know he wasn't putting on an act to try to cheer him up.

"Good, I think," Ash yawned.

"Need anything?"

Ash laughed. How could he, in a place like this, with the kitchen cupboards full of food? "Nope."

"Okay. Gotta go. Let me know if you do."

"Will do," Ash promised. "Bye."

"See you later."

The silence settled over the house again within minutes,

like a wet blanket over his spirits. He still had until tomorrow morning to kill the time.

It was his first time really alone since... that night—early morning, really—when he'd fucked up his life even more instead of ending it.

In the hospital, there had always been nurses to check on him, waking him up in the middle of the night or questioning him on his painkiller use. Since then, Chris had been glued to his side, attending to his every need.

But now, the afternoon dragged on, minute by minute seemingly slower.

To distract himself, Ash tidied up his guest room as best he could from the bed and spent a little while on his laptop watching YouTube videos. His own conscience wouldn't let him sit still for long, though. He had promised himself—and Chris—he wouldn't mope.

But where did he begin putting his life together again? He barely had a home, no job, no boyfriend or family, and no training.

"Start with your passions, they say," he said out loud. It was nice to hear the echoes around the living room, just for the sound.

He opened up a new Google window, then stopped.

What *did* he feel passionate about? Honestly, apart from being around Chris, it was hard to think of anything he'd wanted or felt particularly passionate about in the last few months.

"Depression is a bastard, isn't it?" he muttered, then paused. There *was* one moment he'd felt... free. Joyful.

Standing on that railing.

Thinking about it was almost more than he could stand. He'd avoided those thoughts for the last few days, as if that would make it easier to deal with. As if it would make him less likely to do the same damn thing again, only properly this time.

Ash drew a deep breath. "I'm safe," he murmured. "Safer on the ground."

There was an itch there, though. The city had looked so beautiful from even a little way up, with open air in front of him.

Skydiving? He might never walk properly again. The idea was laughable.

He slowly typed in: *how to feel like I'm flying*.

The answers were predictable: planes, tall buildings, and the likes. One made him pause, though. Hope, fear, and a strange yearning mingled in his mind.

Hang-gliding?

It was the dumbest idea he'd ever had. Probably dumber than giving in to the fucked-up hormones and crushing self-esteem and the drug-fueled whispers in the back of his mind. Premeditating any more in-air experiences seemed beyond the pale.

Chris would probably give him that skeptical expression as soon as he told him.

But, at the same time, it made sense in some crazy way. He didn't want the biggest thrill of his life to be *that* night. He never wanted to feel like that had been the high point of his life.

But in the years since his parents had died in that fucking car crash, it *was* the high point.

"No, it wasn't." He'd been plenty respectable while having fun in more legal ways than that night. "Depression lies," he said out loud, as firmly as he dared. It was his mantra, but sometime in the last few months, he'd forgotten it.

Ash shut the laptop firmly and grabbed his crutches. It was time for a walk around the neighborhood.

The street was clean and quiet. Ambling down the sidewalk on his crutches now, mid-afternoon when everyone his age was at work or perhaps school, was odd. He saw signs of life in some houses, but he tried not to stare.

Now that he was used to his crutches, he was walking on them pretty easily. Ash's mind could wander while he walked. He knew they were sized wrong—the nurses had told him he had to get properly-fitted ones, the right length for him, and these weren't adjustable. They were only supposed to be temporary.

His other leg was getting stronger again, not aching nearly as much. If only he could bear a little weight on his leg... but if he rushed recovery, he might be fucked-up forever. Not that he wasn't already going to be. But *more* fucked-up was worse, so he'd follow the doctors' instructions. Thank God he was such a fast healer.

Funny—little thoughts like this told him he wasn't ready to call it quits yet. Maybe he was ready to fight for his own life again.

The depression was a big problem, but one he could handle. Half of it was definitely situational—he'd always been prone to depressed spells, but it was only in the last few years they'd escalated to the point he couldn't crawl out of bed. He had to change something if he wanted different results.

"Fuck's sake," he murmured under his breath, shaking his head slightly. He'd only met Chris last week and he was already planning a new life course. Chris probably had no idea he was the kind of guy to get Ash thinking about how he could be better.

Ash nodded in passing to a neighbor walking her dog and got a nod in return, along with a sympathetic glance to his crutches.

He was going to deal with those stares forever now, if he

had to use a cane long-term. He'd already been warned he might have to. The doctors had done their best, but his leg had been... shattered, they described it.

No, he wasn't going to dwell on thoughts of the past. Too easy to mope that way, especially just walking and thinking by himself. Ash gritted his teeth with determination and focused instead on the future.

He needed a job he could do from home while he recovered. His internet wasn't awesome, but he could make do with it. When he got home—back to Chris's, that was—he'd start looking up careers he could do online from home. Piecework or freelancing or anything.

In the oddest way, his sudden limitation was liberating. He couldn't throw himself into gas station jobs, retail, restaurants... he *had* to find something better, or at least less physical.

Of course, there were a million tiny annoyances, like fitting through doors and using the bathroom and not putting the damn crutch on his own foot, but he was working on that silver lining.

It wasn't strictly work-related, but one idea kept coming back to his mind. It was dumb, reckless, and the kind of thing Chris would say *no way* to... but it could be fun. He didn't have to tell Chris about his plan yet. It was something that made him smile to think about, and that was important right now.

Was it even possible? He'd have to research it.

Ash turned around, an awkward 180-degree maneuver, and walked home a little faster.

15

CHRIS

"Your hot date is tonight, right?"

Chris drummed his fingers nervously on the steering wheel as he nodded at Ash. "Yeah. Six, for dinner, and then maybe a movie afterward."

"Not just Netflix and chill? You're so old-fashioned," Ash grinned.

Chris chuckled. Ash was starting to crack his own jokes now, like he was slowly unwrapping from the tight ball of emotions and stress he'd been wrapped up into. It was wonderful.

"I can be. Except for the bit where I've had... uh... dozens of first dates in the last couple months."

"*Dozens?* What about second dates?"

"A lot less than that," Chris laughed. "Every time I date someone a couple times, something comes up, or Liam and Dylan don't like him..."

"No," Ash groaned. "You don't let them judge, do you?"

"It's not my *only* factor," Chris defended himself, his

cheeks flushing scarlet. "But they, uh... help me realize stuff. Like, I don't have to sleep with a guy because he buys dinner..."

When he glanced to check his shoulder and merge lanes, he caught sight of Ash's face. He looked incredulous. "You *are* old-fashioned."

"Okay, maybe," Chris conceded, rolling his eyes and flicking his turn signal back off. "I'm never really into most of them, but I think it's always worth saying yes to one date. You never know who you'll click with. And sometimes the sex is hot even if you're not interested in seeing him again," he winked.

Ash hummed. "That's smart. But isn't it a waste of time and money, too? All those dates?"

"Not strictly a waste. There's the chance you'll stay friends with someone, right? And that hasn't happened, but that's... mostly me," Chris admitted. He sheepishly shifted, tapping his left foot against the floor of the car. "I have some guys I know all around town now. I *could* be friends. I've just been too focused on finding a boyfriend."

Oh, man. He hadn't even realized it until he'd said it just now. Ash seemed to sense he was realizing this, because he stayed quiet.

"Huh. Yeah. I'll try to take it easier," Chris said simply after a second of silence. Looking too hard for love never ended well.

Ash nodded to himself, then looked ahead again. "Oh, here it is already."

They were back at the hospital for Ash's one-week follow-up appointment. As they walked in, Chris watched Ash's curiosity and openness melt, his eyes more guarded and shoulders hunched.

The doctors here must have been real dicks. Ash had hinted that they questioned him about the drugs, and he'd watched the doctor act differently himself last week, but Chris was less than impressed at how apparent the change was.

His mind was made up: he wouldn't let Ash come here alone unless he really wanted to.

"Hi. We're here for a follow-up appointment," Chris greeted the receptionist at the arrivals desk. He stepped aside to let Ash give his name while she looked him up in the system and gave them directions to the right clinic.

"I hate this place," Ash muttered as they made their way down the hall. The crutches were always a strange separation—a physical object between them, and Chris had noticed his own instinct to walk a little too close as a result. Ash had only put the crutch on his foot twice before that.

"Yeah? Bad memories, huh?"

Ash's eyes flicked around the hallway before he nodded. "Mom and Dad were taken somewhere like here the night they died. Car crash."

It was such an abrupt statement, but it fit with everything else Chris knew about him to date. He gave Ash a gentle, sympathetic look and patted his back once. "Yeah? Shitty. I'm sorry, man."

"Yeah. And then I almost wound up dead here, too." Ash worked his jaw around, then scoffed as if at himself. "Can't believe it."

That sounded like good news. "You're not feeling that urge now?" Chris asked, trying not to sound too hopeful. He didn't want to rush Ash's recovery, but he wanted him to feel better. He deserved a break.

"I... *want* to... but I'm not *going to*," Ash said carefully, frowning as he looked over at him. His voice was low and intent, like he wanted to make sure Chris knew what he meant. "My depression... wants me to, that is. Like, when I'm low. But I'm working on that. I don't feel totally gone again. *I* want to make it."

Chris let out a breath he hadn't realized he'd been holding.

"Good. That's... that's good. I'm proud of you, man," he added, in case that wasn't clear enough.

"Thanks." Ash offered him a little smile.

In dwelling on how cute Ash was when he smiled and his dimples showed, it took Chris a moment to realize that he'd outpaced Ash, who had stopped. "Oh! We're here."

"Yeah," Ash laughed. They both turned the corner to check in, grab a number, and wait.

"You might never walk the same again."

Arms folded, Chris's nails dug into his palms as he heard the doctor's words ring around the room. His fists were as tight as his chest.

He dared a quick look at Ash. Not even a hint of surprise on Ash's face? He'd been preparing for this, then. "Right," Ash said. "But it should get a little better?"

"The pain will recede, yes." Dr. Green sat back in his rolling chair to look at Ash, who was leaning back in his own seat now that the inspection was done. "It should be stable. We'll get you to come in again for follow-up x-rays in three weeks to make sure you continue to heal well. If all goes well, you could be in a half-leg cast after that. You're healing very fast already." He flipped the file shut and rose to his feet.

"Good for me." Ash cast a quick glance at Chris as he clutched his prescription. "I'll need to pick up the new crutches, then."

Chris didn't want to bring Ash's mood down, so he grinned. "You can get better-fitting ones, yeah. Maybe fancy patterns."

Ash relented and smiled back, though Chris caught a glimpse of frustration there. "Yeah."

"C'mon, then. We'd better go crutch shopping," Chris told

him. "Thanks, Dr. Green. Won't find any fabulous styles around these parts."

Ash grabbed his crutches, and Dr. Green watched along with Chris as he pushed himself to his feet neatly.

"You quickly learned how to use those," the doctor commented, slowly leading the way to the door. "Definitely get those crutches in the right size."

"Will do," Ash nodded. Once they reached the hallway, he did an awkward shift to lean his weight on one crutch and free his hand from it, reaching out to shake hands. "Thanks, doctor."

"Thank you," Chris echoed.

The doctor smiled at them both, his eyes flicking between them. "Pleasure to meet you both. Look after him until he gets the hang of the cane, then, Chris."

"Will do," Chris cheerily promised.

They were halfway down the hall before Ash cleared his throat in what sounded like a pointed move.

"What?"

"You didn't get that?"

Chris furrowed his brow. "Get what?"

"He thought we were... oh, never mind."

Heat crept through Chris's cheeks. *I should be so lucky.* Instead, he cleared his throat, too. "Right. We'll pick this up and then get you home before my hot date tonight," he said loudly—mostly to keep things from getting awkward between them.

I mean, of course it's gonna be a bit awkward. Two single gay men living together all of a sudden. The whole "taking care of him" thing. And he's really good-looking. Nope, not going there.

"Need a han—oh. Well, then. What do you even have me around for?"

Ash had managed to swing himself down in the car seat,

then maneuvered his crutches into the car to slot alongside the door. "Nope," he winked. "Just hurry up and drive like my house is on fire."

"Smartass." Chris shut the door on him and shook his head as he circled to the driver's side and climbed in.

Good-looking *and* smart.

Damn it, no. Still not going there.

16

CHRIS

"You really wanna have coffee again after we just had coffee?" Chris's eyes sparkled with amusement as he watched his date come up with a smooth response, ambling alongside Derek to the street where his car was parked.

Derek hummed, clicking his tongue against his teeth as he eyed Chris. "Something rich and sweet."

Chris winked. "Firefighters don't make that much." He looked him up and down, taking in the skinny jeans and long t-shirt. It was casual, but everyone here was.

They didn't have crazy chemistry or anything, but he really *should* take it a little further than a "see you again sometime" and then months of avoiding each other in chance encounters at the grocery store or on the street.

What about Ash? No, he's cool with it. God, he's not my boyfriend or anything. Why am I even thinking about him?

"Come on," Chris said over his own thoughts and clapped Derek on the shoulder, then unlocked the car door for him. He could at least take him home for a cup of for-real coffee, right? Make up his mind on sex later?

Derek lived in the area and hadn't driven downtown today, so it wasn't like a huge weird thing to bring him home and *not* sleep with him, if it came to it.

Then, Chris furrowed his brow as he climbed into the driver's side. What was wrong with him? When did he ever say no to sex? God, he'd better get laid, or he'd start to think he was getting neurotic.

He had absolutely no reason not to want to fuck Derek.

"You live with the old man or what?"

One of Ash's crutches was leaning in the front hall, like he'd ditched it there. Chris eyed it—he wasn't trying to walk on his own without it? The cast had to be too damn heavy to manage that, and his pain was still too strong. "What?"

"That's not yours, is it?"

Chris eyed Derek and shook his head, leading him through to the kitchen. "Hey, Ash. We're grabbing coffee."

Ash poked his head out of the guest suite as they passed, then nodded at Derek and Chris. He had a crutch under one arm, which answered that question. "Hey."

"Oh. Hey. Skiing or something?" Derek asked, glancing down at his cast.

Ash hesitated for a moment, but before Chris could jump in, he shook his head. "Jumped out a window. Seemed like a better idea at the time."

The way Derek recoiled, it was like Ash had stung him. "Oh. Right." As fast as that, he turned off, ignoring Ash and heading for the kitchen.

Chris's mouth dropped open a little. He looked between the receding back of his date and Ash, whose expression was crumpling.

Oh *hell* no.

"What was that?" Chris frowned, following Derek to the kitchen.

Ash's room door closed.

"What? Oh. Just... isn't it kinda weird?" Derek murmured, dropping his voice. "Was it an accident, or...?"

"Does it matter?"

Derek eyed him, then gave a slow, uncertain shrug as he leaned on the counter. "Guess not..."

"Right." Chris rubbed his chin. He wasn't sure why he was suddenly getting such a bad vibe from Derek after their okay date. Was Derek jealous of him living with this guy or some-thing? "Why be a dick to him?"

"Yeah, that was kinda dickish," Derek admitted, then sighed and pushed himself away from the counter. "I better go, actually."

"Yeah. Probably," Chris agreed. He respected Derek for manning up to it and not trying to worm his way into bed after-ward, but still...

As he followed Derek to the door to see him out, Chris cast a worried glance to his closed door. Maybe he was just trying to give him space... or maybe that weird moment had freaked him out.

"It was fun," Derek told him once he was on the porch, offering a little smile.

He was right. It *had* been fun, before this. "Yeah. See you around."

"You too. Take care."

When the door shut, Ash's bedroom door clicked open. There was always a delay of a few seconds while Ash adjusted himself on his crutches and got out of the room.

Chris shook his head and grabbed the other crutch from the front hallway to bring over to him on his way to the kitchen.

"You really can't bear weight, you know. Don't be a dumbass. Want coffee?"

"Yeah, thanks. Says the guy who let a perfectly fuckable guy walk out," Ash jerked his head toward the door. "Or are you following him somewhere?"

"No, I..." Chris trailed off. He wasn't really sure what to say about it. Was that *relief* coursing through him? At letting a perfectly fuckable guy, as Ash put it, leave?

Why was that?

The first possibility that occurred to him was too obvious: he wasn't crushing on Ash or anything. They weren't even flirting. Not much, anyway.

"I just felt bad."

"I don't want pity." Ash's dark eyes cut across the room toward him, lightning-quick as he was to pick up on nuances.

Chris caught his breath, eager to correct him. "No. I didn't mean that way. It's not pity. But I'm sorry he was a dick."

"You still could have had him. It's none of my business," Ash shrugged, a movement made awkward by the fact that he had to pause his walk to the dining room to lift his shoulders further from the crutches.

"Nah. I'm not gonna reward anyone who's a dick to my buddies," Chris said firmly. That much, he was certain of. "I didn't really like him anyway. I shouldn't be so... scattershot."

"With your dates?"

"Yeah." Chris was still talking through the thoughts as they occurred to him—this wasn't exactly first nature. Relationship discussions never were. "I've... had a lot of fun the last few months, since coming out. You know? But..."

His phone went off, and he slipped it out of his pocket for a look while Ash turned himself around to get settled on the stool at the kitchen counter.

Feeling pretty down :(Wanna meet this weekend?

Of course it was *him*. Chris's heart sank as his finger hovered over the notification, then swiped to dismiss it.

"What was that?"

"Nothing. Where was I?" Chris went on, grabbing coffee mugs for both of them. "Yeah. Gotta be pickier or something. Maybe wait and see what falls into my lap."

"Other than me?"

It took Chris a second before his brows shot up. Was that a joke about—? Yeah, it was. He laughed and brought their coffee over to the counter, pulling up the stool next to Ash. He was careful not to jostle him, since his balance could be precarious. "Yeah. Hopefully with a little less bone-breaking."

"I don't recommend it," Ash smirked. "God, I'd give my right hand to fuck someone as hot as him." He was watching Chris.

Did he want him himself? Chris shrugged. Derek *was* hot, even if kinda rude. "Well, if you want his number..."

"No," Ash laughed, turning to his cup at last and bringing it to his lips. "No, I think I'll manage."

Still feeling like he was only in on half the conversation, Chris sipped his own coffee and nodded slowly, gazing across the living room. "So, not such a hot date. Not gonna date as much. Just as well... maybe I can turn some of those dates into friends first."

"Sounds very healthy. Ugh," Ash shuddered, and Chris laughed. "Will you start running marathons?"

"Maybe. What about you?" Chris nudged the leg of Ash's stool with his foot. "Big plans?"

Ash looked hesitant for a moment, then licked his lips. "I've thought of a few things, but... not much I *can* do until I've got my feet under me. Ha ha."

"It's not how many times you fall, it's how many times you get back up," Chris instantly quipped.

It was Ash's turn to look surprised for a second before his face cracked into a smile. "Yeah. Something like that." Then, Ash slid his hand onto Chris's lower back and rubbed up to between his shoulder blades. "I'm sorry it didn't work out."

"It's *really* okay, especially if it's earned me a back rub. Or..." Chris smirked.

Ash laughed again, richly this time. "Some thoughts should stay behind that filter," he teased. He gingerly turned on his stool to run his other hand up Chris's back while Chris twisted away from him to give him a better angle.

Those thumbs dug into the knots of muscle at the base of his neck instantly, and then the flats of Ash's palms ran down to his lower back and up a few times before he let go.

"That's like, three strokes and a poke," Chris mumbled his complaint.

"Oh, I'm sorry," Ash teased. "I can poke you a lot more."

Chris's cheeks flushed as he twisted to look over his shoulder at Ash. But instead of giving him a shit-eating grin, Ash was watching him with half a smile, his eyes bright and... interested?

Shit. Maybe he's hitting on me, too. Now what do I do? Chris's heart thudded, and he slowly turned to face the counter again, grabbing for his coffee cup. He didn't care if it singed his palms; it was a lifeline to something he could see and make sense of.

He was *not* going to get hard from three strokes and a poke. But just in case, he was going to stay right under this counter for a few more minutes. And why the hell had he said that? It was about the most sexual thing he could have come out with.

Chris's cheeks had to be red. They burned almost as much

as his palms once he loosened his grip on the cup and cradled it with his fingers instead.

"I never learned massage or anything. Properly. I used to give pretty good back rubs... and, you know, all kinds of rubs." Chris was talking now. Shit. Ash wasn't stopping him. "I mean, to girls. Mostly. Then my first boyfriend, but he was a secret between us, you know? Big carpenter guy, not out. He used to get all tense, so I learned to, you know, help with that. Did you? I mean, take a class?"

Chris clamped his lips shut to wait for a response.

Ash's lips twitched into a smile. Thank God he didn't tease him about his run-on mouth. Instead, he nodded. "Sort of. One of my shitty exes taught me how to pick a lock, give a killer massage, and open a wine bottle with my teeth."

Chris stared at Ash. That kind of relationship sounded so far from anything he'd experienced in his cozy suburban life that he didn't even know what to say. "I..."

"Yeah," Ash laughed. "Anyway, what's on TV?"

"Let's find out," Chris suggested. After a quick downward glance to make sure everything was in place, he took Ash's cup and his own to the living room. Once he crashed on the couch, he kicked the pillow down so they could sit there together and watch whatever was on. And maybe forget that weird moment.

But every time Ash's elbow or his knee bumped Chris's body, that same strange crackle went through him—and now Chris couldn't stop thinking back to his not-so-hot date.

Had he ever felt that chemistry? No. And worse yet, he hadn't felt it with any other guy since meeting Ash.

Shit. I've done it now.

17

ASH

"The fuck is that?"

The knocks on the window were a quiet but distinctive rap-rap-rap shattering the relative peace and quiet of the house at almost midnight on a Saturday. No, probably early Sunday by now.

Ash was instantly on-guard. He had no idea what to expect, but if someone was knocking at Chris's window instead of his door...

No way. It wasn't Benny or RJ, was it? Or some other ex he'd pissed off? How did he get to a point in his life where there were *several* assholes it could be?

His stomach tight with fear, he pushed himself out of bed, glad he'd struggled into loose sweatpants and a t-shirt before bed. If he was going to face some drugged-up super villain evil ex, he could at least preserve some dignity and not flash his goods while he leaned on his crutches.

Could he fight with one? Probably.

Getting ahead of yourself there, he reminded himself as he heard another series of taps. He eased up onto one, sliding the handle into his armpit, then the other, and took the few short steps over to the window. He left the room lights off and slowly slid the curtain open, leaning in as far as he could to peek before he kept going.

It was one guy outside, and the way he swayed and leaned on the wall, he wasn't going to be breaking any windows. He'd more likely break his face against the window.

Better yet, he didn't recognize the guy outside, and vice versa. When he hauled the curtain open the rest of the way, they stared at each other through the darkness and the double-paned window.

Ash tilted his head; the stranger pinched his lips together and stuck them out, then tried to imitate it. It knocked him off-balance and he staggered against the window again.

Ash rolled his eyes and cracked the window open just slightly. If this was some drunk kid who lived next door, maybe he was at the wrong place. "Who the hell are you?"

"Who're *you*? Friend of Chris?"

"Yeah. Staying with him."

The guy looked him slowly up and down—as much as he could see of him through the window—and scoffed. "Some gimp? You're why he didn't text me back?" The words were heavily slurred, but Ash still picked out the offensive word. "He there with you?"

"No. If he wants to talk to you, I'm sure he will." Ash shut the window—and the curtains. He was in no mood to stand there and listen to some drunk asshole getting jealous about him.

He knew exactly what was going on.

Chris had dropped enough tiny hints—that he had an ex, that it hadn't ended well, that they'd tried a couple times... And the texts on his phone. It all fit together.

Ash didn't actually expect him to go away. Instead of going

back to bed, he pulled open his bedroom door and leaned on the door jam.

Sure enough, the doorbell rang, and a thump from upstairs heralded Chris's arrival. Ash let him answer, since he knew the guy, but flicked on the hall light to announce his presence.

"Shit, sorry," Chris mumbled, rubbing a fist over his eyes, and... fuck. He looked cute as hell with sleepy eyes and sweatpants, and that was about all that looked cute. The rest of him was fucking *hot*.

The darkness hid the best bits of his abs, but his broad shoulders and the biceps were easy to see even from the back as Chris strode for the door. And that ass. God, what a view.

Of course Chris slept shirtless. No need to wear clothes at all when you were ripped like that. Besides, he probably didn't have to worry about what he'd be wearing if the firefighters had to come rescue him.

Ash realized he was grinning and ducked his head to rub his face and wipe the smile off. *Stop it.* The last thing he needed was a hard-on in his sweatpants in front of this creep he'd just told he wasn't dating Chris.

Chris had the door open and, even from behind, Ash could see the tension in his body. "What is it, David?"

"You're alllllive. Didn't think so. You weren't answering me," David answered. "And what's with the *full name* all the sudden? That's cold. Maybe I don't wanna fuck you now..."

"Good." Chris was trying to keep his voice low. "We can't keep doing that."

"You say every time, but you always fuckin' let me in. I can't drive. Look at the state I'm in."

Chris hesitated, dropping his head in thought.

Surely *that* wasn't going to work on him? Ash huffed out a quick breath and swung his way down the hall, keeping the rubber tips of his crutches close to his ankles so he didn't trip over any furniture in the dark.

"I see you found your way to the front door instead of my window," Ash greeted David—Dave?—when he got close enough.

Chris looked confused. "Davey?"

"You're... fucking him now, aren't you?" Davey answered, jerking a thumb at Ash. "What, you break his skinny little ass? Come... c'mon. I know you miss me, baby."

Ash scoffed and shouldered his way past Chris—no small feat given his mobility predicament. "What you're doing is harassment. You're texting him, too, aren't you? Showing up late at night? Chris, are you two exes?"

Chris looked stunned as he looked over at him. "I... Yeah."

"Ex," Ash repeated firmly, looking at Davey again. "Take the hint. Stop guilt-tripping him into more."

Davey's lip curled. "What's it to you? Chris, tell him to fuck off."

Ash looked him up and down. From frat-boy ball cap to flip-flops, the musty smell of beer around him, and the hatred simmering in his eyes, he hated every inch of this guy. He probably would have hated him sober in the daylight without first meeting him knocking on his window and waking him up past midnight, but that was an aggravating factor.

Chris was silent.

"You're a fuckin' moron still, then," Davey jabbed his finger at Chris. When he started reaching for his pocket, Ash's gaze sharpened and he shifted on his crutches to free one arm. He only hooked his thumb in his pocket, though. "You fucking stupid loser. You never could see a good thing. That's why they didn't give you the—the promotion, you know. You don't deserve it."

"That's fucking out of line," Ash snapped.

"It's the beer," Chris sighed quietly. "He always gets like this when he's drunk. He doesn't mean it. He's still in love with me."

"The fuck I am," Davey mumbled. "With a little... little cocksucker like you."

Ash simmered with rage at the guy who dared to talk to Chris like this when Chris was fucking sweet enough to put it down to alcohol and forgive him—probably over and over. But he wasn't going to give him the satisfaction of getting hot under the collar.

"You about done?" Ash coolly told him. "'Cause some of us have to get some sleep and be mature adults." He backed up, pushing his back into Chris's chest to make him back up.

"You can't just—" Davey sounded indignant as he shoved his hand in the door.

Resisting the urge to bite his wrist, Ash grabbed his little finger, the crutches pushing uncomfortably into his armpits as he leaned on them while Davey tried to yank it away. "Look, asshole. I can break this or you can fuck off, permanently."

Chris's hands rested on his hips—probably just to steady him—but suddenly, even through the anger, he felt steadier. Grounded. Appreciated, even. And he wanted Chris's hands to stay there.

Emboldened, Ash hardened his voice. "And leave Chris alone until and unless *he* texts *you*. Guys like you are dime-a-dozen. He doesn't deserve you."

Davey managed to wrench his hand free at last, shoving his middle fingers toward Ash before he turned to stumble down the porch stairs. He took them two at a time and almost face planted on the pavement, but managed to keep going until he reached the sidewalk.

"I should call him a taxi—" Chris murmured, his breath warm against Ash's neck. He hadn't taken his hands away still.

"No, sweetie," Ash murmured. "He's responsible for himself." He watched Davey head down the street, still mumbling under his breath about how stupid Chris was and what a nosy fucking faggot he was. Then, he eased back a little more to close the door.

Chris's hips pressed into his. It was easy to feel Chris's cock against the curve of his ass, Chris's hard pecs against his shoulder blades.

Fuck. He had to stop thinking about his friend that way. Except that Chris had been giving him these signals of desire before cutting them off every time. On the kitchen stools, on the couch, sometimes bedroom eyes or an innuendo-laden turn of phrase.

There was something else simmering between them as he shut and locked the door. Chris didn't pull back, his hands still lightly on Ash's hips. Ash could feel his heart thudding against his back, could hear the rasps of his breath.

What was going through his head?

Ash eased the crutches away from himself to lean them against the door, sagging slightly as he tried to rest all his weight on his good leg.

Chris's arms slid harder around his waist as if to hold him upright and hug him at once.

Then, he heard Chris's voice catch. Chris pressed his forehead into Ash's shoulder as he squeezed him tightly. "Haven't told anyone about him."

Ash's heart ached. He ran his hands gently down Chris's biceps to his forearms. He squeezed gently, then traced the backs of his hands with his palms until their fingers tangled over his stomach. "Why not?"

"Didn't want to... I mean, he gets into my head. I know it's not good. But he can't help it. He's just... angry at everything."

"The shit he said to you... is that typical?" Ash's other knee was getting sore, but he didn't want to break the moment. Chris was vulnerable now, for probably the first time since they'd met. He wasn't going to scare him off.

"Typical," Chris repeated under his breath, and then, a few seconds later, he nodded. His stubbly chin grazed the bare skin between neck and shoulder where Ash's t-shirt hung loose.

Fuck. His body couldn't help but react to that closeness. Chris smelled good, felt *incredible*, but now was not the moment.

Ash shifted slightly and tried to think unsexy thoughts, tightening his grip on Chris's hands in case they wandered a little too far south. His cheeks burned, but he tried to focus on the more important thing right now. "That's fucked-up," he said gently. "You know that, or you wouldn't hide it from Liam and me, and probably other people, right?"

Chris hesitated for a few seconds, then nodded. "Yeah. I guess. But I'm not innocent, either."

"No matter what you've said to him before... he came at you like that tonight, and that's unacceptable going forward." Ash knew Chris was talking himself in circles—fuck, he'd chosen his own bad boyfriends over and over, he knew what was going through his head—but he had to try to get through.

At least a crack of doubt in Chris's acceptance of the status quo would go a long way.

"Will he come back?"

Chris shook his head slightly. "Prob'ly not. You wanna sleep upstairs, just in case?"

"Fuck that. Stairs in the dark. You sleep downstairs."

"Deal," Chris murmured, but he didn't move just yet.

Then, like a truce lifting, Ash's body burned again. The man holding him from behind, his hands flat on his stomach, his lips so close to his ear...

"Lead the way," Ash murmured, dropping his hands and

grabbing his crutches. When Chris pulled away from him, he quelled the ache of disappointment in his chest by reminding himself that they were about to share a bed. It was going to be a long damn night if he didn't get that semi under control.

Thinking about how sex would even work with a leg cast, and then some detailed thoughts about his still-healing injuries did the trick, but only just.

When Chris climbed under the covers in the dark bedroom and reached out to help him ease himself down, Ash's skin prickled with pleasure.

But try as he might to get the courage to address that moment, no way could he make that first move. Chris deserved so much more than Davey, or him. He deserved one of those model boyfriends who cooked and cleaned and had a high-powered finance career or something.

Being settled next to him, close enough to imagine he felt his body heat, was enough.

Ash reached out to rub Chris's shoulder—careful to locate his body before doing so—and was rewarded with a long, slow sigh.

"Thanks a million," Chris murmured through the darkness.

Despite his momentary sadness, Ash's smile tugged at the corners of his lips. He couldn't guarantee either of them would be able to stay away from the other, but for tonight, Chris didn't have to take it. He was finally able to repay this sweet, gentle, kind man just a little.

"Anytime."

He didn't even remember sleep pulling his eyelids shut.

18

CHRIS

What time is it? Oh, shit, am I supposed to be at work? And who is that?

Waking up with a hand on his back, an arm pressing his shoulder into the bed, was almost unfamiliar to Chris. The more pressing concern—what time it was—resolved itself as soon as he remembered that it had to be Sunday, his last day off before a couple days at work.

That brought him to the smell and sight of Ash, curled onto his side, facing Chris and about as close as he could get without actually touching him.

He is definitely a cuddler.

And Chris liked it.

Then, after the obligatory memory-search to see *why* they were in bed together, it sank in.

Fuck, last night was a mess.

Of course Davey insisted on showing up just as things were going well with Ash—fucking up whatever precarious balance they had.

But Ash was fucking badass. He could barely walk, but

he'd shoved Chris out of the way to send Davey packing at some ungodly hour. He'd even threatened to break his fucking hand while barely able to stand upright.

It had been a long time since Chris had known anyone to be that passionate on his behalf. Suddenly, he understood why Ash gave him that doe-eyed look during his doctors' appointments.

Chris's heart started to race, his palms damp and head spinning as he reached out to rest his arm across Ash, his other arm awkwardly curled under his own pillow.

It's just cuddling. Friends do it.

He tried to ignore the part of him that was laughing hysterically at the idea that this was *friendship* between them. Chris wasn't an idiot, whatever Davey sometimes made him feel like late at night. He'd felt that same spark, standing in the dark hallway holding Ash against him.

But Ash had pulled back, kept it decent instead of pursuing... something. Anything.

"Hey," Ash mumbled, his eyes flickering open slowly. He tensed for a moment and started to pull his hand back from Chris's back, then seemed to notice Chris's hand on him, too. His gaze flicked down to Chris's arm, then up to his face.

The question was in his expression: *what are we doing?*

Chris shrugged slightly. "You're a cuddler, aren't you?"

"I..." Ash's cheeks went red. "I didn't get too close, did I?"

"I'll let it slide," Chris winked, then let him in on it. "Nah."

Ash huffed out an annoyed breath of laughter and flicked his shoulder, resting his hand on his side instead. "Thanks, asshole."

"Anytime." Chris grinned. "It's fun to watch you squirm."

"You're going to start a prank war if you're not careful."

"Who says that's not what I'm going for?" Chris winked, then tucked his elbow against his chest and managed to raise his other hand to his eyes to rub sleep away from them. "God. Last night was..."

Oh, right. Probably not supposed to bring that up.

"Hm?" Ash murmured, his gaze softer now.

It was rare for Chris to feel shame or embarrassment, but his chest was tight and he suddenly couldn't look at Ash's sympathy for him. "I... It's not abusive."

"Mm."

"It's *not*. I'm not that kind of... I'm not..." Chris trailed off, not even sure what he was trying to say. Was he trying to prove to Ash he wasn't some weakling being led by the nose by fear or guilt or whatever?

Unless he was. He wouldn't have dated the guy the first damn time, or the second, or fucked him half a dozen times since then otherwise.

It was like a punch to the gut.

Ash scooted a little closer, his hand running up Chris's side to his back to rub gently. "I didn't say you're a victim or anything. Just that you have blind spots."

Chris's throat was tight, and he closed his eyes for a second to rest them. These conversations were not his forte. He wasn't going to cry all over the damn guy when this was, like, the only problem in his life. Ash had so many bigger things to worry about. "Right."

"You trust people a lot. I... I'm kinda jealous," Ash breathed out a quiet laugh. "But, man, you can't let people fuck you over like that. Doesn't matter how drunk he was—he shouldn't say that kind of stuff to you."

Chris swallowed the retorts as they came to him:

I deserve it after what I did to him.

It's not that bad.

It was the beer talking.

He loves me.

Each time he was about to say one, the uncomfortable gnawing sensation of self-awareness prickled at his consciousness and reminded him that that was the kind of shit abuse victims said.

"You'd never let me go out with someone like that, would you?" Ash murmured.

Chris gritted his teeth. He was too honest to lie about that. "No," he admitted. "Even though I, uh, don't really know you. It's none of my business. But I wouldn't... like to see that." He slowly opened his eyes again, fidgeting and curling his toes into the sheets.

Ash chuckled quietly. "All things considered, we know each other pretty damn well."

Not as well as we could. Chris resisted the urge to say it, or to let his eyes trail down to the bare patch of skin where Ash's shirt had lifted in the night. Too late—he'd already looked. His cheeks flushed, and he nodded again.

Ash winked at him. "Not to make things awkward or anything." But he wasn't pulling back, either.

"I don't want that. Things being awkward, I mean. Not with you." *Oh, God, don't say it.* Chris bit his tongue before anything more could escape, but it was too late. He could feel the ball rolling between them.

Ash's breathing was quick now, his pupils large. Chris couldn't look away from those baby blues. "Are you saying you'd kiss me if I asked you to?" Then, the last bit of persuasion melting his resistance—his pink tongue swiped across his pretty lips.

Chris's stomach tightened with nerves. But he wasn't gonna start lying now. "I would. Are you feeling... um... chemistry?"

Ash nodded slightly.

It was almost a stupid question given that they were lying

in each other's arms, their lips tantalizing inches away from each other. So close he could feel the warmth of Ash's breath, and almost hear his heart thudding. Certainly feel it against his palm, which still pressed against Ash's back.

"I didn't want to... pressure you into anything," Chris breathed out, his voice breaking the moment of stillness between them.

Ash cracked a smile. "Yeah, fuckin' right. I'd tell you to fuck off if I wanted you to."

"But you don't?" Chris smiled slightly, rubbing Ash's spine lightly with his thumb. "'Cause I might be really up for this. But if it's gonna make things awkward... If we both need friends more than, um..." *Lovers? Fuck-buddies? What am I going for with him?*

"I want you, too," Ash whispered. "Kiss me."

Chris slid closer, his hand rising to cup Ash's soft, stubbly cheek as he pressed their lips together. Ash's lips were hot and firm, his tongue teasing at Chris's lower lip already as Chris tilted his head so their noses didn't brush.

Their first kiss was slow and gentle, but it only took ten seconds or so before Ash sucked his breath in. His eyes darkened, and Chris's back stung from the scrape of nails.

Ash pecked his lips over and over, sucking his lower lip and teasing his upper one, then nipping now and then.

His cock was hardening already, his thigh brushing the outside of Ash's as Ash gradually shifted onto his back. Ash's hands settled on his waist, pulling him in closer.

Lying down is probably easiest for him, with the cast. Unfortunately, it's pretty damn suggestive... Or maybe, luckily.

Chris followed Ash as Ash pulled him over him, shifting until he straddled him, those thighs firm against his inner thighs. And, best of all, he wasn't the only one sporting a tent right now.

His cock brushed the unmistakable bulge of a hard cock poking up against soft, loose sweatpants, and almost instantly, the pressure wasn't enough. He settled his weight carefully onto Ash until their cocks were trapped together between them.

"Oh, God, yes," Ash moaned, answering that question before Chris could even ask. He licked his lips and grabbed the back of Chris's head to pull him down for a harder, hotter kiss.

Their lips slid together hard now. In this past week, the simmering sparks between them had built into this insane inferno that Chris almost couldn't wrap his brain around. After —what? Two minutes of kissing?—he would have done anything Ash asked him to.

This was what had been missing with Derek, or Davey, or... all of the guys he'd taken to bed in the last month or two.

Sometimes he'd had chemistry, but no desire to talk to the guy afterward. Sometimes vice versa.

Physical chemistry hot enough to scorch the sun and whatever made him care so deeply about Ash, together? That was rare.

Scarily rare.

Chris pushed the thought aside and sucked on the tip of Ash's tongue until Ash gasped, his eyes sliding closed. Then, Chris pressed kisses along Ash's lips to his jaw, until he reached his earlobe.

"Oh, fuck, yes," Ash whimpered, his hips jerking up to grind harder into Chris. "I'm really—hnnnh."

Chris didn't need him to finish that sentence. He grinned, then gently nipped the earlobe before flicking his tongue back and forth across it, kissing behind the ear and down his neck to the hem of his t-shirt.

Ash was already fighting his t-shirt off, and when it was

tossed aside, Chris took a second to admire his slender body tucked into the wrinkled white sheets.

He was fucking gorgeous. Chris's heart almost skipped a beat at how much he *wanted* him.

This wasn't idle boredom or curiosity or experiments. This was something completely different, and he almost didn't know what to do with it.

"You all right?" Ash's whisper brought him back down.

"Yeah. You're really hot," Chris murmured, meeting his gaze again. He gave him a roguish smile to cover up his moment of whatever-the-fuck-that-was.

Ash's blush deepened. He was red as a tomato, and Chris loved it. "I... thanks. You probably hear it all the time, but you too. The hell do you do to get abs like that?"

"I'll show you," Chris winked, then ducked down to lick one of Ash's nipples. "Eventually," he whispered over the damp skin.

"*Christ!*" Ash whimpered, his hands digging into the sheets on either side of them as his body trembled. The little whines of pleasure that slipped free with each sucking kiss Chris placed on his warm skin were delicious.

Chris could already imagine what it would be like to be inside him, their sweaty bodies barely covered by a sheet as the mattress creaked...

His cock throbbed with need, and he was just about positive Ash was going to be cool with this. "You want more than me kissing you?"

"Desperately," Ash breathed out, and that word choice made Chris's head spin so hard he lost his breath. "Please. Fuck. You can do literally anything."

Despite the pleasure that ran through him at the permission, Chris grinned mischievously. "We can start slowly, you know. A little cock-on-cock action, like the Greeks... Romans? Greeks? Someone like that."

"Don't get distracted now, or I swear to God," Ash mumbled, his hands sliding down Chris's bare back to hook in Chris's waistband and carefully yank them down. Chris fumbled at the same time to deal with the rest of Ash's nuisance clothing, though he had to leave the sweatpants around his knees since yanking them off his feet at this angle would be damn near impossible, and his cock really didn't want any interruptions.

Ash's hard cock bobbed above his stomach, thick with arousal and flushed red. It looked delicious, and... just right for him. Chris watched as Ash's eyes flicked down, naturally, to take him in, too.

"Hot," Ash breathed out simply. "I have condoms in my bag on the bedside table."

"Do we have to—"

"Yeah," Ash said firmly, in a tone that made Chris's skin tingle. *He's so bossy. Hot.* "I haven't been tested lately."

"We'll fix that," Chris breathed out, swiping the bag and grabbing a condom. "You or me?"

"Me. I want you to come on me."

Oh, fuck. It was Chris's turn to stare, his cheeks flushing as his jaw dropped.

Ash winked at him. "Hurry up, then, my sexy fireman. Don't let this fire go out."

It always sounded like a cheesy porno movie when someone tried to riff off his profession in bed, but from Ash, it was just the right blend of cheesy, funny, and... sexy.

"I don't intend to," Chris breathed out. He swiped his hand down the length of Ash's cock to unroll the thin material—and squeezed him as he went, stroking up and down the shaft a few more times just to hear his whimpers.

Ash's fingertips dug into his ass, pulling him close, so Chris stopped resisting. His own hard length bumped Ash's, lining up just right with it.

The sensitive spot on the underside brushed against the head of Ash's cock right as Ash hauled him down for another long, slow kiss full of tongue and promise, and that was about it for rational thought. They hit the flashover point.

Chris rutted their bodies together hard, sweat droplets trickling down the back of his neck, his cheeks flushed with arousal. Ash stayed still to let him get the angle just right, but the rest of his body shuddered and twitched.

"Yes," Ash moaned against Chris's lips, his arm sliding up to wrap around his shoulders and keep their chests close together. Their hearts thudded together, the heat between them so fucking intense. Chris had been in house fires cooler than this.

Chris's body crackled with pleasure, his fingertips tingling and balls drawing tight. He was going to come so fucking *hard*, and so fast.

Ash was bypassing everything he could do to stop it, but Ash's hips were shuddering, his breath growing shorter and eyes sliding shut—Chris was pretty sure he was getting close, too.

Chris pressed a few more kisses against Ash's lips as they panted together, his nipples even brushing Ash's until his stomach drew tight, his arms, even his legs.

He *needed* this so badly he could explode.

But not before Ash, who was breathing out a quiet, "Yes... yes... *yes!*" into his ear. Ash's thighs were trembling, his arm like a vice around Chris's back. Chris ran his hand up Ash's other arm to curl his fingers into Ash's, pressing his hand into the mattress above his head.

"Come on, baby. You're so damn hot. I'm gonna come any

second now. On you—just like you want," Chris managed between his pants for breath.

"Chris," Ash whimpered. "Fuck, this is so... your cock... *hnnh!*" Chris kept that angle of his hips, his own cock throbbing with the barely-restrained need for release as he ground the sensitive undersides of their cocks together, frenulum rubbing frenulum. "Right there... yes! Chris!"

Like a gunshot, Ash went off, his hips arching into Chris's and body squirming under him as he gasped for breath open-mouthed, his eyes screwing up tightly. His hand above his head clenched hard around Chris's.

He was fucking *gorgeous*, coming undone under him and not hiding a second of his pleasure.

Chris kept thrusting, loosening his grip on Ash's hand while Ash's cock shuddered against his. He needed that hand for himself. He couldn't stop staring at every sexy reaction, even as his own chest tightened and head spun. "I'm almost— baby, I'm gonna..."

"Come for me," Ash growled, still out of breath and shuddering, running his nails up his back.

The parallel tiny stings were enough to upset the last ounce of self-control Chris had. His whole body pulled tight and then released in rhythmic shudders as he thrust the head down against Ash's cock and stroked the root of the shaft.

Ash's hand ran up his upper thighs, his eyes fixed on Chris's the whole time. "Gorgeous," he heard Ash whispering into his ear, and his chest tightened with emotion. "You fucking sweet goddamn *sexy*, hot, gorgeous thing."

Chris could almost think straight now that he wasn't pushing against Ash as hard and fast as he could, his shudders slowing to those last few pushes of body against body. "M-Missing another descriptor?"

"Mine?"

The simple word made Chris catch his breath, his head snapping up and jaw dropping.

Ash looked nervous as hell, his body tensing under Chris's as he opened his mouth, maybe to take it back or qualify it —*mine for now.*

He had no reason to worry. Every instinct in Chris's body told him the answer to that one. Ash was right—he *wasn't* stupid, and he *did* know exactly what he wanted and deserved.

It was Ash.

"Yours."

Ash let a long, slow sigh out. "Fuck. I didn't mean to even say that. We don't have to be, you know, exclusive yet... but I just..."

"Want you," Chris supplied simply. It was how he felt about Ash.

Ash relaxed even more, his cock softening slowly as he closed his eyes for a second. "Yeah," he whispered. "Want you."

Until this second, Chris hadn't really known what he was looking for with all those guys. He'd assumed he'd know it when he found it, but... shit.

This, whatever it was, blew everything else out of the water. And it was only a little frot and a lot of making out. Well, that and a week of close quarters, and deep emotional intimacy in a near-death experience.

Ash wrapped his arms around Chris's body and pulled him down for a long minute while their breathing caught up with their lungs and their heartbeats returned to normal.

Whatever it was that pulled him toward Ash, Chris was ready to stop fighting it.

19

ASH

"The fucking asshole wants extra rent next month because the place is unoccupied. Higher insurance rate, apparently." Ash gritted his teeth so hard his jaw hurt as he stared at his phone.

"That's not even *legal*."

Ash sighed at Chris's naïvety. If the living conditions were legal in that place, he wouldn't have been so desperate to escape it.

Weirdly, things hadn't been awkward after their first brief and exhilarating sex. They just felt *easy*—so easy, in fact, that Ash was sitting in the fire station living room right now with Chris's buddies.

"I'm sure it isn't." That was Liam, who was exactly as tall, dark, and handsome as Ash had pictured Chris's best friend being. Then again, their other coworker, Kevin, was pretty cute too for an older guy.

Or maybe it was all the muscles. Ash was kind of a sucker for them. It was almost enough to make him fume a little less at the text from his landlord.

"Okay, no. You're not paying more rent for a place like

that." Chris sprang to his feet and paced this area of the fire hall, back and forth along the space behind the couch, between the kitchen and living area.

"You're already living with him, aren't you?" Liam said casually, and Ash's eyes flickered to Chris. From the way Liam had greeted him, Ash had the feeling Chris had told him there was more up—pun intended—than they'd expected.

"Yeah."

Chris nodded at Liam, and Ash raised his eyebrows to ask what that was about. "So," Chris continued, "move in with me. Give up your lease on that place. You're going to be non-weight-bearing for at least another... what, six weeks? Seven? Plus, partial-weight-bearing for months more. And you can pay off your deductible easily that way, I bet."

It's practical, not a relationship thing. Ash considered it for a few moments, looking around the fire station.

It was more homey than he expected—though he hadn't really known what to expect from a fire station. There were a few cozy couches, and the living room was bright and clean. The open-plan kitchen behind was well-stocked, and there was a big dining table between the two areas. Almost like a big bachelor apartment. The exposed brick walls of the station added an extra charm, though the outside was the same white stucco as every exterior around here.

The actual garage where they kept the trucks was cooler, though. Ash had to admit there was still a bit of the little boy in him that got excited at the sight of the bright red trucks. It was totally irrational—they should have been portents of grave accidents or something, but he'd still snuck a few touches of the clean red metal on his quick tour.

Right. Moving in.

He couldn't lose anything, could he? It was a bit quick, but then, he also couldn't afford higher rent *and* the deductible from his hospital stay. The interest on it would be a killer. So, without much of a choice in the matter, he had to agree.

"Yeah, if you don't mind me crashing for longer... that would be great."

Chris stopped pacing and clapped his shoulder, dropping onto the arm of the chair. "Course I don't mind. After I've slept, we'll start moving your stuff."

"There's not much there I care about," Ash admitted. "Are you sure, though? I won't be much use with this." God, it had taken him long enough just to get out of the house to the bus stop and then up here to the station. Carrying anything was out.

Chris patted his biceps. "What do you think these are for?"

The alarm ringing through the station answered that question, and Ash caught his breath at the speed with which the atmosphere changed.

Kevin, who'd been washing up the dishes and listening in, was suddenly out of the room, and Liam and Chris were right on his heels.

They'd already briefed Ash on what to do—stay out of the way, sit tight and wait here with the rookie today, Glenn.

Chris managed a quick glance over his shoulder and nod, his eyes flashing. It was easy to spot the adrenaline running through his veins—the same as pumped through Ash's, only Ash couldn't do a thing about it. "See you."

"Stay safe," Ash breathed out.

Chris nodded once, and then he was gone. Within a minute, the engine was peeling out of the station.

There were a few minutes of silence before Glenn appeared, raising a hand in a quick wave. "Sorry for the interruption, man."

"No, it's kinda his job," Ash laughed. "I didn't even know I could visit."

"Yeah? At least you're here to see Chris. A lot of the wives —I mean... you know, partners... get pranked by him." Glenn stumbled over his words, clearly trying not to be an asshole. Ash tried not to smile. The effort was appreciated.

"How so?"

"He got Liam's, um, boyfriend. Dylan. Made him think they were eating raw chicken for protein. Dylan *almost* took a bite."

Ash started laughing, the tension and worry in the back of his mind easing slightly. "Ew! No way!"

"Yeah way," Glenn laughed. He was still young enough to have acne. "And sometimes the old bucket of water overhead. Liam threatened to... uh. Well, threatened bodily harm if he did that to Dylan, though."

Ash snorted with laughter. The dynamic between the two guys made him smile. He was glad that despite the stress of Davey hanging around on the periphery of his life, and what he'd said before about not having friends outside work, Chris did have one solid friend both at work and outside it.

He kinda wished he had one, but then, he'd always wanted a best friend. He'd just never lucked into one.

"What's the call for?"

"Sounds like a medical call. A lot of our calls are," Glenn explained.

Ash's stomach twisted. When *he'd* been hurt, the ambulance had been first to show up. Or had it? He couldn't really remember well through the sea of pain, but he only remembered seeing EMTs. "So you do a lot of that?"

"Yeah, especially car wrecks and that kinda stuff." Glenn eyed him for a few long moments. "Uh. I hate to ask, but are you two...?"

Shit. What do I say? Ash licked his lips. Chris had said he was out at work—and his behavior this afternoon supported it—but was he supposed to confirm or deny?

Fuck it. He wasn't going to lie. Chris didn't seem like the type to. Besides, Glenn was clearly fine with Liam and Dylan, if a little uncertain how to talk about it.

"Yeah."

"Oh, cool," Glenn nodded simply. "Well, um... there will be a lot of moments of... you know. Worrying about him. That kind of stuff. My girlfriend found it really hard."

Ash winced sympathetically. "Yeah. I bet. Were you dating before you started doing this?"

Glenn nodded. "Ex-girlfriend now," he added to correct himself, perching on the arm of the sofa.

"Ah. Ouch." Ash wanted to pat him on the arm or something, but he was kind of stuck on the couch unless he levered himself up out of it. "Sorry, man."

"No, no. It's fine. I'm just glad for Chris. He seems like he needs someone around."

"Yeah?" Ash thought he knew Chris pretty damn well, but there was the chance he was a different kind of guy at work. He wanted to know what his coworkers thought.

"I mean, I've been working at a few different stations since two months ago, and the guys here have been... great. Just awesome. Everyone loves him."

Ash relaxed and smiled slightly. "Yeah. Sounds about right, from what I know."

"How'd you meet?"

Oh, there it is. Ash's lips twitched into a slight smile. "He was a first responder."

"No shit!" Glenn exclaimed. Then, his eyes flicked down to the cast, and back up to Ash's face. Ash could see the wheels turning in his head before his eyes widened.

And there we go.

"Oh, yeah. I heard," Glenn said casually. "He got sent home from work a little early after something not long ago, right?"

"Yeah, that was me."

"Shit. You guys move fast," Glenn grinned. "I need to get myself a guy, apparently. Staff party's next week and I don't even have a date."

That was not the reaction Ash had expected. He'd been setting himself up for pity, or worry, or some kind of high-horse judgment about his life and why he'd decided to try to end it.

Instead, Glenn was just grinning easily at him, and he couldn't help but smile back.

Okay. Maybe a few people can be cool.

"Yeah, I recommend it," Ash bantered back, his smile growing. "Okay, I should get out of your hair, huh?"

Glenn nodded. "Need a hand getting out to the bus stop?"

"Nah. I can move pretty well on these now. But thanks," Ash added, and he didn't just mean for the offer of help. His chest had been tight with fear for the first minute after the other guys left, but Glenn had distracted him until he'd found out it was a medical call and unlikely to be the one that took him away from him.

Or something like that.

Yeah. Glenn was right. They had to talk about the danger of Chris's job sometime, but that could wait until after the discussion about them moving in together all of a sudden, and all of *that* could wait until Chris was off work.

"Take care of Chris for me," Ash added once he was in the doorway, Glenn close behind him.

Glenn offered him a quick smile and clasped his shoulder. "I will. Take care of yourself for him. And for you, too, man." His eyes weren't full of pity, though. There was a note of understanding there that made Ash settle.

He knows what it's like, somehow. Ash wasn't gonna ask questions, though. He jerked his chin in a quick up-nod of appreciation. "See you."

He was still smiling lightly to himself as he started the slow walk to the bus stop just down the street. He couldn't pick apart the source of his lighthearted feelings: sleeping with Chris, moving in with him, being accepted by his friends, or all of the above?

But since moving in with Chris, it felt like everything was rolling uphill in the best of ways.

20

CHRIS

"So, in answer to your question..." Chris heaved the last box into the back of his car and shut the door, then wagged his finger at Ash. "No, you are *not* paying rent."

"But..."

Chris shook his head. Ash had been trying to argue that he should all afternoon as they drove back and forth, Chris loading up boxes while Ash supervised. "No. I don't need your money, and I don't want it."

Ash pouted at him, leaning on one crutch as he rolled his head back. "But, man. I don't want to be a charity case."

"Okay. That's understandable." Chris nodded. In his shoes, he'd feel the same. "So, make me food now and then, once you're able to cook again. You know, tidy up a little. That kind of thing. Keep me company. Damn, man, that's more than you know."

Chris didn't want to get all sappy on him, as much as Ash would enjoy that, but these last two weeks were something else compared to the months of... well, boredom... before that.

"Are you sure?" Ash gazed across the hood of the car.

Chris relaxed and smiled. At least he was willing to accept help more readily now, if after a fight. "Yeah. Besides, you know... living with you comes with its perks."

They hadn't slept together since that one time, but holy crap, Chris wanted to try it again. Maybe being in such close proximity so soon after agreeing to date was a bad idea, but his gut instinct told him to get close to Ash and stay close, no matter how hard Ash tried to shake him loose.

All the low self-esteem signs were there: Ash kept looking twice at him when he flirted as if making sure he was serious, and when Chris had suggested Ash be his date for the fire department's staff party for some guy's retirement, Ash had agreed, "if Chris was sure about it."

He had to make sure it wasn't cold feet, though. "You want this, right?" Chris said, lowering his voice so Ash would know he was serious about the question.

"You? Or moving in?"

Chris shrugged. "Both? Whatever?"

"I want both." Ash let out a slow breath as he looked over at his house—in all its decrepit glory. "I just keep waiting for something to go wrong, you know?"

Chris could understand that, after the little snippets he'd heard about his friend's past. "Yeah. But, I know it's cheesy, but... let go of that. See what happens."

"If I spread my wings and fly?" Ash's lips were quirked in a little smirk.

"Yeah. If you like." Chris laughed and nodded. It amazed him that Ash was able to laugh at all, let alone about the non-accidental-fall that had almost ended his life. That kind of strength was awe-inspiring... and Ash didn't even know he had it, did he?

"All right. Speaking of which... Well, first," Ash shifted around to open the car door and lever himself into the vehicle.

Chris knew better than to try to help him. He climbed into the driver's side and waited until Ash had the crutches settled into the car and the door shut. "Speaking of?"

"I want to go hang-gliding."

That was batshit crazy talk, and judging by Ash's laugh when Chris looked at him, Chris had that reaction written all over his face. "You... *what?*"

"It... I can't explain," Ash laughed, buckling up. "I know. But I was... I don't know. I might like it."

Chris nodded slowly as he started up the car. "First, wave goodbye to that hell-hole." He backed down the driveway as Ash grinned at him. "So, is this a conquer-your-fears thing?"

"Yeah. And..." Ash hesitated, clearly choosing his words carefully. "I felt so good for a moment there. I liked the flying. Just not... the bits before or afterward."

Chris kept his focus on the road, but he let the words wash over him and processed them. He could kind of understand that—the adrenaline rush from ignoring every human instinct that told him to back down from a burning building and walk in. Protection or no, there was a significant risk every time he did it, and every time, it taught him a little more about the strength inside him.

The more he thought about it, the more he liked the idea. "So, just randomly doing it? Or for charity?"

"That's... That's a good point, actually," Ash hummed.

One look at Ash told him he'd just given him an idea. And he was so damn stubborn, he wasn't going to be talked out of it.

"Okay, one thing," Chris laughed. "I think it's cool, but you have to tell your doctor what you're doing so he can say *when* you can do it."

"Ugh. I don't want to wait months."

Chris shook his head. "You're not hang-gliding with a cast. It'll drag your legs down and... stall you in the air."

"I'm fairly sure flight doesn't work that way."

"What about running to launch yourself?"

"Some of them are motor-driven."

Chris laughed. "You've been looking this up. How long have you been planning it?"

"Ever since the existential despair started to ease up," Ash half-smiled at him. "Well, I started off looking up jobs..."

"*Jobs?*" Chris exclaimed. "You wanna do it for a living?"

"No! Fuck, no. I'm terrified of heights now," Ash laughed. "Even looking out my hospital window was giving me vertigo."

"Oh. Phew."

"But, you know, it's not like you have a safe job either," Ash pointed out, and Chris couldn't really argue with that.

"Ah. Yeah. That's... a thing sometimes. How are you about that, by the way?" Chris casually asked.

Ash reached out to touch his arm. "I'm okay with it," he promised. "Glenn was telling me some partners get weird about it."

Partners. They had way too many balls in the air to add one more, but Chris decided to bring it up at some point. "Yeah. They do."

"Well, you met me from being a hero, so... you know. Keep saving people." Ash squeezed his arm, then let go. "As long as you try to come home to me."

"And I'll help you go hang-gliding when your dumb ass is healed enough, and not a minute earlier," Chris told Ash, which made him laugh.

"Deal."

"Cool." Chris grinned as they turned the corner to his street. "Okay. Last trip just about over, and just in time. Pizza should be here in... hey, check the tracker app. My phone's in my pocket."

Ash reached into his pocket to grab his phone, and Chris

winked at Ash when his fingers lingered on his thigh a little longer than necessary.

Pizza and maybe something else? He could go for that.

"Twenty minutes."

"That's plenty of time. You take your meds yet?"

Ash started to nod, then hesitated and checked his phone before he scoffed and shook his head. "Yeah, no. That explains the ache. You're like a robot nanny. How do you do that?"

"You get a little gray. It's easy," Chris told him simply. Anyone trained in first aid could read the signs of pain, as much as Ash tried to hide them.

Ash gazed at him for a few moments, then shook his head. "Man. I really like you."

If he'd been trying to get Chris to blush, it worked. Chris pulled the parking brake and hopped out of the car. "Yeah, yeah. You say to get me to haul your boxes around."

"Did it work?"

"Yep." Chris opened the car door to eye the few remaining boxes. "Get your ass inside and take your pills."

Ash circled around the back of the car, and before he led the way to the porch, he stopped to press a kiss against Chris's cheek. "You're cute when you blush."

For once, Chris didn't even have a response for that. He stared into the car to try to calculate how many loads he had left—the kind he had to carry—while Ash's chuckle receded toward the front door.

In life, as well as work, he trusted his gut instinct.

Yeah. This was the right call.

21

ASH, TWO WEEKS LATER

"It's nice to see you boys again. And even better to see your X-ray."

Ash jiggled his other foot nervously as he sat in the hard plastic chair of Dr. Green's office. He couldn't believe, either, that it had already been a month since his surgery.

The last two weeks had been much the same as the week before—filled with sexual tension between them, a couple hand jobs, and lots of making out.

And even more cuddling on the couch. That was pretty much his favorite part.

But, mostly thanks to the clunky cast and his own niggling fears that Chris would find it a boner-killer, they hadn't gone any further.

With luck, today, he got it off.

"Can I switch to the below-knee cast?"

"Jumping right to the big questions, huh?" the doctor laughed, settling back in his chair. "Yes, you can. You progressed much faster than we expected—it's rare to switch casts after just four weeks. But you're going to be on crutches

135

for a while yet, and then partial-weight-bearing for a few more months. A cane is okay at that point if you feel more comfortable with it than crutches. By then, you may be accustomed to crutches."

The breath of relief from next to him was almost as deep as his own sigh, and Ash swapped grins with Chris. "Phew."

"We'll see you again in a few weeks to measure your progress. You're healing very well so far. We don't see a lot of people recover from tibial surgery—especially after the kind of fracture you sustained—this fast. And in general, you've put on weight. Your blood pressure is better, too. Keep up your diet and exercise," the doctor praised. It could just be him, but Ash could swear the doctor was actually talking more *to* him, rather than *about* him, this time. "Do you need more painkillers?"

Oh, now that I'm dating him, I'm not a druggie?

"Yeah. I think for a few more weeks. It's better—a *lot* better —" Ash chuckled, "—but when they wear off... it's still bad." He'd spent so much damn time napping over the last couple weeks, but the alternative of going without medication or taking something too weak to help was nasty.

"Okay, we can do that." The doctor grabbed his prescription pad. "And we'll get you sent down to get your cast off and the new one put on. Then I'll have another look at it to make sure it looks right and we'll get you on your way home."

"Thanks, Dr. Green."

The doctor didn't stand up yet, though. "One more thing: have you talked to anyone about your employment options, and your living arrangements? You mentioned you two living together—I assume you're supporting him?" Dr. Green looked at Chris.

Chris frowned. "That's assuming a lot, sir."

"My apologies—" the doctor began.

Ash sighed to himself and interrupted. He was right, after all. "Yeah," Ash nodded. "No, I haven't yet."

Chris frowned, looking between them.

"I'll make you a referral for that, too. A lot of my patients struggle with integration into life again, especially after several months of unemployment. Are you searching for another career?"

It had only been a matter of time, really, before the bliss of a vacation from work and living expenses lifted. Ash dug his nails into his palms and shook his head. "No. I worked restaurant jobs and odd jobs before," Ash murmured, his mood sinking again. That was all he was good for, anyway. "I don't think I'll be able to do them. So I don't know what's next."

The doctor hesitated, his expression falling into a carefully-practiced neutral smile. "That's a good assumption. I'm sorry, but... your leg will never be the same. There's still every chance you'll have to use a cane even after you've healed. Remember, you still have a long time in recovery before you can reliably walk or stand for a long time. And you may be healing faster than expected to go from non-weight-bearing to partial-weight-bearing, but... surgery recovery takes its sweet time, and nobody can rush it. You'll remain partial-weight-bearing for at *least* one month, and I'd be surprised if it's not closer to three."

Ash nodded, clasping his hands together tightly.

"Now's a good time to brush up on other career skills or look into education."

The idea was terrifying. Ash wasn't good at anything, didn't have any kind of training, and wasn't going to accept Chris's money to go get education for a job that probably wouldn't hire him anyway.

Ash looked at the ground and nodded.

"And if you need it, I can make a referral to mental health services," the doctor said carefully.

Yeah. My crazy isn't just going to go away overnight. "If I get depressed from being disabled and unemployed? Can't imagine how that would happen," Ash managed a joke, half-smiling at the doctor, who smiled slightly back.

"We'll get it figured out." That was Chris sounding cheerfully determined as ever. "Thanks, doc."

Chris waited until they were settled in the next waiting room before he looked over at him. "Hey. That didn't go badly."

"No. Except that last bit," Ash murmured.

Chris slid his arm around his shoulders. In public or not, he hadn't hesitated to do so over the last few weeks, and the touch did soothe Ash a little. "We *will* get you sorted out," he promised. "And if you need antidepressants or therapy or anything, we'll do that, too. Your insurance should cover it."

"I dunno. Therapy won't fix my job situation. It was... one of the things that really pushed me over the edge last time," Ash admitted as his chest tightened and cheeks flushed. "I don't have any skills. I'm not smart enough to just... pick up a new career."

Chris snorted, and Ash tilted his head in confusion.

"Not smart?" Chris asked. "Who's your Davey?"

Ash opened his mouth, then closed it again, his cheeks burning harder.

It's no one in particular. It's just me.

Yeah, maybe he was hard on himself, but someone had to be. Nobody looked out for him, so he had to push himself.

Before he could answer, the nurse called his name.

"I'll come in with you," Chris told him, letting the previous threads of conversation go and rising to his feet. "But we'll get you working on something important."

You're assuming I even can.

"Yeah."

"Like coding, or languages, or... lots of things. You're smart."

"I'm really not."

"You'll see." Chris sounded smug, and irritation flared up in Ash's chest. Chris didn't know when to stop pushing it. He was eager to live his life for him, and sometimes it helped push him out of his depression. Other times, it just reinforced that he didn't have that kind of drive to care about himself.

Somehow, Chris thought he was smart enough for those things? When he found out the truth, he was going to be sorely disappointed.

Eventually, he'd expect rent or him to move out, and Ash couldn't see a way to provide either, but he wasn't going to be a burden.

Ash wasn't naive enough to believe that the first man he met after his not-accident would be The One for him. And when this ended, one way or another, he'd be right back to square one, only he'd have to work even harder to find a way to make ends meet.

"Ash?"

"That's me."

"Congratulations. Let's get your cast off."

As the saw whirred a few minutes later, the nurse told him to relax, so Ash let himself close his eyes and imagine that moment again—the one where he'd stopped worrying about absolutely anything.

It was bound to happen. This is the bit where real life sets in again.

22

CHRIS

"Oh, Jesus. I thought I was living with a zombie."

It was true on two levels: Ash had been nearly comatose for the last week, between sleeping off his painkillers and what even Chris could identify as a depression rebound after that asshole doctor's commentary.

But also, that color really brought out the paleness in Ash's cheeks.

"Jeez. Thanks," Ash snorted.

"No problem. You might wanna touch up on that tan first," Chris grinned. "I mean, I'm no expert. Maybe you're going for the, uh... Walking Dead look..."

Ash flipped him off and retreated to his room again. "See if I'm on your arm again," he called out. "Next party, your ass is alone at the party."

"More champagne for me," Chris cheerily answered, leaning in the front hall to await Ash's next choice of shirt for the fire station's autumn staff party.

"When *is* the next one? Ow. Jeez."

"Just before Christmas. We try for one every quarter." Chris winced at the noise of pain. "You all right?"

"Yeah. Smacked my leg."

Chris winced harder. "You'll never be able to make me casseroles at that rate."

"Thanks, Dr. Chris." Ash hobbled out of the room. "Glad you have your priorities straight."

"Anytime. *Something* about me should be straight," Chris grinned. "Hey, much better." The dark green brought out his eyes. "I like having a live date."

He didn't get in Ash's way, just put up his hands and backed away as Ash barreled down the hall toward him. The rubber tips on those crutches *stung* when they were applied directly to a foot, even through a shoe.

"So, this is a date?" Ash tossed out there.

I'm not sure what the right answer is. Chris frowned. They hadn't even messed around in the last week, mostly because Ash was napping or seemed too down. But that didn't mean his interest had faded.

No, he could still bring himself to be *very* interested in Ash, even if his sexy little ass and gorgeous cock were drowning in those dark, loose jeans he had to wear to fit over even the smaller, nimbler cast.

"Um. Do you want it to be?" Chris asked, zipping up his sweater and checking his pants again for his wallet and keys. He shot a quick look at Ash.

Ash looked nervous. "Do you?"

"This is going to go in circles. Yes," Chris answered. No sense in dancing around it, after all.

Ash relaxed and offered a quick smile. "Okay. Yeah, then. If people ask...?"

"You're my date... and a friend, too. Anything else is our own business." Chris hoped that answer sounded right. It wasn't like they were boyfriends; friends-with-benefits was way too much information. And they had more of a romantic spark than FWB...

When did his life start to require dating profile acronyms?

At least he wouldn't be the only one at the party bringing a male date. Liam and Chief Williams were both gay—and he kind of wanted Ash to see that he didn't have to be hidden away.

"Okay. Good." Ash was clearly worried. His brows pinched as he shifted on his crutches, then nodded at the door to indicate that he was ready to go. "Are they gonna be weird?"

"No. Well, some will," Chris admitted. "You gonna be okay? I can't punch them, but... be a smartass back."

Ash cracked a smile. "That's not a problem. As long as I won't be, like, exiled for it."

"Nah. You know the dynamic at our house? It's a lot like that. Except without over half the firehouse being at least half-gay."

Ash paused for a moment, leaning on his crutch while he fumbled to get the car door open. "Half-gay?"

Chris shifted from one foot to the other, then shrugged. "Bi, if you like."

The perceptive look Ash shot him made him almost squirm. But Ash climbed into the car and stowed away his crutches, waiting until they were both buckled up before commenting. "You think of yourself as half-gay, not bi?"

"Um." Chris hadn't really wanted to put that much thought into it. "Well, it's not exactly fifty-fifty, if we're talking... I guess sexual versus romantic... I don't really know. Do I qualify? I used to date women more, but now I've been catching up on men, like I said..."

"Whoa, whoa." Ash laughed under his breath, and then Ash's hand was on his thigh.

Chris took a breath and grounded himself before turning the car on. He shot Ash a look. "Sorry. Still don't really know what I'm doing, I guess."

Ash nodded. "It's up to you what you wanna call yourself. I don't have a problem with you being bi, if you go that way. In case you were saying half-gay so I'll... you know. Accept you."

Ah. Yeah. Chris winced. He could still remember the Grindr messages he'd gotten now and then, telling him to pick a side or that this was a site for gay men, not guys like *him.* Luckily, other people's idiocy didn't tend to bother him, but Ash was sweet for making sure of it. "Thanks. Are you?"

"Nope," Ash shrugged. "I've only been into guys. I tried really hard for about two years of my life, and then my parents died, and..." he trailed off.

Chris made a face. "Ouch."

"Yeah, I kinda stopped trying to be anything other than... me. That was hard enough."

Ash started to draw his hand away, and Chris put his own hand on Ash's to keep it there for a moment. Ash gave him a startled look, and Chris murmured, "Sorry."

"No, sorry," Ash echoed. "Don't wanna bring the mood down."

"It's not. It's part of your life," Chris said with an easy shrug. Yeah, it hurt his heart a little to hear Ash's past when it was full of so much worse than he deserved, but he wasn't gonna say he shouldn't talk about himself.

"I..." Ash trailed off, then chuckled quietly. "I like your style, man. Thanks."

Chris had to pull his hand away to flick the turn signal, but he cast Ash a quick smile. "I'll listen to anything. Never worry about that."

"Do they train you all in, like, counseling?"

Chris laughed doubly hard at the idea of them being counselors in the middle of the situations they were put into and the idea of *him*, of all people, being chosen as one. When Ash gave him a questioning, almost wounded look, he grinned. "Sorry. Not laughing at you. But *me*, a therapist? Can you imagine?"

Then, Ash cracked a smile and started to laugh, too. It was gentle, subdued, but it was something. "So you're just a surprisingly good listener, for all you come off as... brash."

Chris's heart soared. *I knew getting out to this thing would be good for him.* He snickered. "Brash. That's a carefully-chosen word."

"Very carefully."

"Hey."

Ash grinned and smacked Chris's thigh lightly, then pulled his hand back. "You can't deny it. So, is this just some random party? Retirement? Do I need to know anything else?"

"Nope. Oh, it's our Labor Day party."

Ash gave him an odd look, then pulled out his phone. "Jesus. I thought I was missing a month all of a sudden there."

Chris laughed. "The fire season goes longer and longer every year now, for brushfires. Crimps our style, you know? So we pushed the party back a month and it's more of a... pre-Halloween thing."

"Mmm. You mentioned that before," Ash nodded. "The longer season. But you don't have much of the hills in your territory, do you?"

"We have some," Chris said. "And this is a party for the whole district."

"Right, right." Ash drummed his fingers on the edge of his cast through his jeans. "I never really thought about different fire stations having different territory."

Chris nodded. "It's a challenge, actually. We've got residential, commercial, large buildings, little ones, some parkland..."

"So you're pretty good if they put you here."

Chris blushed and closed his mouth, offering a humble half-shrug. He didn't think of himself as a genius in a crisis or anything, but he was steady and dependable, and he thought fast on his feet. The same quick wit that held him back from promotions—because of how he used it—was actually a big advantage in a situation where he wasn't afraid to throw out oddball solutions.

"Oh, look. There's a blush. I'll just have to ask your coworkers," Ash teased.

"Please don't," Chris groaned. "Williams will think I've sent you angling after he passed me up for promotion."

Ash frowned. "That's bothering you, still, I bet."

"Yeah. It's been... well. Whatever. Okay, nearly there." Chris brushed off the reminder and set his focus on what mattered: enjoying himself and bonding with his coworkers.

It was important to do that not just for team morale, but safety. He hung out with some of the guys outside work, but as far as he was concerned, he had to be at least vaguely familiar with the other guys around town. If he was called in as backup, he didn't want to walk in blind and put his life into the hands of a stranger. Nor did he want to be a stranger to them.

If they knew each other's families, they'd all be a little more careful to bring their teammates safely home to them.

"Hey, Chris! Oooh, and this is the man I've heard so much about?"

Chris's second blush of the night was at the hands of Liam's boyfriend, the perky little twerp. Dylan was beaming at him, making it clear his intent was to embarrass.

Ash cast Chris a curious glance, a smile tugging at his lips, then looked at Dylan and smiled. "Hi. I'm Ash."

"Dylan."

They shook hands, and then Ash glanced at Chris. "So, you've been talking about me?" he winked.

Chris had no defense. He might have mentioned Ash a few times to Liam at the station that week... or a lot, come to think of it. But Ash was the new, exciting part of his life, so of *course* he was going to talk about him.

He opened his mouth, then just shrugged helplessly. "A little. I'm gonna kick Liam's ass."

"What now?" Liam came up behind Dylan, sliding an arm around his shoulders and pressing a cup of punch into his hand. "You can kiss my ass if you want."

"*Kick*," Chris threatened. "You gossip."

"Oh, that. Sorry," Liam grinned at him. "So, Ash, how's it going? Happy you moved in with this loser yet?"

Chris flipped Liam off while Ash laughed and nodded. "Yeah, it's been great," Ash told him. "I mean, I've been still sleeping a lot, but when I'm awake and he's not at work... we occasionally see each other."

That was pretty painfully accurate. Chris half-smiled and nodded.

"Good. You're healing fast, though, right? Chris was all proud of you for switching casts," Liam told Ash with a beam despite Chris's glare.

"He was?" Ash smirked, and Chris knew he was gonna get it later. "Thanks. Yeah, apparently I do something right. It must be his diet plan."

Chris shrugged. He *did* have a pretty strict diet to keep himself in shape and boost his energy, so all he'd done was double the portions to feed two. Ash was essentially on a speedy track to regrowth with his protein ratio and calorie intake. And maybe weight gain, but the few pounds he'd put on were good on him. Made him look a little more like he belonged in this neighborhood, at least.

"Good," Dylan agreed, smiling. "That must be a pain in the ass, though," he gestured at the crutches.

"Better than I expected. I've gotten fast on them," Ash told him. "But I'm hoping to switch to a cane after six or eight weeks. Could be up to twelve..."

"More exercise," Chris told Ash firmly. He couldn't be lying around sleeping all day if he wanted to keep his legs strong.

Ash rolled his eyes at his friends. "Yes, sir."

"Ooh," Liam winked. "Don't blow up his ego too much. Oh, hey!"

It was Chief Williams, and Chris's chest tightened.

"I'd love to reward your hard work, but... I just can't overlook the whole picture."

Chris's throat was tight, and he swallowed hard past the lump. "Such as?"

"Your conduct in the fire house has to improve. I get that pranks are part of life, but sometimes..."

"I take it too far." Chris knew what he was going to say, because he'd heard it before—from lovers, teachers, friends.

Fuck it. He wasn't going to pretend to be someone serious and boring just to get a promotion. If that was what it took, he didn't want it.

He gripped his cup a little harder as he nodded casually at the chief and his husband. "Hello."

"Evening, boys. Liam, Chris. Dylan, right?"

"Yes, sir. Good to see you again," Dylan told the chief with an easy smile.

"You, too. And you must be new?" Chief Williams addressed Ash with a curious smile. "I'm Chief Williams."

"Oh. Hi. Ash." Ash was suddenly nervous, fumbling with the grip of his crutch to shake hands. "I'm here with Chris."

Chief Williams glanced at him, the question in his eyes: *with* him?

Chris nodded firmly, straightening up. "Yeah, he was the only guy who wanted to be my date, so..."

"Oh, so I'm not your first pick?" Ash smirked, knowing the answer to that one.

Dylan and Liam grinned as one while Chris's cheeks heated up and he tried to deflect. "Well, since David Beckham wasn't answering the phone."

"Uh huh," Liam snorted into his cup. "*Ash* this and *Ash* that..."

Even Chief Williams was grinning now. "That's a nice color you've got there," he complimented Chris, then looked back at Ash. "Glad to meet you, then. This is my husband, Mike."

Chris wasn't that observant, but even he noticed something was a little wrong with Ash as he reached out to shake hands with the guy—his gaze skittered off him too quickly, back to the chief.

"Good to meet you," Mike answered. He was short and stocky, and of all the times Chris had seen him at parties and functions, he rarely smiled. Still, it had to be a strain on their relationship to have been the first, and top-ranked, openly gay couple in the department. He didn't envy them a bit.

"I'm sure Mike will tell you it's rough to date someone in this line of work," Chief Williams brought up, while Chris rolled his eyes and shifted. It was a good speech, but almost mandatory.

Ash nodded jerkily, his eyes still on the chief. "I'm aware. You guys all do good work, but... yeah. I've heard."

"Good. It's not all joyrides," Chief Williams told him, then lightened up and smiled. "Though it can be. Don't let me catch you doing that again," he added to Chris with a wink.

Something in Chris's chest squirmed as he remembered *that* incident last summer, with a girl he'd been trying to impress. No harm done, and he hadn't taken their main rig, but... "No, sir."

Liam, bless him, intervened to change the subject. "So, if this is our chance to tell all our embarrassing stories, we should probably make him look good now and then."

Oh, never mind. Don't bless him.

"Oh, yes. That'll embarrass him more," Chief Williams agreed with a wink, then took Mike by the shoulder to lead him on. "I'd better make the rounds. Talk to you later. Pleasure meeting you, Ash."

"You, too." When he was gone, Ash glanced back to Liam. "So, do I get to hear about him being a hero?"

"I'm heading off for snacks," Chris grumbled and did exactly that while the others laughed. Not that he didn't like hearing good things about himself, but it was always a little embarrassing to hear praise and not know how to respond to it.

It wasn't like he did the job for these moments. It was the acts that mattered, not having them retold.

The snacks table was good this time, too. He hovered around it as he worked his way down the table, trying one of everything from the little sausage rolls to the weird olives. He was just figuring out where to put the pit when the rhythmic thumps of Ash's crutches announced that he was joining him.

"Hey, big hero."

"Oh, God." Chris rolled his eyes. "Whatever they said, it was probably fifty percent exaggeration." Ash leaned on his crutch, awkwardly trying to grab a plate and figure out how this was gonna work, so Chris took the plate for him. "Tell me what you want."

"Thanks." Ash winked at him. "I won't mention what they said, then."

Once the plate was loaded, Chris started to lead him to the side of the table, but caught him staring across the room at Mike.

Okay, something was definitely up.

"You don't like him?"

"What?"

"Mike?"

"Oh, shit. No, that's not it." Ash wouldn't meet his gaze. He was much too busy shifting to stand against the wall and lean one crutch there, then cradled the plate awkwardly in his spare hand against his chest to eat.

Chris stared at him with a raised brow until he looked up.

"Fine," Ash murmured, his voice almost too low to hear under the babble of rising and falling voices and laughter. "I, um. Recognize him."

Chris looked at Ash.

Ash didn't drop the gaze, just worked his jaw around slightly.

Then it hit.

"Oh, shit," Chris breathed out, almost dropping his own plate. Mike wasn't sleeping around, was he? That was the awkwardest fucking possible problem. "Maybe they're... open?"

"No." Ash didn't elaborate, just looked back down at his plate at last. "I like these cookies."

What the fuck was he supposed to do? Chris stared at the couple—Chief Williams, ever the calm and grounded presence, seemingly never rattled by a thing, and Mike, who had seemed like the loyal husband in the background.

"Do we...?"

"*No.*" Ash's voice was sharp.

Chris shifted from foot to foot and drew a breath, then nodded. No, he was right. It wasn't his business, anyway. "I want that promotion sooner or later..."

At last, Ash chuckled slightly. "Yeah. That, too."

"Wouldn't want to commit career suicide. No windows in here anyway." It took Chris a second of silence from Ash before he looked over at him.

Ash was still staring at his plate, and this time, his body was tense.

Oops. Chris kicked himself mentally, then awkwardly put his hand on Ash's shoulder. Yeah, maybe he ought to leave the suicide jokes to the guy who'd tried it.

Ash shrugged off his hand and tossed his plate in the trash, then grabbed his crutches. "Anyway. Better get back to Liam and Dylan, huh?"

Chris swallowed his sigh as he watched Ash's retreating back, stuffing a few more taco bites in his mouth. Might as well indulge, since he was so *not* gonna get laid tonight.

23

ASH

"Okay. I'm off to work," Chris called out, his voice ringing through the house.

It was early in the morning, but night and day weren't that concrete for Ash anyway. He woke up when his meds wore off, and slept when he was tired, depressed, frustrated, or just didn't feel like living.

Sleep was better than jumping out a window. A little less permanent. That was about all the progress he felt like he'd made, though.

He pushed himself off the bed and grabbed his crutches to hobble to the doorway of his room and look down the hall at Chris. "Okay. Until... God, what day is it?" He'd been living in a daze for too damn long. The only thing to keep him on track was Chris's work schedule, and it was two-on, four-off, putting him permanently a day out of sync with the days of the week.

Chris, in his sexy fire station t-shirt and trousers, looked over at him. His expression softened for a moment as he shoved his shoes on, then wandered closer.

He was keeping a little distance, clearly trying not to

approach too closely. And no wonder—Ash had been kinda pissed off about the joke, but then Chris had spent the rest of his days off awkwardly joking about who else Ash might "know" like it was some kind of weird thing he was trying to process.

Ash had no interest in clarifying the exact nature of the relationship—it was none of Chris's business, after all—but it was looking like he might have to, sooner or later.

After Chris came back from work, that was. For now.

"It's Wednesday, so I'm on until Friday morning," Chris answered. "Um, Dylan's coming by the station with lunch tomorrow if things are slow." He hesitated, the nervousness easy to see on his expression. "If you wanna come…"

Ash let out a sigh, then smiled a little. He couldn't hold a grudge at Chris for opening his big mouth now and then and saying something dumb. It was Chris's nature—unfiltered, raw commentary. At least it was incredibly easy to tell what bothered him.

"I'd like that. It's getting pretty isolating here at home. I don't think that helps my brain," Ash admitted, offering him an olive branch and a nugget of information at once. Not that it was hard to guess, but at least he said it out loud.

"Mmm. Braiiins," Chris countered with a light smile, then stepped forward into his personal space. "Don't go full zombie on me, okay? Call me anytime."

God, he was hot in that t-shirt. Almost hot enough to stir Ash's libido—temperamental these days—and make him want to make him late for work. Ash leaned in the doorway so he could reach out, tentatively resting his hand on Chris's shoulder.

When Chris didn't shrug it off, Ash pulled him in for an experimental kiss, light, just… testing the waters. "Thank you. I know it's been rough the last few weeks."

"You can't help it," Chris murmured, his hands automatically going to Ash's waist. "But you're making progress. Don't forget that. When you're off the damn sleepy painkillers, it'll help. Your next appointment's Friday, right? Late?"

"Yeah. I know you'll be tired out that day, though. Don't stress. Dylan offered to drive me."

"Did he? Awesome," Chris smiled. "I'll leave it to you two, then."

God, it felt good to hold and be held. Of course he'd figure that out right before Chris was gone for two full days.

"When you get back..." Ash trailed off, then cleared his throat meaningfully.

Chris's grin was instant. He checked his phone and groaned. "Oh, you cheeky bastard. I gotta go."

"I know. Just giving you something to look forward to," Ash winked. *And me.* But that went unsaid.

Chris's shiver as he let go of Ash was visible. Then, he leaned in, cupping Ash's cheeks instead to pull him in for a long, slow kiss. Ash barely kept his balance, pressing his hands to the doorway to support himself.

The heat crackling through his body made him curl his toes into the floor and kiss harder, their lips warm and wet.

Fuck, apparently all it took to ignite that chemistry again was a second of touching each other. Good to know.

Ash's stomach tightened, his dick stirring against his thigh as he sucked the tip of Chris's tongue suggestively.

His brain reminded him that he wasn't wearing underwear under his sweatpants—no point, with him always waking up and going to sleep at weird times, and how damn annoying it was to get it on over his cast.

Chris noticed, too. When he let go of Ash, he snuck a quick grope in. "Save it for me, hm?" he winked.

Ash eyed him suspiciously, waiting for the second half of that sentence. If he made one more crack about Mike...

"No... other hot firemen." From the second of realization and panic on Chris's face, he *barely* recovered that one.

Ash cracked up and shook his head. "Nice save. Now go save people, my knight in shiny yellow armor."

"I'll try," Chris winked and pecked his lips once more, then strode for the door. "Later, gator!"

"Bye," Ash laughed, watching the door close. God, Chris was such a weirdo. Why was he grinning so hard his cheeks hurt?

He glanced down at himself. Oh, yeah. That was why.

Well, might as well ride the wave while it hit him. Chris had picked up a bag of cast covers for him last week so he could start showering again instead of awkwardly lying in the bath.

He had all day to figure out how to jerk off and not near-kill himself with a slip and fall in the shower. Having Chris rescue him from *that* would just be embarrassing.

"Okay, *fuck* this." Ash flipped off the mixing bowl with both fingers. It was damn near impossible enough to do any cooking and baking with these fucking crutches, and now the recipe he'd chosen for cookies was not cooperating.

Of course he was going to bring food to the firehouse, especially if Dylan was. But fate, and the mess of dishes across the counter, and the near-liquid cookie dough, told him that he was not going to show up with his own cookies.

Fine. He'd schedule in extra time for the grocery store, and he'd clean up this mess later today... slowly. Cleaning took just as long as cooking, if not longer.

It was maddening when he thought about how much faster

he could do *everything* if he'd just had an extra couple hands, or use of his existing ones.

"What doesn't kill you only makes you stronger?" he muttered, bobbling his head this way and that with annoyance as he made his way to the door, grabbing his wallet from the hall table. "Bullshit. My character is no better now. I'm just angrier."

He huffed a sigh and flopped onto the stairs to put his shoes on, then made his slow way out of the house to the bus stop at the bottom of the street. His car just sat there in the driveway taunting him.

No driving until he'd been switched to a cane. Only fair, but annoying? Oh, yeah.

Buses were shit. In fact, so was his mood now, and it was only the reminder that he was supposed to be acting nicer so Chris didn't get totally frustrated with him that kept him on track.

Grocery store, then fire station.

When he finally got to his first stop—and getting a seat on the bus before it started moving was a fucking talent in itself—he chose the bucket of cookies. It was the only container he could really carry. He could kinda grip the handle with his thumb while he curled his fingers around the grip of the crutch. He managed a smile for the cashier.

At least I'll appreciate that small stuff when I can do it again.

The second bus took him straight to the fire station, and when he made his way up the sidewalk to the door, it was already open for him.

"There's no buckets of water, right?" he asked Dylan, who was beaming at him from the door.

Dylan chuckled. "Nope."

"Good. How are you?" He turned slightly sideways to get

one crutch inside first, then the other, careful not to crush Dylan's foot. It was almost natural by now.

"I'm great. Oh, you didn't have to bring food!" Dylan exclaimed.

"He brought food?" That was Kevin from the engine hall. "He's a keeper!"

Ash chuckled. The visit was already lifting his spirits a little, at least. He wasn't faking the smile now. "Hi," he greeted whoever was around—Kevin, poking his head in now to see what he'd brought; Dylan, who was taking the bucket of cookies from him (thank *God* because his thumb was about to break); and there he was. Chris.

God, Chris was even cuter after a day without him around.

"Hey. How are things?" he asked Chris, making his way through the hall to the open living area. He looked calm and uninjured—both good things.

"Good. Slow. We like that," Chris smiled. "You?"

"Not bad. I might have made a disaster in the kitchen."

Chris eyed him. "You're not still trying to cook, are you? I left three days' meals in the fridge—"

"No," Ash assured Chris with a chuckle. "I was gonna bake cookies. The cookies disagreed."

"Oh, no." That was Liam from the living room, chuckling richly. "Good, is that everyone? I'm starving."

"Yep, it is. Dylan, you serving?"

Everyone bustled around Ash, walking back and forth to grab plates and serving utensils. He'd learned how to tune out their movement and just focus on where he was trying to get to —a seat at the table.

He pulled out the chair and swung down into it, then leaned his crutches against it and drew a breath. Sitting down was always a relief.

When Ash looked around for Chris, he spotted him in the

kitchen, a spatula in one hand, pulling his phone from his pocket. Chris frowned at the screen, then pocketed it again.

Ash tried not to let his mood drop. Chris had lots of friends; maybe he wasn't texting Davey while he was at the station.

Or maybe he was.

His business, Ash reminded himself.

The moment passed as fast as that when Dylan started serving up casserole to the laughter and jokes of the other guys. Ash let it go and lost himself in idle conversation for these few minutes, mostly listening to the guys bullshitting about football and manly things like that.

Once they were done eating, Chris nodded at Ash. "Hey, you two wanna keep Kevin company while we wash up? He's checking the rigs over."

"Least likely to appreciate the company of two hot young guys: Kevin," Liam sighed. "Such a waste."

That broke the moment of calm that followed a good meal as they all laughed and started to get up.

"I heard it's purring weirdly. Before the mechanic gets here, I'm checking out the engine," Kevin told them. "I'll appreciate getting a hand—oh, wait."

Dylan made a face and slid his hands into his pockets. "I don't know engines."

"I know a bit. I had to keep my old beater running," Ash shrugged. "But I can't give you a hand..."

Kevin laughed as the three of them headed to the engine room. He seemed like a cool enough guy—a little older than Liam and Chris, maybe in his late thirties, but just as cool-headed and laid-back. Was that a firefighter personality in general?

Oh, man. The engine was *cool*, though. Diesels were so pretty, even if Ash didn't know a lot about them. Dylan looked bored, but he leaned on the side of the car and looked down dutifully into the mechanics while Ash and Kevin eyed them.

"So it's making a rattle? What kind of rattle?" Ash asked. "Not the radiator or air filters or something?"

"I'm thinking not. Sounds like an exhaust issue," Kevin told him.

Ash grimaced. "Oh, yeah. So you do all this yourself?"

"Only the basics. We have to have mechanics do the real servicing unless it's something real easy, and even then, they have to sign off on it." Kevin started fiddling with the diesel pump, then checked the oil on autopilot. "I'm a fire engineer, so I'm in charge of the rest of the equipment on the truck. I drive, and I communicate with other districts. I handle stuff like water flow rate, supply lines, hydrants. That kind of stuff."

"Ohhh." Ash raised his brows. "So engineering in the sense of handling all the equipment."

Dylan snickered, then cast Kevin an apologetic look.

Kevin cracked up as he shook his head at the engine, then closed the hood. "Yeah. I do that, too."

"Huh." Ash glanced back toward the kitchen at the sound of raised voices and laughter. There was an idea in the back of his head for a career, but he didn't dare to think about it yet. He could barely get out of bed, let alone make big life decisions for himself.

Dylan straightened up, too, and followed Kevin back to the kitchen. "Okay, we'd better get out of your hair. Ash, you want a ride somewhere? Or better, wanna hang out?"

Ash blinked at him. "You wouldn't mind?" After all, Dylan had a job, like everyone else here. And he didn't know him very well.

"Yeah, I'm off today," Dylan shrugged. "If you wanna, that is."

"Yeah. Sure."

Chris grinned at them. "Oh, uh oh. Here's trouble. Now the guys are going to conspire against us," he told Liam.

"We're forming secret plans to become BFFs already," Dylan dryly told him. "In fact, we already are. Heart eyes, motherfucker." He gazed, doe-eyed, at Ash, who mirrored his expression.

Kevin laughed and rubbed the back of his head like he didn't even know how to address that, then shook his head and headed back to the engine room. "Thanks for lunch. See you guys soon."

"See you!" Dylan strode over to Liam and pecked his lips. "Stay safe, babe."

For a second, Ash envied him. Then, the inevitable moment where he looked at Chris and both of them felt awkward about what they were supposed to do.

Chris raised his hand in a little wave, then moved into hug him.

"You could be more awkward," Liam commented.

Ash rolled his eyes. "You chose to be best friends with this asshole?" he countered to Chris, shaking his head as he pulled back. "God."

"Touché," Liam smirked. "See you later."

"Bye!"

Dylan strutted out first and headed around to the passenger side of his car. "You need a hand?"

"No, I've got a rhythm now. Watch me fall on my ass," Ash chuckled. Luckily, he succeeded at swinging himself into the low car and stowing his crutches.

"Back to my place? Oh, I'm up a flight of stairs... Yours? Or a coffee shop?"

Ash waved a hand. "God, I need to get out of my place. Yours is fine. I can do stairs."

If he counted Liam and Chris, that made two friends.

Making a third? He'd hang out on the beach in an awkward cast wrap if he had to.

"Sold."

And besides, hanging out with the partner of a firefighter made him feel a bit more like he had a chance. He was stumbling into a few people who accepted him, who wanted him around. That did wonders toward clearing the fog from his brain, if only for a few hours at a time.

Just as Julie had said when teaching him to use crutches: small steps.

24

CHRIS

"Well, who's the popular guy in school today?" Liam's voice echoed around the living room, disturbing Chris from his crossword.

Chris looked over at Liam and put the book down. "Huh?"

"Someone here to see you." Liam shrugged, then stepped aside to let him into the firehouse.

Davey.

What the *fuck?* Chris's heart dropped at the exact same moment Davey caught sight of him and smiled.

"Hey. Uh, can we talk?"

Something was stirring in the pit of Chris's stomach. Annoyance? To say the least. "We sure can." He tossed the book aside and strode for the door, shoving on his flip-flops. He steered Davey outside, then shut the front door.

Not that it did much good—the bay doors to the engine room were open, so every word was going to echo through there.

"What are you doing here?" He could see Davey's car down by the bottom of the driveway. Chris nodded down at it.

"You can't park there, either. Not within a few feet of the driveway."

Davey snorted and looked around. "Pretty place here. I can't believe I never visited you here." The pathway was lined with a few flower beds tucked in against the building.

"I can. I never invited you. I didn't invite you over that night a couple weeks ago, either," Chris told him. He didn't even try to hide the annoyance that sharpened his voice.

Davey looked hurt, his thick brows pinching together as he recoiled. "Oh."

Chris drew a breath, then let it out. He couldn't yell at him when he looked like he'd only just realized it was inappropriate to be here. Maybe the guy just had the worst boundaries known to mankind. "I'm kind of at work."

"Doing crosswords? What are you, eighty?" Davey laughed.

Chris eyed Davey and didn't smile.

Davey's laugh faded, and then he fidgeted, shifting from foot to foot. "Look, man, things are getting... pretty wild where I'm living."

"The rampant booze has nothing to do with it, right?"

"No. It's my roommate," Davey frowned, carrying on despite the interruption. "I don't want to live there anymore."

"So move out. Why do I care?" Chris asked. It was starting to get real old to see Davey hanging around here.

Still, there was a part of him that felt bad. But that was the part Davey was counting on.

The impulses were at war within him: *let him in, help him out*, and *Ash is right, kick him the fuck out*.

"Look. We're done," Chris told him clearly and slowly, his gaze flickering between Davey's eyes. "Our first try was sweet in a... stupid college kid way. The second, this summer, was dumb. A third time would be a fucking disaster. I don't make disasters for myself."

"We don't have to *call* it anything," Davey wheedled, raising his voice into a whinier pitch. "I miss you, baby." He tried to slide his hands around Chris's waist, but Chris jerked away and backed up, his foot sinking into a flower bed. "Don't you care about me?"

"I do. I *did*," Chris muttered. "Now, you're coming to my place of work to make a scene and try to embarrass me into *whatever* this is. You called Ash names, and you texted me and visited over and over when I said not to..."

"But then you liked it," Davey whispered.

Instead of the little thrill of anticipation Chris was used to feeling at that hoarse, suggestive tone, he just felt... numb. Shit. He had no sympathy for the guy at all... none. Had that ever happened, with anyone?

Chris scoffed. "Not really, no. Let it go, David."

"Don't call me that."

"Don't call me," Chris countered. He pushed Davey's shoulder and pointed down the sidewalk at his car, then pushed him again to get him moving. "Go. Move it before I call the cops. And if I see your face again—if you bother Ash, me, or any of my buddies—make no mistake. I will. This is it, Davey."

Davey stumbled and looked over his shoulder. "Really? You're really gonna...?"

Chris said nothing, just folded his arms. Behind him, he heard the door crack open.

"Whatever." Davey scoffed, looking Chris up and down as his lip curled. "I didn't want you anyway. Ugly cocksucker. Hope your muscles keep you warm. That gimp won't."

The door opened the rest of the way now, and Chris knew without looking that it was Liam, probably putting on his menacing look.

The way Davey stumbled back a pace confirmed it. Then, he scoffed and stomped down the driveway to his car, but he only succeeded in looking like a petulant child.

Thank God. It was good to see his retreating back. Why hadn't he done that *months* ago?

Chris shifted his weight to one leg and stayed where he was, watching Davey until he'd actually driven off, then sighed and turned to the door.

Liam leaned there, his expression sympathetic. He eyed Chris carefully. "You never told me what it was like with him."

"No." Chris moved for the door and Liam stepped aside to let him in. As Chris led the way to the kitchen to grab a snack, Liam tailed him but kept a distance. "I... let him get to me, that's all."

"When I was just starting to see Dylan, you said you were dating a guy from your past."

Chris wasn't going to beat around the bush. "Yeah. Him."

"Right." Liam leaned against the counter. "That's the end of him, right?" His tone told Chris there was only one right answer.

Chris cracked a smile as he tore open a bag of chips and dumped them into a bowl. "Yeah, it is."

"Good. You have a lot better to look forward to," Liam told him, grabbing a handful.

About that... Chris's gut tightened as he glanced at Liam. "Actually..."

Liam pointed a chip at him, then shoved it in his mouth and talked around it. "You are *not* getting cold feet and dumping that man."

"Gross. Don't talk with your mouth full." Chris anticipated the inevitable and looked away so Liam couldn't open his mouth and gross him out, shoving a few chips in his own mouth instead before carrying the bowl to the couch.

"Fine." Liam flopped next to him on the couch. "Are we going to have to talk about your feelings?"

"No," Chris scoffed. That would have embarrassed them both.

Liam grinned. "Good. So, what's really going on?"

"He told me something about..." Chris glanced around the room and dropped his voice. Not that he didn't trust Kevin, but the fewer people who knew, the better. "Something about a coworker."

"If someone's a kiddy-fiddler, we've got an arson toolkit out there," Liam jerked his thumb at the garage, his expression suddenly serious.

Chris cracked a little smile. "No. Not like that. Just... something that would hurt them if they knew, or... knew I knew."

"Right. So not really about them, even."

Chris nodded.

"And you resent Ash for telling you that?"

Chris opened his mouth, then closed it. Actually, that was about right. He hadn't been worried about trusting Ash, or the truthfulness of anything he'd said, until this. "Um. I guess. Fair enough."

Liam eyed him. "And you haven't talked about it, because that would be *gay*."

"No," Chris laughed. "Just, you know. It's not my forte. Took me goddamn long enough to figure out we both wanted to..."

"Too much information."

"Fine," Chris laughed. "And hey, you weren't exactly the best when you and Dylan..."

"I know, I know. Okay, man. Honestly? Why the fuck aren't you telling him whatever you're thinking? You tell everyone everything," Liam shook his head. "What's the problem *now*?"

Chris narrowed his eyes. *Because... it's not his fault for telling me. It's... Oh. Shit. I'm jealous.* "Ah."

The thought of Ash with Mike wasn't just distressing because he wasn't sure if Chief Williams knew about it. It was thinking about Ash with someone else.

Which meant he wanted... more than friends. More than friends-with-benefits. Shit. What if Ash didn't want that?

"Is whatever it is important enough to lose him over?" Liam quirked his brow.

"No. God, no."

"So don't be a chicken. You walk into fucking burning buildings. Pretend the feelings are a burning house or whatever. Tell the man how you feel. Goddamn," Liam scoffed at him.

Chris's cheeks flushed, and he nodded. "Yeah."

"And, man? I like that you give everyone a chance, but..." Liam trailed off, nodding toward the front door. "That guy? He was bad news. Yet you don't trust Ash about whatever this is? He*llo*?"

"I know. I'm not doing that again," Chris nodded. He hesitated, then added, "Thanks."

When Liam smiled at him and paused to formulate whatever the sappy response was going to be, Chris took the chance to shove a handful of chips down Liam's shirt to break the mood.

"You ass!" Liam laughed, then tried to shove chips in his face while Chris wrestled him off.

He couldn't wait to get home tomorrow. He had to figure out how not to fuck things up with Ash, and if he had to man up and ask what had happened between him and Mike, and whether he could be the most important man in Ash's life...

Well, he had nothing to lose.

"Hey, boys."

Liam and Chris nearly jumped out of their skins at the same moment. It was Chief Williams poking his head into the living room.

"Holy shit! Didn't even hear you," Liam exclaimed, clutching his heart and laughing.

Chief Williams' eyes were on the crushed chips all over the couch.

Of course he would show up now. Chris's cheeks flushed as he smiled at the chief, trying for a sheepish expression.

"Chris... could I have a word with you, if now's a good time?"

Shit. I hope it is. Chris brushed off his front and pushed his hand back through his hair. "Of course, sir." He followed the chief to his office, his heart thumping. "Is this about the chips?"

"No," Chief Williams laughed, then showed him to the office. "Close the door."

That's never a good sign. What have I done now?

25

ASH

"Hello. This is Ash. I'm looking for a... um, Charles?"

"That's me. How can I help, Ash?" The voice on the other side of the phone sounded perky and energetic. Definitely outdoorsy.

"Hi. I saw the thing on your website about hang-gliding for charity once, and I had a question."

"Sure."

Ash drew a deep breath and looked around the living room. "I'm looking at—after I've recovered from some injuries right now—doing a charity hang-gliding thing to get over a... really recently acquired fear of heights. I saw some stuff on your website about disabled hang-gliding... so I wondered if you might be able to accommodate it."

"That's awesome. Yeah, man, we can definitely talk about that." Charles sounded enthusiastic. "What kind of timeframe?"

"I'm not sure. I have to get in touch with some charities and see what to expect. Most people do sky-diving and stuff, but this seems almost... harder in a way. I don't know. It speaks to me," Ash laughed sheepishly. "God, that sounds lame."

"No, no. I get it. I've done paragliding and skydiving and all kinds, but hang-gliding can definitely be more of a challenge if you're afraid of heights. You're not falling, but you're just hanging there..."

It sounded like at once the best and worst idea ever. A shiver ran down Ash's spine. "Right," he agreed breathlessly. "Um, for full disclosure, I've got a shattered leg right now. I should be full weight-bearing in a few more months, but maybe with a cane."

"That's no problem for us. Our tow can accommodate it," Charles assured him. "Can I ask how you broke it? Must be pretty extreme."

Ash winced. "And that's the other thing I wanted to say. I totally understand if you didn't want to work with me, given... things. I, uh, jumped out a window. Deliberately."

If he could have paced, he would be right now to try to burn off the fearful energy racing through him. He was positive Charles was about to hang up on him. He should have lied. Should have told partial truths. Should have... given up on this whole damn idea.

There was a moment of silence—hopefully surprise, probably at the nerve of him for daring to call and say that—from Charles's end.

"Things are a lot better now, but I kinda picked up a... healthy fear of heights from that," Ash chuckled nervously. It felt like a hand was squeezing his heart. God, no sane person would want to be strapped to him now. "So I wanted to challenge that and also... do something to raise funds for a male suicide charity. You know. Something to keep other people from... doing the same thing. You can put me in a straitjacket up there or whatever," Ash weakly joked. He had to stop rambling before he pulled a Chris.

Charles chuckled. Then, he hummed. "Okay," he said slowly. "I appreciate you being honest, man. I'll wanna meet you and go over what to expect and stuff, but I'm not ruling you out."

"Really?" Ash exclaimed. "I figured nobody sane would want to—I mean, sorry." *Don't piss off the guy who might actually take a chance on me.*

Charles laughed. "Yeah. For a good cause, I'm a little crazy. But we'll meet and talk, all right? How's tomorrow?"

"Tomorrow... is good. As long as it's within bus range of Santa Barbara."

"Downtown on the pier? Say, one?"

"Perfect. Thanks, man," Ash told him as relief washed through him.

Charles chuckled. "Of course. Everyone deserves a second chance, right?"

Ash's chest felt warm. Before this—before meeting Chris, before all these crazy, sweeping changes in his life—he never would have agreed.

Now, he was starting to see why Chris was so optimistic.

"Yeah. We do."

"Great. Send me a text when you're there, and I'll see you tomorrow," Charles told him.

Ash was smiling now, so wide it hurt. "Yeah. See you tomorrow."

As he hung up, he wiggled on the couch in an impromptu little dance, then pumped his fist.

He did it. He actually called a guy about this stupid hare-brained idea, and told him everything, and he got a *good* response after all that.

Then, he turned his attention to the other tab on his browser: *Santa Barbara mechanic courses disability accommodation.*

May as well ride that wave, right?

CHRIS

"Hey! How was your shift?"

Holy shit, Ash sounded *perky* as he looked up from the couch, smiling at Chris. And damn if it didn't feel good to be welcomed home like that.

"It was good! Well... you know. As good as a shift is."

Chris's chest was still tight, but he was home now. He could forget about that whole damn shift, and all the weirdness with Davey and Chief Williams, and... everything.

"Good," Ash grinned slowly. "'Cause I've been waiting for *days* to follow up on our promise."

As distractions go, that'll do.

Chris dropped his keys on the table and locked the front door, then tossed his sweater in the direction of the closet as he kicked his shoes off. "Oh?" he asked, trying to stay casual. "Which promise was that?"

"The one you made when we were sucking face in the hall. Right before you grabbed my dick and then walked out the door on me."

"Sorry," Chris grinned, approaching the couch as Ash

levered himself to his feet. "I assume you were able to... *handle* that."

"You could put it that way," Ash murmured with a grin. He tilted his face up and to the side, so Chris did what came most naturally and leaned in for a kiss. "You look like you could use some stress relief before bed."

Chris was always exhausted at this time, around nine in the morning, from his last evening. There hadn't been much sleep last night after that fucking meeting, and then the call to that idiot who'd lit his own damn car on fire, and then...

None of that mattered. He was home now, and here with Ash. And Ash was hitting on him so hard that his head was spinning.

"Good guess. You should accompany me up to bed," Chris smirked. "Have you taken your painkillers?"

"Yes," Ash grinned. "So I have, like, half an hour before I conk out."

"I can think of ways to put that to use." Chris so wanted to scoop Ash up off his feet, but Ash was already on his crutches and leading the way to the stairs. Shit, he could move quick when called to do so.

As Ash worked his way up the stairs, Chris got to enjoy the view from behind, and did he ever. He lost his patience about halfway up the stairs and started groping that hot little ass.

"Oh, you're handsy," Ash laughed, glancing over his shoulder at him and sticking out his tongue.

"And you're a handful. Two, even." Chris stepped up to the stair below him and managed to catch that tongue before it disappeared behind Ash's lips again. He sucked slowly, still squeezing Ash's ass and digging his fingers in.

"Dude," Ash moaned when he pulled back. "Let me get up the damn stairs without falling."

Chris reluctantly pulled his hands off Ash and held them up. "Fine. As you wish."

"Those hands better get busy in, like, ninety seconds."

Chris snorted with laughter. "If you'd let me carry you, I could get it down to twenty."

"And leave me stranded without my crutches."

"Says the man who tries to cook with only one crutch when he's *supposed* to be non-weight-bearing."

Ash turned red and scoffed as he reached the top of the stairs, then swung himself down the hall. "Which room?"

"Oh, shit, right." Chris had kinda forgotten, what with Ash living here for so long now, that he'd never even been upstairs before. "The one at the end."

"Nice place up here."

"Says the man trying to pretend he's not still non-weight-bearing," Chris grinned, ignoring the glare Ash threw at him.

"I swear. Push your luck once or twice and you never live it down. I'm being good now," Ash sighed dramatically.

Chris dropped his voice as he closed the bedroom door behind them. "Not *too* good, I hope."

The way Ash shivered, his back straightening and lips parting, was unmistakable. He eased himself onto the bed and leaned his crutches next to it, then scooted up to lie along it. "*Very* good, I've been told."

That, in turn, sent a shiver through Chris. He was warm now, forgetting all that teasing on the stairs in favor of focusing on what mattered: tearing their clothes off and killing the stress that had been building between them for weeks now.

If Ash was in the mood now, so was he.

He straddled Ash in one quick move, shoving him flat on the bed with one palm to his chest and leaning down to catch his lips and suck them in a long, slow kiss, ending with a filthy flick of his tongue along Ash's lower lip.

"God, you're a good kisser," Ash moaned when he pulled back for breath.

"Wait 'til you feel me kissing somewhere else," Chris breathed out, still keeping his voice rough and low with promise. He mouthed at Ash's neck, kissing and licking his way up to tease Ash's ear and throat until Ash trembled under him.

"Oh, fuck, yes," Ash moaned within a minute. In fact, every damn time Chris kissed behind his ear or that spot on his throat or his collarbone, he squirmed. He was so damn easy to get going, apparently.

Perfect. Chris loved them that way: responsive and ready to let him please them.

And fuck, Ash was hard already. The tent in his sweatpants was impossible to miss.

"You skipped underwear again for me?" Chris murmured, grinning as he ran his hand along the bulge through the fabric, cupping and stroking. "Bold."

"I'm never in them these days. I've gotten out of the habit of wearing it," Ash confessed with a laugh. "I'm... ah... hnnh. Gonna get into trouble from that."

"I hope so," Chris whispered. He brought both hands up to strip Ash out of his t-shirt, then kissed his chest, admiring the slender form on his bed.

They'd stuck to handjobs and grinding and tame stuff after that first hot time, and yeah, Chris liked it, but he wanted more. He wanted Ash writhing under him, moaning in pleasure.

"My results came back," Ash whispered. "You get yours?"

"Oh, yeah!" It had been so long ago now that his text message came through—but Chris hadn't wanted to bother Ash when he'd seemed totally out of the mood for it. "All negative."

"Mine, too." Ash seemed tense for a moment. "And I haven't slept with anyone else. Can we go without condoms for, like, blowjobs?"

Chris grinned. "More important question: you want me to swallow?"

The exact shade of pink that flushed through Ash's cheeks as his dick twitched—visibly!—in his sweatpants was totally worth it.

"Yes," Ash moaned, grabbing his hand to guide it down to his cock again. "Fuck."

"So impatient," Chris whispered, but he was feeling the burn, too. It had been *ages* since they last fooled around on the couch after some TV show. He wanted them naked, now.

He leaned back to strip off his own fire station t-shirt and grinned when Ash wolf-whistled.

"I like that view," Ash approved.

"Take some more." Chris kicked off his jeans at the same time, bracing himself with an arm by Ash's head.

Ash turned his head and kissed the inside of his forearm, up to his elbow, and Chris's smile grew.

"Cheeky," he teased. Once he was naked, he could turn his attention to the only remaining clothes between them.

He hooked his thumb into the waistband of Ash's sweatpants, but despite the way Ash bucked up into his touch, he didn't pull them down yet. He still had too much to tease. Ash pushed at Chris's hand a couple times, but Chris didn't budge.

"Fucker," Ash mumbled.

"Just the way you like it." Instead, Chris kissed from his throat down the middle of his chest, pausing to lick and mouth at each nipple before he continued his slow, steady trail down to the waistband.

By the time he got to Ash's stomach, Ash was shoving his hips up against his hands, trying to grind against his chest. Chris ignored him and kept him pinned to the bed.

Chris was enjoying mouthing at his stomach too much,

letting his tongue trail along the side of the V to his hipbone, which he sucked lightly.

"Wha—fuck! That's... good?" Ash sounded bewildered.

"Don't tell me nobody's ever tried that," Chris mumbled, flicking his tongue along the thin skin over the jutting bone. It was just such an obvious move for a skinny guy like him. "It'd be fun to grind on, too..."

"You better be planning more than that, buddy," Ash muttered, trying to push up against his hands again. "Fuck. You're strong," he panted. Instead, he resorted to grabbing his sweatpants himself to haul them down.

Chris laughed and let him do it, pulling back to help Ash haul them down. His cock looked so fucking raw and hard just bobbing in the air there, the tip already wet. He was *desperate*.

And Chris wasn't going to leave him hanging.

He settled on his elbows, keeping one hand flat on his partner's stomach, and lapped at the tip of his cock. Oh, fuck, the taste and feeling of it were addictive. The velvety soft skin under his tongue throbbed with need, the veins standing out along the shaft. He kissed them, right down to his balls, and then licked to the tip again.

"Ohhh, God," Ash groaned as Chris flattened his tongue on the head and swirled it around once. "So good."

"I'll show you better." Chris closed his lips around the tip and bobbed his head slowly down to take in every inch, letting the tip slide across his tongue to the back of his throat.

Ash shuddered under him and in his mouth, his thighs going tense as he caught his breath. "Yyy—hnnnh." The noises from his lips were tight, high-pitched whines of need now, and Chris could tell he was already getting close. Hearing every little gasp and whimper was rewarding, but it reminded him of the need aching between his own legs.

Chris pursed his lips tighter, then bobbed them to the

bottom of the shaft once more. That was all it took for Ash to clench and shudder, the hot wetness coating his tongue. Chris made sure Ash saw him swallowing, pulling his lips slowly up the shaft while he kept the edge of his fingers against his lips.

When Ash was done, his eyes shut as he gasped for breath, Chris pulled his mouth slowly off and grinned. "That was fun."

"You fucking tease."

"I can be. Worth it?"

Ash groaned and nodded. "Oh, yeah." His chest heaved for a few moments more before he met Chris's gaze. "You'd better roll over quick."

"Aye aye." Chris pressed a kiss to the side of Ash's neck, then levered himself off, careful not to kick the cast. He flopped on the bed, his back upright against the headboard. "Are you sure you can do it?"

"Dude, it's only my shin now. I'm not in a full-body cast." Ash rolled over, too, and scooted himself along the bed until he was settled between Chris's thighs.

Chris tangled his hand in the hair at the back of Ash's head, rubbing lightly with his thumb. "Fuck, you look hot there," he breathed out.

"Mm?" Ash's lips were wet and parted as he pressed a slow, teasing kiss at the bottom of his cock. The hot, open-mouthed, gently sucking motion with the lapping of his tongue made Chris catch his breath.

When he repeated it all the way up his shaft to that sensitive spot where the head met the shaft, Chris's arousal only built. His cheeks were hot now, his stomach and legs tense from the effort it took not to just slide himself into that hot mouth and go to town.

"Speaking of... fucking teases," he managed breathlessly. Ash tapped the spot a few times with his tongue. "Jesus!"

Ash smirked at him, then slid his top lip across the head at last and bobbed his head down.

Oh, the hot, wet tightness around him was hard to describe and impossible to forget. Ash bobbed his head all the way down and Chris lost track of everything except those gorgeous lips and the wide blue eyes that stared up at him, drinking in his reactions.

Chris's skin sparked with pleasure and his hips pushed lightly, but he kept himself against the bed as much as possible to let Ash do the hard work.

He was so close already, a knot of pleasure in his stomach throbbing as the orgasm built up under his skin. And then he came, groaning Ash's name and pushing his head back into the pillows as he twitched and shuddered involuntarily.

When Chris went still and gasped for breath, Ash's hand slowly ran up his stomach to his chest and he shivered. He was so overwrought that even an innocent touch had him on edge.

"You're sensitive," Ash whispered, the hard cloth of the cast rubbing against one of Chris's legs as he pulled himself up the bed to nestle against Chris's chest.

"Can be," Chris agreed breathlessly. "Fuck."

"That was good, too, huh?" Ash teased.

Chris opened his eyes and chuckled when he saw that Ash was grinning away. He looked so damn proud of himself, as well he should be. "Yeah," he laughed. "It was good."

The stress and fatigue of his last few days at work made his limbs and eyelids heavy. Ash shifted to lie on his side next to him, and he wrapped his arm around Ash's shoulders as he let his eyes close again.

This is good. I want this.

Chris had never had trouble getting out of bed, but suddenly, he understood why Liam was so much slower to get out the door these days.

"How was work?" Ash's voice was quiet. The late morning sun streamed through the bedroom in strips of light across the rippling sheet. A lot like an eye test, all wavy and straight lines.

"Good," Chris murmured automatically, and then reality sank in. *Ah. Yeah.*

"You looked pretty stressed."

Chris winced. "I talked to the chief."

"I've been thinking more about your promotion. You're one of the best men we have, and your conduct has become more professional in the last month."

"Sir?" He wasn't sure where this was coming from, or what the chief was trying to say.

"What I'm saying is: keep making it easy for me to promote you, kid."

Chris let out a long breath of relief. "Really? I will."

"I'm not sure engineering is the right choice for you yet. It is a safer career choice if you have someone you want to get home to, though."

"Oh." Chris frowned. "You're saying I should do it?"

"Ash made quite an impression on myself and Mike."

Chris straightened up. Shit. Whatever went on between him and Mike, maybe he was the only one in the dark now. Was it good or bad? Why hadn't Ash said? "Yeah...? I mean, I admire what you and Mike have. Mostly. I want something like that."

"Mostly?"

"And?" Ash prompted.

Chris avoided Ash's gaze. "Um. I might have accidentally... said a few things."

Ash let the silence draw out until Chris looked over at him, then raised his brow slowly. "Like?"

He was making him say it. Chris sighed. "Um, that you knew Mike from *something*..."

Chief Williams was staring at him from the other side of the desk. He'd been capping and uncapping a pen, but he was just holding it midair now, his jaw dropped.

It was hard to startle him, but he'd managed it.

"Are you asking if I'm in an open relationship?"

"No! Just, like, that's not up my alley."

Chief Williams was silent.

"And the guys here would probably, you know, think it's stereotypical or something." Chris was sweating now, but that was it—his mouth was running. "They accept us as it is, but if they knew... not that I'm going to tell them about you guys or anything."

"Setting aside the boundary issue... what would make you think we are?"

The way he was watching him, Chief Williams knew what he was avoiding saying.

"Ash... recognized Mike."

"No." Ash groaned, straightening up and pushing himself against the headboard to sit up. "You didn't!"

"It kind of came out!" Chris defended, rubbing a fist across his eyes as he pushed the covers away from himself. "Fuck. I didn't mean to. But you know me."

"Yeah. I do." Ash snorted.

Chris ignored the grumble. "He... kinda didn't believe me."

"Great. So now your chief hates me," Ash sighed, sliding

out from under his arm and fishing around on the bed for his clothes.

Chris flicked his shoulder, but he grabbed his own clothes to bundle them into the laundry basket, pushing himself to his feet out of bed. "Uh, and *me*. I'm the one actually working there."

"Why did you even—how did that come up?" Ash exclaimed.

Chris glanced over his shoulder. "I think he was saying I should be more careful at work with you around or... something."

"Does he think we're boyfriends?"

Yeah, I think so. Chris shrugged slightly.

Ash paused, then tilted his head. "Do *you* think we're boyfriends?"

Whoa. He had no idea how he was supposed to answer this one. "Uh."

"That's why you've been so weird about Mike. You think I fucked him," Ash surmised. He squirmed on the bed to pull his sweatpants on, then his shirt.

Chris wasn't sure he liked Ash being so damn insightful. And he thought he wasn't smart? Bullshit. "Um."

Ash didn't give him a chance to answer, his shoulders rising as he pushed himself to his feet and grabbed his crutches. His gaze was guarded. "Are you jealous?"

"Territorial." A second later, it occurred to him that that could be a bad word choice. It wasn't like he *owned* Ash or anything.

"Right..." Ash trailed off in a slow drawl, getting his balance on the crutches. "For your information, *I* never fucked him. You wanna know who did?"

Chris nodded slightly.

"Benny, my druggie ex. The day I kicked him out, I walked

in on him naked with RJ and three other guys and a shitload of drugs. One of them was Mike. I don't even know if he remembers me coming in. They were all high as kites."

Chris's mouth hung open. "...Oh."

Ash wasn't giving him any time to think about that. "But we should probably have the relationship talk."

Chris's chest tightened with nerves. Yeah, it was a relief to know his potential future boyfriend hadn't been in bed with his boss's husband, but the stress was only just starting.

He was *not* going to fuck up with this guy by demanding some lifelong relationship out of the blue when they'd only been fooling around now and then for a few weeks.

"If you want. I mean, I think... I know... I *do* want more with you. But clearly, you know, we're a little different. I don't want to fuck up and hurt you, and you're sensitive."

Ash raised his brows.

"Like, at the party, and... other times..." Chris trailed off at the withering look he was getting. "Not sensitive without reason, but..."

Nope. Quit while you're only a mile behind.

He shut his mouth.

Ash let the silence linger for a moment more, then pressed his lips together. "Right. If you call me some wilting pansy who can't stand being in a relationship with a working man—"

"That's not what I said."

"—then I'll tell you to fuck off." Ash nodded at the door. "I have to have lunch before I meet a friend downtown."

"You have friends?"

Then, Chris's cheeks flushed. That came out way, *way* wrong. He just gave him a helpless look.

Ash's brows couldn't have raised any further. "Really," he stated more than questioned.

"Um. I didn't mean. Yeah." Chris *had* kinda meant it, if he was honest. Half the reason Ash was so depressed was that he didn't have people around him. But of course he must know *some* people.

And honestly, it would be good for him to be around people who weren't constantly putting their feet in their mouths.

"Have fun," Chris lamely supplied. The tension between them was entirely new, and he didn't like it. Even he couldn't ignore it.

"Will do." The clicks of crutches against the floor receded down the hall as Ash left the room.

Chris flopped onto his back on the bed and covered his face. Well, of all the ways to fuck up, he'd probably found several new ones. He'd basically implied Ash was a friendless, delicate butterfly who wasn't strong enough to be with him.

And some small part of him might have believed it, wrongly. Ash *was* strong. A hell of a lot stronger than Chris might have been in his shoes.

Then, he checked his phone and dropped a quick group text to Liam and a few of the guys he went out with more often —Harry and Royce, from the station in the next district over. *Wanna go out tonight? I could use one or three beers.*

Royce responded first, and so did the others as Chris lay on the bed and listened to the clattering from the kitchen.

Really, what he needed wasn't a drink to escape the consequences. It wasn't just the pranks that needed to stop... he needed to work on getting a brain-mouth filter. He'd been kind of a dick there. It shouldn't be up to Ash to brush off everything he said.

Chris groaned and rolled onto his front. Better to let Ash cool off before he approached him again. In the meantime, he'd get a full morning's sleep and try to figure out how to be less of a dick.

27

ASH

He was *not* some *sensitive* weakling.

Ash gritted his teeth as he waited for the bus to make its slow way down the street. He still had a twenty-minute walk facing him, but he was dosed up on just the right amount of painkillers—enough to numb the pain but not enough to make him sway on his feet with exhaustion.

He'd like to see Chris deal with *this* while figuring out what the hell they were going to do together.

There was more than enough time to stew in his own thoughts as he made his slow way down State Street, grateful for everyone who moved aside for him and glaring at those who didn't.

And then Chris had been amazed that he had friends? Sure, technically Charles wasn't a friend yet, but... he could become one.

Part of him knew he was being too hard on Chris. Chris just said whatever came to mind. Otherwise, he wouldn't have gotten himself into hot water with his boss.

Everyone had their faults, and at least Chris's was that it

was impossible *not* to know what he was thinking. Worked a lot better than things with Benny, or... well, most of his boyfriends before that.

When he finally found the coffee shop near Stearns Wharf, he drew a sigh of relief. He'd been worried tourists would be crowding the place, but now that the popular months of July and August were done and students were back at their own universities instead of bumming around surfing here, it was tolerable.

"Ash?" Charles's voice was easy to recognize, even from the phone conversation.

Ash spun and found him sitting at a table in the corner of the outdoor patio. "Oh. You're Charles...?"

The guy looked to be in his mid-thirties, and he was scrawnier than he'd expected. He was wearing a baseball cap backwards, and in a casual t-shirt and jeans. "Yep, that's me. Wanna grab a coffee and sit here? They'll deliver it to the table."

"Perfect," Ash smiled awkwardly.

God, he'd forgotten the initial awkwardness of meeting someone like this. He hurried through the transaction and back outside as fast as he could, leaning his crutches against the metal rail and drawing back his chair.

"Jeez, that looks like a pain," Charles commented.

"I can't wait to get it off," Ash sighed. "But it'll probably be another month or so. I've got an appointment soon, and I'm hoping to switch to a cane or one crutch. Then we'll see what they say."

Charles nodded. "I've busted my leg a few times. Takes a long time to come back from."

Abruptly, Ash remembered what he'd admitted to the guy. God, what he must think of him. He licked his lips and nodded nervously. "Yeah. I'm glad it wasn't worse."

"Me, too," Charles agreed, but he wasn't leaning in and giving some kind of inspirational sermon about life. Thank God. "You been doing better since then?"

"Yeah. Yeah, way better," Ash nodded. "Except for the... new fears. Which is what brought me to you."

"Gotcha." Charles leaned back in his chair as a waiter brought out Ash's coffee, then folded his hands. "How about I take you through what you can expect in a typical session?"

"Okay." Ash listened intently as Charles described the process: he'd get out to the field and lie in a harness, letting Charles strap them both in securely. The glider would have wheels, and it would be attached to a motor.

"Then, it pulls us along until we get airborne. There's a line that attaches us to the ground, and when we're about vertical, maybe a hundred feet up, I disengage that. By that point, people are pretty small below."

Okay, now he was starting to go a little faint. The view from a couple floors up had to be nothing compared to a hundred feet over the fields near Santa Barbara.

"You all right?" Charles smiled.

"Yes," Ash quickly burst out with. "I mean, maybe. I might have my eyes closed for a while."

Charles laughed. "I can warn you before I disengage the line. The glider shudders a bit, shifts the balance in the air, but then... it's just like flying. Maybe not comforting to hear..."

"Not really," Ash laughed weakly, tightening his grip on the coffee. His fingers were shaky at the imagination of what that view was like. "But safe?"

"Very. I've had a few minor bumps—hard landings, that kind of thing. But we take all the precautions we can," Charles promised. "I ride the currents and control the glider, taking us up in drafts of hot air to give us a great view, gliding along on whatever the winds give us that day, until it's time to go down.

Then we slowly spiral down again, in nice lazy loops. Not fast at all."

Okay, a gentle descent sounded okay. Much like the videos he'd seen of gliders in the air.

"Do you deal with a lot of people who are afraid of heights?" Ash asked, sipping his coffee. The slightly burnt taste helped ground him, even if his lips were almost scalded.

Charles chuckled. "Yeah. Most people are, to some extent. But most people are surprised at how easy it is once they're up there. Have you ever done anything like it? Aside from..."

"Not aside from that," Ash muttered, awkwardly shifting. "Um, and that doesn't bother you? Like I said, I'd... expect it would."

"You seem to have your head on straight," Charles told him, shaking his head. "Besides, the way you're strapped to me, there's not much you can do. If you're really afraid of heights, you might just be paralyzed with fear anyway," he winked.

Ash burst out laughing. "Thanks!" he exclaimed, but that broke the tension. His palms were a little less clammy now. It sounded like something he could *maybe* do.

"Anytime. So, you want to do it for charity?"

"Yeah. I found one that I think would work." Ash drew a breath. "I just have to figure out fundraising, and... go door-to-door. Obviously, after my crutches are off. It's not as exciting as, like, jumping out of a plane, but..."

"If you say you're afraid of heights, most people will still be impressed," Charles grinned. "Besides, it's a little more disability-friendly."

"Right," Ash murmured. It wasn't like he could forget about the cast on his leg or the bone-deep *wrongness* he felt even on painkillers. He was positive the doctor was right—he was going to be disabled.

But alive. Gloriously free and *alive*. And, for perhaps the first time in his life, he was glad of it.

"I know a lot of guys who get into this to try to escape something or other," Charles said slowly, sipping his coffee. "It's kind of addictive, I'll warn you."

"It's not the unhealthiest addiction, is it?" Ash countered.

Charles nodded. "Better than a lot of things." Something was troubled about his expression, but he brushed it off. "You're recovering, though? You got friends around and stuff?"

"A few," Ash admitted.

"Good. Hold onto them," Charles told him with a quick smile. "Put down roots."

"I'm trying," Ash promised. Then, he hesitated. "If it's not too nosy... you're really... insightful."

"Yeah. I've had my own... brush with death," Charles told him, clearly picking his words carefully. "I'm doing a lot better now. But it's hard sometimes. And we don't always talk about it like we should."

Ash shifted and nodded slightly.

"I was pretty... intrigued, actually, that you did. And I respect that, man." Charles reached over the table to fistbump, so Ash smiled and returned the gesture.

"Thanks. I figure..." Ash trailed off, then shrugged. "It's part of me now. I have bigger things to worry abou—huh." Wow. He hadn't expected to think that in a million years.

Charles watched him with a smile. "Hm?"

"I... just realized that's true. You know. Putting down roots, like you said. And relationship stuff. This guy..." Ash trailed off, testing the water.

"That's the other thing I thought," Charles half-smiled. "I am, too."

Oh, thank God. Ash relaxed and grinned. "Yeah? I wondered, but sometimes..."

"...it's hard to tell around here?" Charles laughed.

"Yes!" Ash laughed. "God, the skinny-jeans hipsters, or the students... everyone looks like they kinda *could* be."

Charles chuckled richly. "I know." Then, he nodded. "If you ever wanna hang out and watch how things are done, before you're healed up, you can watch some of my flights."

"Oh, I'd love that!" Ash broke into a smile. That was definitely an offer of friendship. Maybe Chris *had* been right about him not having friends, being a little too sensitive to his ill-timed suicide jokes, but not anymore. He was going to be more than that.

His phone went off and he glanced at it, expecting a message from Chris. Instead, it was Dylan.

Wanna hang out before I drive you to the hospital? Vee made cookies :)

Ash's shoulders sank and he smiled. "Sorry," he apologized to Charles and quickly messaged back.

That'd be awesome! Give me half an hour.

The warmth in his chest was still hard to get used to. Ash caught a glimmer of a thought for the future: studying mechanics, maybe, or something else practical that caught his eye along the way. Dating a man like Chris. Hanging out with Charles, maybe hang-gliding regularly. Having friends and hobbies.

That was something worth fighting for.

And if Chris was being all weirdly argumentative... well, maybe that was his own issue to sort out. Ash could wait for him to figure out if it was jealousy or something else.

Ash knew the real Chris already, and he was worth waiting for.

28

CHRIS

"Hey, man. You have the worst timing ever."

Chris furrowed his brow as he nearly ran into Liam outside the laid-back bar near State Street where they liked to hang out. "What?"

"You slept? No pre-drinking?"

Shit. He knew where this was going. Chris straightened up and patted his pockets. He didn't even have his car keys, but a rig could pick them up on the way by. "Yep. Where is it?"

"The mall."

Chris didn't even have to ask which one he meant. They'd find out the rest of the details on the way to the scene, but they both knew what he meant.

The plaza by the 101 and State was crammed full of shops from Macy's down to Sears. On the other side of the road were a few more large stores.

And if they'd been called in on overtime, it had to be a big one.

"Shit," Chris whispered, then nodded. "Are you good?"

"Yeah. I'd just ordered when Williams called. Royce and

Harry got here half an hour ago, though. They're toast." Liam typed out a text, probably to let the guys know there was one more on the way.

"Bet they're pissed," Chris grimaced. The regulations were strict—no sleeping medications, alcohol, a certain amount of sleep. Hell, even some painkillers ruled you out. It made everyone safer, and there were enough trained firefighters in the city and county that they could afford to do it that way, but it was frustrating when a sip of beer was enough to sideline you.

Some guys deliberately cracked open a beer if they saw a C.O.'s name show up on their cellphone, but none of the guys he hung out with were like that. They didn't exactly leap into harm's way, but they weren't *that* kind of guy.

"Hey, you heard the news?" Royce came out, tailed by Harry. "Fuck, I wish we hadn't just gotten started without you."

"Yeah, yeah," Chris bantered and slapped Royce's shoulder. "That's what they all say."

"They picking you up on the way by?" Harry asked, and Liam nodded. "Cool. They say much?"

"Not much. It's... bad."

There was a moment of silence between all of them, acknowledging what that probably meant, before Chris leaned over to check out the horizon. They weren't that far from the fire, and if it was that bad...

"There," Harry whispered. The trail of thick smoke rising from just behind the buildings pinpointed the location.

A chill ran down Chris's spine as he slid his phone out of his pocket. He typed out a quick text.

Work called me in. Stay away from the plaza. Love—

Then he paused and caught his breath, backspacing over the word. It had been automatic. He didn't have time to think about that.

Work called me in. Stay away from the plaza. TTYS. xx

He sent that, and Liam squeezed his shoulder. There was an approaching siren—their ride was nearly here. "I already called Dylan. He's with him."

"Oh, thank God," Chris breathed out a sigh of relief, then nodded. "Thanks for telling me." He trusted Dylan to look after Ash.

He and Liam silently watched the trail of smoke for a moment, then exchanged looks with the unspoken agreement: now they just had to keep themselves safe.

29

ASH

And it had been such a good afternoon.

"You're kidding! No, we hadn't heard." Dylan paused, looking at Ash for a second. "Ash is over. Yeah. Okay, I will. Stay safe, baby. Call me when you need a ride. I love you."

None of that sounded good. Ash's chest was knotted as he watched Dylan in the kitchen, pacing back and forth as he talked. He could only be talking to Liam, and he was on the same shift as Chris, which meant they were both supposed to be off.

And that meant... something was wrong.

He pushed his chair backward against the Juliet balcony and turned in it, half-expecting to see the building across the street alight.

No such sign, but as Dylan hung up, his heavy sigh brought Ash's attention back to him.

"What happened?"

"Mall fire. You know the plaza?"

"Shit. Big? I guess it would be."

Dylan nodded tightly, already grabbing the TV remote and switching to the local news channel. They were talking about some dumb park revitalization program, but the banner scrolling across the bottom of the screen was talking about a major fire in Santa Barbara.

Ash's heart squeezed with the sudden realization that this was happening. And maybe Chris was going to be involved. "Is this... common? Um, do you know if Chris is going, too?"

"Liam said he will, if he's fit."

Ash's phone went off with a text from Chris.

Work called me in. Stay away from the plaza. TTYS. xx

"Fuck," he whispered. "Yeah, he's going to it, too."

Dylan suddenly seemed to realize he'd asked another question, looking over at him. "And no, it's not common. Not at all. The vast majority of what they deal with is mundane. Relatively. Medical emergencies, car crashes, someone setting their deck just slightly on fire."

"Slightly on fire," Ash smiled weakly. "Right."

Dylan eyed him, then patted the couch. "Stay with me until they send Liam and Chris home. Oh, right. Dude, what about your appointment? I can still drive you."

"Yeah," Ash murmured, easing himself to his feet to hobble across the cute, light-filled, hardwood-floored apartment. He dropped heavily onto the couch. "I won't be any use, but I'll stay here. Fuck the appointment. I'll reschedule."

"I won't be any use either," Dylan murmured, only half his attention on Ash. He was intently watching the screen still. "Last big incident was..." he trailed off, then cleared his throat. "A frat house down in Isla."

"Of course. Dumb frat kids," Ash mumbled.

"I was in it."

Ash recoiled. Dylan didn't seem like the fraternity type at all, even though Ash knew he was a student at the university there. "Shit. Sorry."

"No, s'okay. Wasn't me lighting the place up," Dylan snorted. "Or lighting up in the place." His expression was distant for a moment. He drew a breath and nodded, then let it out. "But at least here, there shouldn't be any drunks to handle. Hopefully everyone cleared out fast..."

Ash nodded jerkily. His mind was already racing, though. Then, he grabbed Dylan's arm as the news channel changed.

There was a news helicopter or drone or something over the scene, circling the column of thick black smoke. It looked like it was coming from the restaurant side of the mall, but it had definitely spread along more than one shop on either side.

"Holy shit," Dylan whispered, and for the first time, he seemed rattled.

The drop in Ash's stomach made him clench his hands tightly. Still, Dylan needed support, and for once, he could give it. Yeah, he was as scared for everyone—not just Liam and Chris—as Dylan was, but he hadn't had *that* experience himself.

Dylan was fidgeting, tapping on the side of his hand with his fingers, his shoulders tense. He barely seemed to feel Ash's hand, so Ash rubbed slowly, trying to get him to relax just a little.

He could only imagine what was going through Dylan's head.

"Okay. I'll get us both something sweet. Don't go into shock," Ash told Dylan, grabbing his crutch to lever himself up.

"Yeah," Dylan mumbled. His breathing was too quick. Ash would talk him through that next.

As Ash rummaged in the fridge for something, he was suddenly glad he was staying with Dylan. He didn't even want to think about his mental state if he were alone, and looking after Dylan could give him something to do.

It was all he *could* do.

30

CHRIS

No wonder they'd called in backup. Rigs from at least two other districts were here, and Chief Williams was already on hand, striding around the edge of the scene to check in on the engineers. The wind was high—not stormy, but even ten miles an hour made a huge difference in conditions.

They worked as a well-oiled machine, nobody panicking despite the heat that already pressed against Chris's skin when he jumped out of the truck and headed for the familiar deep red of *their* engine.

"Kyle," Chris greeted B shift's engineer, who was grabbing a supply line from the rear compartment. "How's it looking?" Getting his turnout gear on was a quick process, as heavy as it was. It went so fast he didn't even notice each step of the fasteners and buckles.

"Bad. It's right in the middle of the complex. They just finished clearing this side of the mall, but there's civilians trapped and it's moving fast. Williams will give you the briefing in a minute, I'm sure." Kyle was working fast, and Chris didn't want to break his focus. The engineer was the source of all water, after all.

"Shit," Chris whispered as he pulled the fireproof hood over his head and settled one of the rig's spare helmets on his head.

The briefing was bad. Though Chief Williams was calm, it was clearly a measured, deliberate response. And thank God, there wasn't a hint of tension between the two of them as the chief assigned him to the crew in charge of the most delicate and dangerous work on the scene—rescuing the handful of people suspected to be inside the huge, almost windowless clothing store.

The smell was the worst. He'd had a few lungs full of choking, dark black smoky air before getting his mask on, and even through it, it was impossible to miss the smell. Chemicals and strange, toxic compounds were released when anything burned, and a huge industrial-scale fireground was far more volatile than someone's cedar back deck.

They couldn't fuck up this one. The rules they all lived by —and hopefully would continue to live by—were playing in his head even as he listened into his assigned channel.

Having Liam by his side was the best possible scenario. They knew each other's blind spots inside and out.

The wind was still blowing side-on to the building, mercifully sheltered by the secured side, but they were all conscious that a subtle shift in wind direction could drive the flames further in and kill those awaiting rescue. Word had it there were three, so Chris and Liam were accompanied by two of the other guys, Vince and Ron.

It was risky, but the crew was barely holding back this fire, the wind whipping up sparks in the modern construction. They only had minutes.

"You know this place?"

"Oh, yeah." Chris glanced at Liam, then drew a breath through his mask and reached up instinctively to check the lines. Didn't need to tell him he'd come here with a date a couple months ago. "Good sandwiches."

"Toasted?"

"Hah." It was a fraction of a moment of levity, at least.

"I've got it." Liam stepped behind him, and Chris trusted him when he said he was good.

They waited for the signal, watching the spray from Hans and Ron. These new fucking builds had nothing on old concrete buildings. Then again, they were less likely to walk into an oven, so... swings and roundabouts.

The fire fought back, clinging desperately to the window frame as Chris fingered his tools.

He'd hooked up with a British guy who'd used that phrase once. Hadn't even wanted to look at him in the morning.

They were receding, but someone was talking on their radio channel. The wind was shifting, ash blowing against them and the side of the clothing store, where the canopies and overhangs were sparking alight. Chief Williams was already pulling guys off the rest of the plaza.

He wanted to see Ash's smile in one of those rare, unguarded moments between them when Ash got to forget for a second everything his brain set up against him.

For the first time, he had someone to come home to. Chris looked at Liam when the order came over the radio channel. It was now or never, and there were at least two confirmed missing.

Chris stepped inside and crouched, getting a clear line of sight under the thick blanket of smoke that clung to the ceiling.

The floor was still hot. The line of flame ate at the chewed-up blackened wood, but it was dampened.

There. Across the room. The kitchen door was alight and

two men were slumped on the floor in identical green aprons. Sparks were dropping -- no, melting -- on them from the doors. Fucking plastic.

"Got them." The firefighters with them took charge of them, striding forward. They'd probably passed out from oxygen deprivation when they tried to make a run for it. He couldn't waste time wondering if it was a rescue or recovery.

There was still the report of one possibly missing, and he knew where civilians hid from fire in a restaurant.

Liam was thinking along the same lines. "Fridge?"

"Yes." Chris didn't waste breath, picking his way over the fallen beams.

Shit. There was internal trussing, and the flame had eaten through the fucking wall, hungry as ever for more. It was licking up toward the trussing -- had already claimed that beam and a post.

"Internal trussing giving way," he reported back as Liam found the fridge and checked it for heat. No worse than was out here. "It's getting unsafe."

"Retreat the moment you feel unsafe," Chief Williams was already responding. "Is the front your nearest exit?"

"Yes. We're checking the fridge. Doesn't look like anywhere else for someone to hide--shit."

The girl in the fridge was just a kid. Where the fuck were her parents? They should have had a report. Hysterical parents were easy to find.

She was screaming, and no wonder. The fucking cooling unit was the weak point, and it had just exploded, sending a shower of sparks and hot liquid across the room.

Liam had it. He was good at using body language to gain trust instantly. He approached and crouched, but he didn't have time to waste. The second he radioed it in, the chief ordered them out. "Liam--" Chris started.

Liam heard him. He had her over his shoulder while she gripped tightly.

There was a crunch and a roar from outside the fridge.

Chris turned to face their next problem. That was a beam, and the whole thing was poised to come down.

Flame was building along everything outside the fridge. Kitchen supplies. The flour was igniting, fed by oil jugs. The counters. The damn appliances.

No training could prepare him for the chill. He spotted two facts at the same time: there was a pair of red sneakers, barely visible under a pile of rubble, and flashover was near.

Liam was the one who called the mayday, and Chris reported the new victim.

Chris moved as one with Liam, sheltering the others from the door and eyeing the kitchen back door. He couldn't go after the other victim yet. They had to get this girl out, and between them and the door was a pile of debris. He could clear it, but he'd have to lift the beam against the door away while Liam forced the door open as best he could with one hand.

"Kitchen door's jammed but I can lift a beam away. Need someone outside helping get the door open. Close to flashover."

"You've got it."

It was a risk, but they might have ten seconds or less, and they couldn't make it to the front door in that time.

They didn't stop to think--they just moved. Chris went first, wedging his metal tool against the door to get leverage against the wooden beam. When he had enough, his muscles straining and cheeks burning--fuck, the heat!--he grabbed it with one hand, pushing it away from himself and kicking at the door's metal opening bar.

The fresh air was going to feed the fire in here, and probably flashover instantly. That was the only reason nobody outside was opening it up yet.

But Liam had a civilian, and there was someone still inside. Chris had to go for him if he could.

"Go," he told Liam, listening to the hiss of water and shouts from the rapid response unit. They were trying to get through the front toward them. A supply line, his kingdom for a supply line. "Get close."

The wind in here was worse. The front windows had blown, then. It pushed the flame back toward them. They were in an oven now.

The fucking beam was jammed up against a counter. He couldn't lift it high enough to drop it there, and he couldn't step over it to push it the other way. He was a sitting duck.

The girl against Liam was weak now. Fainted or starved for breath. Liam must have felt it, because he didn't stop to question Chris. He moved up to the door.

"Three, two, one."

Air billowed in, and the flames roared past Chris as the wind rushed past him.

It was sunny outside. He could see blue skies, and someone in yellow through the sheet of flame that was building along the doorframe. Why was it so tall?

He wasn't holding the beam. He was on the ground. He was so hot.

So hot.

31

ASH

"Is this Dylan Waters?"

With his arm wrapped around Dylan's shoulder, Ash could hear everything: the catch of fear in his breathing, the gentle yet firm voice on the other end of the line.

"Yes. Is it Liam? What happened?"

The news copters had caught the sandwich restaurant building's collapse, the flurry of activity outside. The cameras on the street had caught two firefighters coming out minutes before with a victim each. But one was too short, the other too broad, to be either of their lovers.

Ash didn't catch all of the words from the other end of the phone, except, "...to come to the hospital..."

His brain supplied the rest: to identify the bodies.

To identify his parents.

Fuck. No. Not Liam—not poor Dylan, too.

He barely heard Dylan's words, but they were enough to snap him back into it. "...gonna be all right? Fuck. Okay. I'm on my way. Thanks. Bye."

What? Ash caught his breath. "He's not...? He's okay?"

"His injuries are minor, they said," Dylan breathed out as he pushed himself to his feet. "Did you want to come, or...?"

"Hey. This way, I might make my appointment," Ash smiled weakly.

Dylan managed a quick laugh, waiting until he'd pushed himself to his feet. He led them to the door, then down the stairs, and poked his head in the side door of the knitting shop. "Vee?"

"Yes, darling?"

"The fire uptown? Liam and Chris were called in for it. Liam's at the hospital right now, I'm taking Ash. By the way, this is Ash, Chris's..." Dylan trailed off.

Ash's cheeks flushed and he glared at Dylan. "Friend."

"Mmhmm," Dylan winked and swayed out of the doorway so Vee could come over. The craft shop beyond was cute—light-filled and spacious, with racks of supplies from ribbons to papers and yarns. Chris could see why Dylan fit in there.

Vee herself was already beaming at him. She was older, probably in her fifties or sixties, with laugh lines and steel-gray hair. Instantly, Ash felt more at ease. "Hi. You must be the man I keep hearing about."

Ash directed an accusing glare at Dylan, who laughed. "Only good things," Dylan promised.

"I hope so," Ash managed a smile. Half his attention was taken up by the still, silent weight of the phone in his pocket. No news had to be good news, right?

"Do either of you need a ride or anything?" Vee asked, directly a concerned look at Dylan now.

"I'm okay to drive," Dylan assured her with a quick smile. "Thanks, though."

"Of course." Vee tugged him in for a quick hug, then touched Ash's arm. "Don't let them hide you away. I have to tease Chris about you, you know. For all his muscles, he goes so shy when he blushes."

Ash laughed this time, his worry pushed to the side for at least a second. "He does. I can be on board with that," he agreed. "Okay, we'd better go." Dylan was fingering his keys already, the light jangling distracting.

"Take care," Vee told them both, lingering in the hall doorway of the shop while Dylan held the street door open for Ash.

Reality didn't take long to set in after that: if Liam had minor injuries and Chris had been with him, what had happened?

It was a lot more waiting than Ash expected. They'd been on these hard plastic chairs in the waiting room for twenty minutes already, hoping Dylan was about to get the go-ahead to see Liam.

And there was still no news on Chris. When Dylan had tried to ask on Ash's behalf at the desk, they'd fobbed him off with the usual *patient privacy* line. That in itself was worrying —that they wouldn't even confirm he *wasn't* there.

Ash tried a text.

Hey xx. Just worried about you since Liam's hurt. Text me back if/when you can?

"Dylan?" It was a young male nurse with earnest brown eyes and a furrowed brow. "Is there a—"

Dylan sprang to his feet. "Me. Can I see Liam?"

"Yes, come this way."

Dylan looked at Ash, and Ash waved a hand, managing a

smile at him. He needed to be with his lover right now. "Go on. Be with him."

"Thanks, darling," Dylan breathed out, squeezing his shoulder before he hurried off after the nurse.

It was so damn sweet to see the way he was totally attached to him.

The TV screen in the waiting room was playing the local news, the same damn aerial footage of the fire while anchors talked about how devastating this was. The fire was under control now, but the news crew still wasn't being allowed close.

Ash glowered at the TV when he saw the employees of the other plaza businesses still waiting. Their bosses probably wanted to milk a few hours of work out of them if possible. Fucking retail.

Then, he saw it: a scrolling banner across the screen.

One firefighter from the city of Santa Barbara department confirmed dead, reports continue...

He didn't see the rest of the banner, his eyes glazing over.

No. It couldn't be Chris. It had to be some other guy. It had to be...!

Oh, shit. The closed captioning had caught up to the announcement in blocky black boxes with white letters.

—the victim and at least one other firefighter were thought to have been rushed to the local hospital after a failed rescue attempt. News crews are being kept away, and officials aren't talking about the circumstances that led to his death. Fire officials are keeping quiet on the victim's identity until his family has been notified. Unspeakably tragic, Linda...

"Shit," Ash whispered. Only now was he aware that his

hands were shaking in his lap, tears welling in the corners of his eyes.

It made sense. If Liam was the other firefighter brought here, and if they were usually paired up...

That was it. He had to ask the receptionist.

It took him a fucking eternity to get over to the desk in the corner of the room, and his breathing was labored by the time he got there.

"I need to see Chris Black. He has to be here, I know he is."

"What's your relationship to the... to the patient?"

To the deceased. I bet she nearly said it. Ash's shoulders and throat tightened as he heard the phrase echoing in his memories. "His... I live with him. I just need to see him."

"Are you listed as his next-of-kin? Or a relative?"

"Not yet," Ash muttered, his fingers closing into tight fists. "I came here with Dylan, the next-of-kin for Liam... um..." Shit, what was his last name? "Liam, the other firefighter they brought. Look, I saw the news. I just need to know..."

"I'm sorry, sir. But according to the patient privacy act—"

"If he's alive!" Ash snapped, trying to keep his voice quiet. "Just tell me that."

"I can't share any information with—"

"Shit." Ash was hyperventilating now, the same familiar grief flooding through him. He'd been here before.

Not *here* here, but close by. Further up the coast, in NorCal. In a hospital a lot like this, with a receptionist who had a sympathetic gaze and let him in because he *was* their relative. Their only son.

A police officer by his side, telling the receptionist that this was the victims' son.

He couldn't remember anyone else. No, there was a coroner's officer or something. He hadn't really known *who* the people around him were. All he could remember was the image of *them*.

"Sir?" She was talking loudly and clearly now, half-rising to her feet. "You need to sit down and stay calm. You may experience shock—"

"No. I know shock," Ash whispered. "It's fucking grief, actually. Thanks for *nothing*." He regretted the words instantly, but he couldn't stop them slipping from his mouth as he made for the door.

Thank God he could could walk so damn fast on these things now. He needed to get out, to get fresh air.

He was outside and gulping breaths of the clear air from the annoyingly shitty blue sky. It was almost windless now, which the TV had told him had helped.

Not in time, though.

"Not Chris," he whispered, his lips numb as he sank onto the bench outside, in the little garden for anxious relatives and loved ones to pace around.

Ash grabbed for his phone when it went off, but it was Dylan.

Liam just had smoke inhalation. He's awake and OK. Have you seen Chris? Staff aren't telling Liam anything.

Ash put his head into his hands for a minute. The slim chance that it *wasn't* Chris was melting away by the second.

The screen was blurry when he answered.

No. They won't let me in. HIPAA.

He didn't even know how to approach the news about the firefighter confirmed dead. That was too much to repeat right now. He'd have taken a photo of the headline if he'd thought about it. But... no. Liam had to hear about it from someone better than him.

Oh babe. Thats fucked up. You OK?

A weak laugh escaped Ash's throat as he pocketed his phone. He didn't know how to handle that.

No, he wasn't.

Just earlier that day, he'd seen a life he could live. A guy he could love. A guy he *did* love.

"Fuck, fuck, fuck," he whispered, his palms digging into his eyes as the tears spilled out of his eyes again.

It was too fucking soon. He'd barely grown able to handle his own life, let alone their relationship. They hadn't even properly *started* one. He couldn't handle it ending.

He wasn't sure how long he sat there while the loop played in his head: *don't love people, don't trust people, you're not worth it, you'll end up dying alone.*

It was the same damn loop that had been playing that night. The same one that had led to him meeting this man, and starting to get his life under control.

It was an unwanted thought, so unwanted that he sat up straight, wiping his eyes and gritting his teeth: Chris wouldn't want him thinking like this.

Fuck that. He was going to mourn what and how he wanted.

But the more the thought played at his mind, the more it rang true. Chris wouldn't want him crying and feeling helpless until he slid into the same fucking depression death spiral.

And after saving him once, Chris wouldn't want him to fuck it up.

His phone went off with a different buzz pattern than a text. Not a call, either. It took him a few moments to stir himself into action, but he took his phone out again, then squinted at the screen.

It was a reminder alert for a calendar event. His leg appointment was in fifteen minutes.

He almost laughed at the absurdity. Here he was, mourning this guy the hospital wouldn't even let him see, but he was considering going to some fucking stupid, useless follow-up appointment?

Ash closed his eyes for a few moments as he swiped to dismiss the alarm.

But if he wasn't going to end it over this—if he was going to carry on, like he was certain Chris would want... he couldn't sink into his shell and ignore the outside world.

He had to see if the doctor would let him switch to a cane, so he could get a job easier, so he could get a new place to live... shit, the details were enough to make his chest seize up with anxiety.

Ash breathed in slowly and out again, letting the details of the garden around him ground him.

"Okay," he whispered to himself. His hands shook, but his gaze was drawn to the door of the hospital.

Maybe this was the right thing to do. He had to take care of himself, now that there was nobody else to do it.

He blinked away his dry, sore eyes, pushing himself to his feet.

As he entered the hospital, he let his brain go on autopilot to get him to the right clinic.

And he was in the waiting room, slumped in the corner.

And he was waiting for x-rays.

And he was waiting for Dr. Green to see him.

And he was waiting for Dr. Green to stop talking.

Who knew what time it was? Or where he was? He was ignoring the texts from Dylan, after the first concerned text he'd dismissed. He couldn't lie and say he was okay, or that he'd even fully committed to... not just jumping off the roof of this building.

"...partial-weight-bearing for some time now. Just because you recovered this quickly doesn't mean you can ditch the cane yet."

Ash was pretty sure he was nodding at the right moments, his brain far too caught up in everything else.

He hadn't met Chris's family. Had Chris told them about him? Was he even entitled to feel this distraught when he hadn't known him for more than a couple months?

Dr. Green had asked a question about antidepressants. Probably whether he needed support or something. It was just that word that had caught his attention, so he'd missed the context.

"Make the referral you told me about," Ash found himself saying, his voice quiet. Not broken, but rough. "Things... have changed."

"Okay." Dr. Green was watching him carefully. "We'll be in touch very soon with appointment details. Are you in crisis?"

"No," Ash lied, and then he was lying his way out of the office, bullshitting the doctor with a smile and reassurance that he'd get through it. Jokes about his cane making him look like a supervillain. Whatever it took to get the doctor not to look at him so suspiciously.

The last thing he needed was to be tied to a bed in a ward here. At least on the outside, living was his choice to make.

"Ash! You graduated."

It took Ash a second to recognize his name. He was out of the office, so who knew him?

Then he smiled slightly at the warm smile of the woman approaching him. It was Julie, the nurse who had talked him through using crutches in the first place.

He was walking slowly and awkwardly again, the crutches in one arm while he leaned his weight on the cane. A whole new learning curve.

"I... did," he agreed, managing a slight smile.

She saw through it in a second. "What's wrong?"

Ash paused, and then shame burned his cheeks. As hard as he tried to keep it on the inside and steel his face, the tears welled up behind his eyes. "Remember Chris?"

"The handsome fellow checking in on you? I sure do."

"He... He's a firefighter. The fire today." Ash hated dancing around it, but fuck, he couldn't say it out loud.

Julie's eyes widened. She was holding a brown paper lunch bag, and it crumpled in her fist as she flinched. "He was hurt?"

Ash couldn't answer. His gaze dropped to the floor as he blinked rapidly a few times, his throat too tight.

"Oh, darling," Julie whispered. "Oh, no. I heard them come in, but..."

"They won't let me see his... him. HIPAA. Fuckers," Ash whispered, the white-hot anger melting away the grief for a second. He preferred it. Easier to lash out than linger on the gash inside him. "But I saw it on the news."

"They released his name already?" Julie murmured.

Ash paused mid-nod and shook his head. "Not 'til his family... I don't know if they know me... it's a mess. I don't even know what happened. I don't... They told me nothing. Not even his fucking work partner, Liam. They're not telling anyone anything. That's why I figured it's him. When my parents..." he trailed off, then bit his lip hard. "I've seen it before. Not until someone IDs him. I could do that, but..."

"Come on, sweetheart." Julie had the crutches from him in a second and under her arm, holding his arm. "Let's get you some answers."

"You... don't have to," Ash managed. She was probably on

supper break or something. He was enough of a fucking burden on his friends, let alone nurses who had others to look after.

"I want to," Julie told him firmly. "Come on. The elevator's this way."

Ash didn't try to stop the tears rolling down his cheeks this time. All he could manage was a quiet, "Thank you."

Yeah, maybe Chris had been right all along to be an optimist. Most people were okay.

32

CHRIS

"Chris? Hi. You're awake now. You're in the hospital."

Fuck. His head was killing him, and his lungs... shit, breathing was a struggle. He could already tell it was an oxygen mask on him, so he didn't try to rip it off his face, as much as he wanted to.

The adrenaline jolting through Chris's body settled as it registered: he wasn't waking up in that building.

And... holy shit. He was waking up? He hadn't thought he would wake up again. The last thing he remembered was sunshine and red sneakers.

"Did he make it?" he mumbled, cracking his eyes. White, sterile walls around him, and a brown-haired nurse standing by the bed, a hand on his arm. "The other guy. The..."

His head was fuzzy. Painkillers or something. Morphine? Something in an IV. Shit, something ached, but it was mostly numb. Definitely painkillers.

"The guy. I wanted to go back for him. Did he make it?"

"I don't know, honey." The nurse squeezed his shoulder

lightly. "You got badly hurt in the line of duty. Do you remember it?"

How could he forget? Chris managed a jerky nod. "Liam got out okay? And the little girl?"

"Yes." Something sparked behind her eyes—anger? That was weird. Chris blinked at her once or twice. It settled and she offered a quick smile. "Yeah, he's okay. They both are. They weren't letting him know your condition, so I've told him."

Chris managed a sigh of relief. It ached to breathe too deeply, but he was starting to relax into the mattress. Then, he squinted slightly. She looked familiar. "Do I... know you?"

"We met before. I was looking after your friend, Ash."

Chris gasped, and his lungs ached despite the painkillers at the sudden breath. "Shit. Is he okay? Where is he?"

"He's waiting to see you." There it was—anger again, and determination. She was carefully keeping it under control, though. "Wires... were crossed. They weren't giving him any information. He assumed the worst. Honey, I have to tell you something."

That wasn't helping. Chris struggled to sit up, and she slid a hand under his back to help prop him up. He was grateful for the help. "Did he hurt himself? Is he okay? Shit."

"He's okay, he's fine," Julie quickly assured him, settling him against the pillows. She checked her watch and winced. "I'm sorry. This isn't my department. I need to head back, but... I can send him in."

"Please. Please do," Chris breathed out, then caught her hand as she pulled back. "Thank you," he murmured. He had the feeling she'd been there for Ash when he couldn't be. "And... what did you have to tell me?"

"They're reporting a firefighter—not your friend Liam, he's okay—but another firefighter was killed at the scene."

...*No.*

It hit like a ton of bricks, and Chris's head spun. He froze for a second as he processed it, names instantly running through his head. Hans? Glenn? Sam? Chief Williams?

Who the fuck was it? How? Why?

"I'm so sorry, honey," she whispered, squeezing his hand. "But that's why he..."

"Assumed it was me," Chris finished, pushing the mask off his nose and mouth to talk better. God, it was hard to breathe without it, but he tried it, slowly and steadily. "Oh, God. Poor Ash. Please do send him in."

Julie nodded and headed for the door.

Chris's eyes sparked with hot tears. He didn't even want to think about who it had been. He felt selfish for being glad it wasn't Liam, because... it didn't matter who it was. They were all a family. It was like losing a brother or sister of his own.

"Baby. Oh, my God."

That was Ash, dragging his attention back to the present.

Chris found himself smiling despite everything, his heart aching at the sight. Ash was in tears, too. Chris's left hand was taken up by the IV, a heart monitor on his right finger, but he raised his arms as much as he could to hug him when Ash flung himself at him.

The smell and feeling of Ash pressed into him... everything was bearable with him there. He never wanted Ash to pull back, even if the bandages he could feel around his chest were prickling now. The painkillers must be wearing off.

Then Ash loosened his grip, catching his breath. "Oh, shit. Are you hurt? I'm sorry."

"It's okay," Chris quietly laughed. "That nurse is cool."

"Julie? Thank fucking *God* for her," Ash whispered, pressing his nose into Chris's neck as he leaned down awkwardly over the bed. "I thought... They weren't telling me..."

"She said," Chris whispered, then swallowed hard. "Don't know who it was yet?"

"They haven't said. I'm so sorry," Ash whispered, pulling back and kissing his forehead. He looked tense and anxious still, gazing at Chris.

Chris avoided his gaze for a second, his chest tight. It sank in that Ash wasn't holding crutches, but a cane. "You... You went to the appointment?"

Ash smiled sheepishly and ducked his head. "I did. Fuck. I thought you'd died. I was... Dr. Green must have thought I was having a mental breakdown."

"But you didn't have a total one, did you?" Chris murmured, pulling Ash in for another light hug before Ash sank into the chair next to his bed. "You still went."

"Barely," Ash admitted, his voice quiet as he looked around the room rather than at Chris. "I thought you'd have wanted me to... to keep going with my life, you know? I almost lost it. Fuck, I was... I love you, and I never got to..." Then, his voice caught and he quickly looked back at Chris, his cheeks flushing.

He was so fucking cute when he blushed. "Me, too," Chris whispered, reaching out to grip the side of Ash's hand with the side of his own. He flicked the plastic monitor on his forefinger with annoyance. "This fucking thing, I swear."

Ash leaned in slowly until his head rested on Chris's shoulder, and Chris closed his eyes. "Your heartbeat spiked to, I swear to God, like, 100 just then," Ash murmured with a quiet giggle.

Chris was blushing now. He laughed under his breath. "Yours did the first time I walked in."

"Oh, now, that's not fair. You can't use that now," Ash muttered in complaint.

Chris grinned and pressed a kiss to the top of Ash's head. "Totally can. But, yeah." His heart was still racing, but he wanted to properly say it. "I... I'm so fucking glad I didn't lose you. One way or another. Before I went in..."

Was that something he should share with Ash? Or was it something for the other guys to understand? But Ash was waiting for him to finish that sentence.

"I realized I wanted to come home to you."

Then, it hit him again, his spirits sinking despite the joy of telling Ash at last, out loud, what he meant to him: one of the other guys wasn't going to get that chance. He prayed to God it wasn't whoever had rescued *him*. And he had no idea if that other guy had made it. How many fucking casualties were there in this?

Ash was holding him tightly, his arms wrapped around his shoulders. "I'm so sorry," Ash was whispering, rocking him gently. Chris suddenly became aware of the hot tears running down his own cheeks, but he couldn't have stopped them if he'd wanted to.

They stayed like that for a few minutes, Chris's nose buried in Ash's hair or the side of his head while Ash rubbed his shoulder or the back of his neck.

When Chris could breathe again, he swallowed a few times and tried to wipe his eyes with his hand. He had to duck his head to do it with the fucking heart monitor hand. "Don't need this thing," he grumbled, pulling it off so he could grab tissues from the box at the side of the bed.

The shrill alarm that went off made both of them nearly jump out of their skin. "Holy shit! Okay, okay, fuck," Chris grimaced.

Before he could jam it back on, the curtain was pushed aside by a worried male nurse striding into the room.

Chris blushed even harder now as Ash pulled back from him. "I'm okay!" He held up the heart monitor.

The nurse took a deep breath and nodded, his eyes flickering between the two of them. Was he one of the assholes who had let Ash think he was dead? Chris was suspicious. "It's usually a false alarm, but you never know."

"Right," Chris nodded, and when he looked at Ash, Ash mouthed, *Not him.*

Ah. His annoyance was clear.

"It's good to see you awake, though." The nurse grabbed the clipboard from the foot of his bed. "Thank you for your service."

Chris managed a quick smile. He didn't want to fucking think about his service—and the risks thereof—for at least another few minutes. At least, not until he knew *who* it was. "The reports. Someone died. Is that true?"

The nurse hesitated, then nodded. "Yes. I'm sorry to say."

"Who?" Chris raised a hand. "Don't you *dare* bullshit me with *I can't release his name.* My chief is going to come in here and yell until he's hoarse that you kept my boyfriend in suspense already. Trust me. You don't want him even more pissed. So... tell me who."

The nurse yielded. "He was ID'd as Hans by his family a minute ago."

Chris's chest clenched. They weren't on the same shift, but of course he knew him. "Shit. Oh, God," he breathed out, closing his eyes. "His family knows? Okay. Good."

"There will be counselors available—"

Chris started to raise a hand to wave him off, and Ash's grip closed around his wrist to keep it down. Chris stared at Ash for a moment.

Ash's jaw was firm, his eyes understanding. "Your boyfriend is vetoing your veto."

Fuck. He almost couldn't stand being looked at with that much understanding, but once he got through the uncomfortable second, it made sense. Ash had lost his damn family. He knew grief. He wanted Chris to have support.

And if he was going to insist that Ash get help, it was only fair that he give this a chance.

"Fine," he murmured, but to Ash, not the nurse.

Sensing the conversation, the nurse looked deliberately busy taking Chris's vital signs.

Ash let go of him, and Chris managed a smile at him. "Guess you get to play nurse now."

"Damn straight."

Chris was gazing at Ash, watching his blue eyes intently focusing on the nurse, watching the way he asked questions— when will he get out? How extensive are the burns? What's the care going to be like?

Only after the nurse was gone did Ash look back at him and smile. "You've been staring," Ash accused in a light, teasing tone.

"Course I have." Oh. Wait. Chris was feeling woozy. When he'd told the nurse that his lungs hurt again, and his back, and most of his shoulders, he'd given him more painkillers.

That might explain why he just wanted to smile at Ash until his eyes drifted closed again. He couldn't keep his eyes open, in fact. "My new boyfriend, hm? Don't go anywhere," Chris managed to whisper when he realized that he was about to sleep.

"I'm not going anywhere, darling," Ash whispered. Lips pressed against his forehead. "Never."

Chris smiled and slept.

33

ASH, ONE WEEK LATER

"Not sure I want you driving me."

Ash burst out laughing as he pulled to an admittedly abrupt halt at the red light, then flipped Chris the bird before he looked over to him in the passenger seat. "Wow, thanks. The car jerks when I stop."

"Welcome. And yeah, I drove it too," Chris smiled at him. "It does."

"I've been studying up, watching videos and stuff," Ash told him. "I think I figured out how to fix it."

"But you haven't done it yet?" Chris asked.

"Well," Ash drawled, offering a cheeky smile as the light turned green again. "I kept having to stay with and visit *some* gorgeous man in the hospital."

Chris hummed. "What a lucky man. Is he your boyfriend?"

"He is," Ash agreed with a straight face. "I even made him steak, since I was supposed to pick him up today."

"Oh my God, *not* hospital food." Chris sounded so thrilled that Ash smiled. "Hey, look at you. Take away a crutch and you're unstoppable."

Ash laughed. It was true—after over six weeks of restricted mobility and movement, he was cooking, cleaning, and walking around as much as he could handle. His pain had been going down every day, and his painkiller use, too. That wasn't an addiction he was prepared to have. His first appointment with the psychiatrist to see about antidepressants was next week, and that was quite enough medication for him.

"But my course starts soon," Ash added. "Because while that sexy hunk was in the hospital, I was applying to colleges..."

"Holy shit!" Chris straightened up and twisted to face him. "No way!" He sounded delighted. "Congratulations!"

"Mmmm." Ash grinned at the pride in Chris's voice.

"I think your sexy hunk should reward you for being so adult all week. In an adult way. There's something that goes with steak..."

Ash couldn't deny the shiver of heat that coursed through him. It took him a second to push aside the visual of Chris's mouth around his cock and come up with an answer. "He's welcome to, *if* it won't hurt him."

"Bullshit," Chris snorted. "I'd fuck on a bed of coals if I had to right now. I'm horny as fuck, you know. No jerking off in the hospital... a week of that. A week!"

"Thanks for the information," Ash grinned teasingly at him. They pulled into Chris's driveway—*their* driveway—and he got out first, grabbing his cane.

Driving after so long being unable to was weird, but he'd figured out the knack of it. Thank God it had been his left leg injured, and he had an automatic transmission.

Chris climbed out himself, and Ash frowned at him. "You're supposed to let me help."

"I didn't break anything!" Chris protested with a laugh. "I'm just a little scorched."

Ash rolled his eyes. His man was just as stubborn as he was, and... then he was smiling at the thought: they were a perfect match.

As Ash unlocked the front door for them, Chris sidled up behind them and slid his arms around his waist. "It's so good to be home."

"I bet," Ash murmured. "It's good to have you home."

They pushed the door closed behind them with their hips, and Ash leaned back against it to let Chris pin him up against it.

"Oooh," Ash breathed out, heat running through his veins again. His cheeks flushed at the firm chest against his own, the half-hard cock pressed into his hip. "It's *very* good to have you home. You weren't kidding about that week."

"A week!" Chris lamented, leaning in and lipping at his ear. His forearms were braced on either side of Ash as he nipped his jaw.

"Are you sure? We can just cuddle, you know. The burns—"

"Shhhh," Chris instructed and nipped his neck sharply. "You didn't let your broken leg stop you before. I want you."

Ash was breathless now, sagging against the door as Chris's hands ran slowly up his hips and over his stomach to his chest.

Fuck. Chris had him in three words.

And then there were three more.

"I love you."

Ash leaned forward to catch Chris's lips and kiss him hard. He sucked on those warm lips, relenting and running his hands carefully up Chris's sides to grip his shoulder blades.

Chris's grip tightened on his waist, and then he was hoisting him up against the door.

"Me, too," Ash whispered, locking his good leg around Chris's waist. It was harder to lift the other with the half-cast he had to keep on for another couple weeks, but Chris didn't seem to have any struggle locking his arms around his ass and around his back.

His cane was abandoned by the door, but he didn't care. He trusted Chris to get him where he needed to be.

Chris didn't even falter on the stairs. "God, you can't get better than a man with biceps," Ash dreamily sighed as he pressed kisses into Chris's neck.

"Perks of dating a firefighter," Chris chuckled deeply. "Not to mention the abs."

"Shut up," Ash grumbled, but he laughed, too. God, he was glad he'd hit on Chris all those weeks ago, even if it had been about the least sexy way possible to meet.

Least sexy, maybe, but most emotionally intimate. Chris had seen everything—the fear, the hopelessness, the desperate, animalistic attempt to cling to life despite his desire to end it...

Chris had been there for him, and now he'd been able to return the favor. And he could help him through this—the grief about his coworker, about not being able to save the guy he'd been told Chris had stayed inside to save... all the guilt and hurt? He could help with that.

They hit the bed together, and Ash scooted up the bed on his back, his arms still locked around Chris as he kissed him over and over.

He never wanted to stop kissing. His lips tingled with raw, sensitive nerves by the time Chris pulled his mouth away to press kisses to his skin, all the way down to the neckline of his t-shirt.

Fuck, he could skip kissing for *that*.

Chris was in charge of yanking their clothes off, and Ash's eyes fell to the light bandages still wrapped around his shoulders and lower back, where the worst of the burns were.

Ash still hadn't found out who had saved Chris, but everything would come out now with the investigation.

Whoever it was... he owed them casserole for life. The fact that he'd come out of it with such minimal injuries after such a dangerous incident was a miracle in itself, Chief Williams had told him.

And Chief Williams hadn't even looked like he hated him, which was another win.

Everything was coming up roses.

Bare skin against skin, except for the graze of cloth here and there, felt heavenly. He hadn't been able to share Chris's hospital bed, but having the man here—safely here, and *with* him, and pressing him into the bed and gently cupping his face to kiss him again...

Ash's chest was tight with emotion as he ran his thumb along Chris's cheek.

Chris was a hero, and *his* hero. And he wanted to reward *him?* It was insane.

"I hope I can give you enough," Ash whispered when Chris pulled back, running his hand gently down his back to rest in the small of his back. "You deserve so much."

"*You* deserve the world, too, darling," Chris murmured with one of those huge, genuine smiles. It was impossible for him to carry a lie anyway, but when he looked at him with those huge brown eyes, even the voice of depression whispering lies in the back of Ash's mind had to believe it.

He'd found his world in, and then through, Chris.

Chris didn't let him get emotional yet, though. His eyes were glinting with mischief as he shifted down the bed to slowly press an open-mouthed kiss over Ash's nipples, one at a time.

Each flick of Chris's tongue wound Ash up a little more, his fingers digging into the sheets as he rolled his head back.

Oh, fuck. There might as well have been a direct line from each nipple to his cock. He was so hard he could feel himself throbbing by the time Chris's stubble finished grazing the skin of his chest, and the burn of trailing lips traveled further south.

"Oh, my God," Ash moaned when Chris kissed his hipbone, then the inside of his thigh. "Fuck, fuck, *fuck.*"

Chris moaned his appreciation. "You're so fucking hot."

And Ash believed it. He lit up with a smile, opening his eyes just so he could see Chris.

It was breathtaking: the sight of the gorgeous man who hadn't left his head in days—weeks, now—between his legs, looking up at him like *he* was the world.

He wanted to remember that sight forever.

And his stomach was tight, his thighs twitching as Chris pressed two more slow, teasing kisses against his stomach.

"Okay, I love you and all, but if you don't suck my cock soon, I am going to be pissed," Ash moaned.

Chris's laugh rolled through the room as he grinned broadly. The tip of his tongue slipped between his lips, and Ash shuddered with anticipation before it even made contact with the root of his cock.

His whole body burned with so much need that it *hurt* as Chris licked a wet, warm stripe to the tip of his cock, then around it.

"Oh, my God, *yes!*"

The warmth and wetness of lips tightly enveloping the head of his cock were impossible to describe. He shuddered again, burning from head to toe as Chris sucked his cheeks in.

Ash could only manage whimpers of pleasure as Chris bobbed his head down to the shaft, his smooth tongue sliding along the underside of the shaft. "Mmnh!"

Fuck, he lost himself and every worry he had about *anything* with Chris looking at him like this, sucking slowly and gently and taking in every inch of him like all he wanted to do was taste him all night long.

Ash couldn't imagine how on-edge Chris was—he'd been able to jerk off in the shower here over the last week, at least. And his toes were already curling into the mattress with how hard it was not to just thrust up into his boyfriend's mouth.

"Fuck me," Ash whispered. "Please."

Chris's eyes lit up as he slowly pulled his mouth off Ash's cock, kissing the tip one more time before kissing his stomach. "You wanna?"

"Yeah," Ash whispered. He ached with need now that he was left aching, but he wanted Chris in him before he came. "No condom? If you're... cool with that."

Chris gazed at him for a moment, then nodded. "I've never done that. Never dated a guy I..." he trailed off, his voice catching for a second before he cleared his throat. "Yeah. I want to."

Ash beamed at him as he grabbed the lube, snatching the tube out of his hand and spreading his legs to show him how he did it. Chris stared at him as he pushed his fingers into himself, and Ash had to breathe out deeply to try to relax. He was so fucking pent-up with desire that his body was tense.

"You are the hottest fucking man I've *ever* known," Chris whispered. And in that tone, Ash could believe it, too.

"Yeah? Funny, 'cause *I'm* dating the hottest man I've known."

"Listen to us," Chris snorted. "It's ego-swelling hour here."

"You know what else is swelling?" Ash smirked, and sure enough, Chris's eyes widened and darkened with desire. Ash let his fingers slide out of himself and grabbed the sheets under him.

Chris brought a hand down to himself, his knee pressing into the bed by Ash's hip as he pressed the tip to his opening.

And then he was inside, and Ash's body was flooded with bliss.

He raised a knee and slid his foot over Chris's leg, locking them together as Chris pushed slowly into him.

Chris's lips were on his neck and ear again as Chris kissed him.

Ash twisted his head away to get Chris to stop, only so he could kiss his lips instead. The tip of his tongue played against Chris's as Chris burned inside him—filled every fucking empty part of him.

And that black hole inside him... for the moment, it was gone. He was fucking burning with everything—love, need, joy. Even optimism.

"Come on, baby," Ash whispered. "Go as hard as you need."

Chris laughed breathlessly, catching his lip to suck it for a second as he pulled his hips back and pushed in again. "Not for long, baby. Like I said... a week."

"Next round can last longer, then," Ash mumbled against Chris's lips. "I am not letting you out of bed all day."

"Deal," Chris moaned, thrusting into him harder.

There. That spot. *That* spot that made Ash's back arch and his cock throb with need. "Oh my God, there. Yes...!"

Every muscle tensed up until he even had to squeeze his eyes shut, moaning his need for Chris as loud and often as he could.

"Yes...!" Chris grunted into his ear when he had to stop kissing for fear of their teeth clashing. "Oh, fuck, baby. Yes...! I'm almost..."

"Me too," Ash managed, his nails digging hard into Chris's back. His cheeks burned, his stomach was tensing, his thighs twitching... he couldn't stop himself. "Oh, fuck, I'm gonna...!"

The blissful darkness of forgetfulness. The world ceased to exist, except for one focal point: Chris's body around him, sheltering him, pushing into him, driving him onward.

And Ash came, his cock pulsing with quick, sharp jets of stickiness between them while Chris's breathing caught. He clenched hard around Chris, barely managing his name.

"Ash! *Yes!*" Chris was coming, too, his thrusts short and stuttering as his nails dug into Ash's hip. "Oh, holy fuck, Ash... s'good. Perfect," he whispered.

Just the expressions of bliss crossing his features were enough to turn Ash the fuck *on*, almost painfully so now that his body was settling, his cock softening and body melting across the bed.

But Chris's cock buried deep in him felt *perfect*. He didn't want his new boyfriend to slide out, so he ran his hands down Chris's back to grip his ass for a few more seconds, slowly relaxing around him and the slick claim he'd left inside him.

Chris had collapsed on top of him, and the pressure and warm weight against him was so wonderful it made Ash's head spin.

"Fuck," Chris breathed out. "Crushing you?"

"Nope," Ash whispered. "This is good."

Chris did slide out, but even when he did, Ash wasn't left as empty as he'd expected. He still had him, right here.

He wasn't leaving.

They didn't say a word as they cooled down, just pressing into each other as they found a comfortable position to lie in. Ash ended up on his side, his hand on Chris's chest.

And, of course he was going to feel up the goods now that they were right there.

Eventually, Chris's voice broke the peaceful silence between them. "You know, if you keep doing that, I'm gonna get hard again."

Ash smirked at Chris as he ran his hand slowly down Chris's stomach again to feel every single ab, one at a time. "Oh, no."

"You're gonna make me feel eighteen again. Jesus," Chris moaned, then laughed.

Ash dramatically sighed. "Oh, *no*. However will we burn off that energy?"

Chris chuckled and pressed a kiss to his forehead. Something was on his mind, though, judging by his frown. Maybe the wake for Hans, which was tomorrow. Or something else completely. He knew better now than to assume.

Ash gave him a minute before nudging him. "Hm?"

"I... I don't know. I'm not gonna be the same, I think," Chris said carefully.

Ash rubbed his side gently, watching his expression. Chris didn't seem sad about it, necessarily, but grief and trauma were complicated. Only time would tell how he reacted. "I know. You may change, but that's okay. We all change, all the time."

Chris paused, gazing up at the ceiling for a moment before he looked over at him. "Hm. Guess so."

"I worry, too," Ash offered after a few moments of gazing at him. "You know. The depression thing. Maybe it's just meds I need. Maybe it was all situational. I don't know. I might never be perfect."

"Oh, baby. I never asked you to be," Chris murmured, cupping his cheek.

Ash's cheeks burned with pleasure and relief. Chris had been there every step of the way. Of course he wasn't gonna freak out and run. "Yeah. My brain just lies sometimes."

"About?"

"You getting fed up, mostly," Ash admitted. "Or losing you."

Chris ran his hand slowly down Ash's shoulder, then back up to his cheek. He pressed a light kiss against his lips, then murmured, "Whatever the hell your brain tells you, it's just a fact that I love you, okay? You're worthy of... everything. I'll keep trying to tell you that as long as it takes."

Ash didn't expect to well up. He quickly looked away, biting his lip.

"Oh, baby. I'm sorry," Chris quickly breathed out. "Did I say something...?"

"No. No, it's in a good way this time," Ash mumbled after a moment, his cheeks burning with embarrassment. "And this is good. I'm... feeling things."

Chris gently swiped his thumb along Ash's cheek, then kissed his lips once. "Okay."

Ash's heart was still racing, though. "But with your job and all... I'll keep being afraid of losing you. That's... the thing I worry most about, with people. Losing them."

"Well," Chris murmured. "If I get that promotion to engineer, there's a little less... direct involvement. And look. You made it through your greatest fear this time, before Julie got involved, right?"

Ash winced and nodded. Fuck, he'd come close, but... Chris was right. He *had* pulled himself through. It wasn't just about Chris. He wanted to live for himself now, too. "It just triggered me. My parents and all."

Chris frowned and rubbed his back lightly. "Yeah. I'm sorry about that. I wish I could have met them."

"I wish so, too," Ash murmured, closing his eyes. They would have loved him.

For years, he'd tried not to picture his parents right there, judging his choices, but now... he was doing okay now. They'd be proud of him. He could already see it: his mother welcoming Chris inside for a meal. His father talking about motorsports and football with him.

"And you can meet mine. I know it's no substitute, but they'll love you," Chris assured him. "It's a shame your paths didn't cross in the hospital, visiting me. I don't see them much, normally, but they'll want to see me a lot now, I think. And you, too."

Ash's eyes stung again, but he smiled nonetheless. "Okay," he murmured. For the first time, it didn't feel like he was bringing nothing to the relationship.

He was bringing *himself*, wholly and fully, to meet Chris. And even if he started with almost nothing—poor health, no home, no job, no friends or family—they could build something together.

"There it is again," he murmured under his breath.

"What?"

"Optimism. Damn you," Ash sighed. "I even like people sometimes."

Chris chuckled deeply and pulled him in for a hug. "See? People are usually great."

"Hmph," Ash snorted. "Other than you, they're okay. I'll only give you *that* much," Ash muttered, pressing his face into Chris's neck for a moment.

"And Liam?"

"He's pretty great, too."

"And Dylan?"

"Shut up," Ash moaned, shoving Chris while Chris laughed.

"I'll work on you," Chris promised. "If you stick around while I try to be what you deserve."

Ash chuckled gently. "Go right ahead, love. I'm here to stay."

34

CHRIS, THREE WEEKS LATER

"Here she is, guys. And," Chris said sternly to Liam, "no crying until she leaves."

Liam didn't look convinced, but he nodded sharply. "Only if you don't cry, bro."

"Deal." Chris clapped Liam's arm on his way to get the front door.

In reality, it was a promise he wasn't sure they could keep. They, along with Chief Williams, had been anxious all week since Sophie's foster parents had called up the station and asked to visit.

The worst fucking part of the whole fire, aside from losing Hans, was that they hadn't been able to save the little girl's father. He'd been trapped inside when the beam collapsed across the back door. Getting his little girl to the fridge had been the last thing he'd done.

It fucking ripped Chris apart to think about her being left without her dad at this age. He and Liam didn't usually talk about that stuff, but it was clear Liam was taking it hard, too.

Since rescuing Sophie—all of six years old—from the fire,

Liam had been talking a little more about kids. About him and Dylan wanting them, too. He'd always been the fatherly type, but something had been shaken loose inside him.

Chris hoped this visit would give him some kind of closure, and that it was really what Sophie wanted.

He put on a cautious but warm smile when he opened the door to the sight of Sophie and her foster parents—Melissa and Kumal, if he remembered right. "Hi, guys! I'm Chris." He crouched to kiss Sophie's hand. "And this little lady is Sophie?"

Sophie relaxed into a giggle instantly, and Chris relaxed slightly. Maybe she was too young to really understand what had happened. Good. That would make it easier for her, for now. She was shy, looking down at first, then up at him. "Hi."

"Come on in," Chris welcomed them, holding the door open for them while her parents stepped inside.

"Wow," she breathed out, immediately looking to the left at the open door to the fire trucks in the garage. Then she paused, staring at them.

Chris held his breath. She had to remember most of that day—being carried out, and then probably straight to an ambulance with fire trucks all around.

She turned and trotted for the living room, and her foster mom swapped worried looks with Chris.

While Liam went ahead with Sophie and Kumal, Chris hung back with Melissa. "How's she doing?" Chris murmured.

"All right. Better than we expected. We don't think she fully understands yet," Melissa murmured back. "And she doesn't have any relatives who can take her in..."

"Thank God you and Kumal were there for her," Chris murmured, squeezing her shoulder. "Thank you."

Melissa looked surprised as she smiled. "Oh. No, thank *you* for what you do. If it weren't for you and Liam..."

"She remembers most of it, right?" Chris asked. "I mean, memory in kids that young..."

Melissa nodded. "Most of it, yeah. Her nightmares are getting a little better. She's resilient, though. She's the one who wanted to come here, ever since her dad's... funeral."

Chris flinched. As much as Melissa tried to word that carefully, it was a slap in the face.

They hadn't found him in time. He knew now they hadn't even been in the building in time, but it still felt personal. Like he could have done something more—something faster, or better-planned—and Sophie would still have a dad.

"I'm sorry," Melissa added, lingering in the front hall. Sophie was giggling at whatever Liam said, which was no surprise. He'd always been amazing with the kids on their class trips here. "And I'm so sorry about your colleague."

Chris took a deep breath and nodded once to acknowledge it, and Melissa seemed to sense it was a raw nerve. The memorial was this afternoon, and he wasn't sure he was ready.

"Anyway, we'd been trying to talk her out of it..."

"She doesn't seem easy to talk out of anything," Chris suggested with a smile, listening in as she interrogated Liam on why they didn't wear their "fire costumes" around the station.

Melissa laughed. "Very right." She headed into the living room with Sophie and came up behind her to touch her shoulder. "Honey, didn't you want to say something to Chris and Liam?"

Liam shot her a look of gratitude, and Chris fully intended to tease him later on being caught off-guard by her repeated "why"s.

"Oh." Sophie rocked on her toes, her spirits flagging a little as she stared down. "I made you something."

Chris instantly wanted to make her feel better, and Liam flinched at the same moment.

"Yes, ma'am?" Liam smiled gently. "What is it?"

She peeked up at him and smiled again, then looked at Melissa, who handed her an envelope that she passed on to Liam. "It's a card."

"Oh! A card for us?" Liam, who was crouching with her, rocked back on his heels to tear it open with a finger.

It was a thank you card with a hand-drawn picture of a few yellow stick-men in front of a red blocky thing that looked kind of like a fire station, and another red blocky thing with wheels.

Liam looked delighted. "Is it us in front of here?"

Sophie bobbed her head in a shy nod.

"It's good! I could tell right away." Chris smiled, waiting for Liam to open the card.

There were only a few words scrawled in messy handwriting that rose and fell across the card, and Chris quickly realized why Liam was looking down all of a sudden.

Thank you for bieng my heros.

Damn it. Chris was going to break that oath any time now.

Sophie spoke up, her voice shy again. "I wrote it myself."

"It's great." Liam's voice was surprisingly steady as he handed Chris the card, then reached out to sweep her close in a long, tight hug. "Thank you so much."

"Before my dad went away, he said he loved me and there would be men to come help me. And then you came in."

Fuck. Chris had to wipe his eyes, looking up and away for a second before he blinked a few times. *Keep it together, man,* he scolded himself.

"Yeah. That must be hard," Liam said softly, finally letting go of Sophie so she could hug Chris. "I bet you miss him."

Sophie nodded, her shoulders slumping before she hugged Chris. "I wish he'd come back."

Chris took the chance while hugging her to wipe his eyes once more and sheepishly glanced up in apology at her foster parents. They weren't dry-eyed either, though.

"I'm sorry, sweetheart. Your foster mom and dad are great, though, aren't they?" Liam offered, clearing his throat as he rose to his feet.

Sophie nodded, her face brightening into a smile. "Uh huh. Can I come see you guys again? Please?" she asked her foster parents.

"You'll have to ask the nice firemen," Kumal told her.

"We can set up a time to visit again," Chris agreed, not even needing to look at Liam for agreement on that. "We'd love that."

"Can I see the rest of the fire... stay... station?"

Chris laughed. "Yeah. Of course you can. Let's give you a tour," he agreed.

Kumal paused, his hand on Liam's shoulder. "You guys go ahead. I'll be there in a minute."

Chris glanced at Liam but didn't ask, just led Melissa and Sophie around to show them the fire engines, the locker room with their gear, and the bunks where they slept at night between calls. Kevin and the other guys who were on shift today stayed out of the way.

By now, Sophie was smiling and giggling again, and even if Chris's heart was heavy, he smiled along.

Then, Chris grinned at the pair of them. "Hey. I have an idea you can help me with, Sophie..."

It only took them a few minutes, and it made Sophie laugh a lot while Melissa relaxed and chuckled along.

"Hey, Liam! Let's come show her what happens when we get a call." Chris climbed into his bunk, stretching his arms above his head as he grinned at Sophie.

It only took a minute for Liam to show up in the bunk

room, smiling broadly. "Yeah? Okay."

Chris lowered his voice for dramatic emphasis. "It's the middle of the night, and this kid... let's call him Chris... is doing chemistry experiments."

Liam gasped at him. "You did not."

"Oh, yeah. I set the kitchen tablecloth on fire. Mom grounded me for months."

Sophie was about rolling with laughter now, and as Kumal leaned in the doorway, he caught Chris's eyes with an appreciative smile.

Liam flopped on his bunk and tried to shove his feet under the covers. He almost kneed himself in the face as he frowned with confusion. "Wha—What the... How..."

Then, Liam noticed Sophie giggling while Chris snorted with laughter.

"Oh, you—" Liam glared at Chris.

"Wasn't me!" Chris winked.

"Sophie! How could you short-sheet me?" Liam dramatically pushed the covers down.

"Wasn't me! My foster mom."

"Sophie!" Melissa exclaimed, laughing.

Liam clicked his tongue as he rolled off the bed. "Good one, guys. You got me."

"Okay, sweetheart." Melissa still laughed as she approached to brush Sophie's hair back and put a hand on her shoulder. "We should let these guys get back to work."

Chris wasn't about to point out that they'd come in on a day off for this. He just bounced out of his bunk and grinned. "Yeah. You can come back and see us, that's for sure. We'll get him even better next time."

"I dunno about this," Liam groaned as they headed for the front hall, elbowing Chris. "He's a bad influence."

Chris gasped at Liam. "*You're* a bad influence!"

This time, as they hugged goodbye, there weren't any tears. Sophie was beaming at them as she ran down the driveway to the car, followed by Melissa.

Kumal lingered on the path up to the door. "Thanks so much, guys. I can't say how much I appreciate this."

"Of course," Liam nodded. "We want her to have good associations with firefighters. She's already bouncing back so well. It's incredible."

"It'll be hard, when she gets older..." Kumal trailed off, then cleared his throat and nodded. "Anyway, thanks."

"Anything we can do," Chris promised, and he meant it.

Kumar nodded. "I'm sure there'll be something."

"Yeah." Liam reached out to shake hands with Kumal, and then Chris took his turn. "Thanks for coming by."

Once the door closed, Liam smacked the back of Chris's head.

"Hey!" Chris protested and shoved Liam back. "What's that for?"

"You broke the promise, man. You buy lunch."

Chris shook his head as he checked for his wallet and keys. "Like you weren't bawling before me."

"Lies," Liam snorted.

"Well, *I* got her to laugh more."

Liam grinned. "Yeah. You should look at fostering, too, you know."

"*Too?*" Chris stared at Liam. "You're not thinking of...? Holy shit. You are."

"Well, not while I'm working in this role, but if that changes..." Liam was blushing now. "You know I'm gonna propose sooner or later, and then... at some point... Dylan and I do want kids. I don't think the timing will work out for Sophie, exactly, but we can be godfathers or something. You know, try to give them a hand with anything."

Chris clapped Liam's back and opened the door to lead him out to his car. "You sentimental bastard. Brings a tear to my eye."

"Shut up. You're still buying lunch."

"Thank you for coming," Chief Williams was saying to one of the other guys. He was working his way around, shaking the hand of all the guests and talking about their memories of their fallen comrade. They'd already said their condolences to Hans's family, and now the guys were trying to keep themselves together for their sakes.

He'd picked up Ash before coming here, and Liam had brought Dylan. A lot of the guys' partners and families were there to support them. Everyone felt the loss, no matter how new they were to the fire station family.

But, uncharacteristically, Chief Williams was alone.

"Ash, Chris." This was the moment Chris had been dreading. Chief Williams turned to them, shaking hands firmly with each of them. "How are you doing?"

Chris swallowed hard and nodded once. "You know." He'd never lost a guy like this before. And he hadn't even been awake when it happened. He couldn't imagine what it was like for Chief Williams.

"Yeah." The chief gave a small nod of agreement, then looked at Ash and nodded. "On a personal note... I'm glad you passed along what you did." His lips twitched slightly. "Even if I'm not sure Chris meant to say everything he did about it."

Chris ducked his head, feeling thoroughly embarrassed at the memory once again. "Sorry again. Um... you here alone?"

Chief Williams paused, and that mask of cool calmness lifted for just a moment. It wasn't hard to see the pain of losing one of his men, but if Chris was reading that right, it was more than that.

"Yes," the chief answered, then offered a slight smile. "But I wanted to say: no hard feelings."

Ash let out a breath of relief, his shoulders sinking. "Thank you, sir."

"Thanks," Chris echoed softly. "And I'm so sorry. For everything."

Chief Williams reached out to clap his hand and half-hug Chris again, then hugged Ash more gently. "Get home and rest up. It'll be a pleasure seeing you around the station, Ash."

Chris rested a hand on Ash's shoulder as he led him out to the parking lot. The chief was right. Chris was worn to the bone. He understood Ash's life and his old attitude that much better now. Meanwhile, Ash hanging out at the station and coming to this service had probably helped him understand Chris's life.

It was a huge fucking choice to make now to go to work every day ready to leave this man—this incredible, sweet, gorgeous, kind-hearted, healing man—and save someone else. He made it gladly, but he was grateful every day to have found someone who understood why.

"No way, Chris. I'll drive," Ash told him, crossing to the driver's side and patting his arm to push him around to the passenger side.

"Bossy, aren't you?" Chris managed a smile.

Ash winked at him. "I know you like that."

"Love it," Chris corrected with a gentle smile. Once they were settled and Ash had tucked his cane by the car door, Chris leaned over for a quick kiss. "Thank you for being here."

"Of course, babe," Ash told him. "I'm here for you. Every step of the way."

EPILOGUE

ASH, ONE MONTH LATER

"This is... amazing."

It was a far cry from the first few seconds; now, Ash couldn't close his eyes as he stared around at the scenery below.

He hadn't been able to breathe, his eyes tightly closed as the mechanical line pulled them along. Takeoff could scare even veterans, Charles had reassured him beforehand.

But he couldn't help but look as they lifted off the ground, as much as it scared him. This was what he'd raised pledges for, after all. Watching the ground recede, his heart pounding, helpless in this harness... he'd wondered for a minute if he was actually crazy to do it.

And then, a minute ago, they'd detached from the line with the sway and bob Charles had warned him about, rising high in the air and then seemingly going still as Ash's fear melted away.

Bliss and awe warmed his chest now, and a smile stretched across Ash's face. "So amazing."

"It's special. It never gets old." Charles was looking around, sometimes shifting his weight in the harness slightly to make the glider bank left or right.

When Ash looked down, it was stunning to realize how tiny the little crowd of eight people looked. He could barely make out the colors of their clothes below.

Chris, of course, was there to watch. Liam and Dylan had been with him the whole way. Even some of their friends from the fire station and Ash's mechanics course had insisted on watching. And, of course, Charles's assistant was there to help them take off and land.

"It's so... peaceful," Ash said, looking up and around. The horizon stretched out, an endless, curved bubble. "I can see the curve of the world!"

Charles was smiling, he could tell from his voice, even though he couldn't see him from this angle. "Isn't it incredible? It's so gentle."

"I thought it'd be a lot rougher and... I don't know. I didn't think we'd be able to talk up here. I don't know why."

Charles laughed. "Yeah. A lot of people are surprised by that, too."

It took Ash a minute to work out why his cheeks hurt so damn much, but he hadn't stopped smiling since he first felt the fear melt away.

He didn't have the words to describe the glow that suffused his whole body, from head to toes. He was *flying*, and it felt like he could see into the very future from here. The world was a patchwork of fields, roads, and houses, with the Santa Barbara harbor and coastline in the distance. The mountains stretched out behind them, the foothills rolling gently into the horizon.

No matter which way they banked, there was something to stare at—not to mention staring up at the sky, which seemed so much bigger from up here. "We're close to space, aren't we?"

"Yep," Charles answered.

Holy shit. This was the freedom, the release he'd sought, but it lasted for minutes on end instead of a few glorious seconds followed by indescribable pain—easily the worst of his life, and then months of more mental and physical pain.

Not that he had much to escape these days. Chris had been promoted and was on track to make engineer, and he'd gladly shouldered the extra responsibility of looking after his guys with his engine. Most days, he was as happy-go-lucky and mischievous as ever, and even Ash had learned to play a prank or two.

Sure, he had his bad brain days, as he called them, but Chris knew how to help now. The light at the end of the tunnel was never switched off.

And now he had his apprenticeship at a local garage to look forward to, starting next week. He was starting a new phase of his life, so what was one more new thing?

It was an impulsive decision, but he'd never known a fiery joy like this. It felt utterly right. "Charles? I want to do this."

Charles laughed. "To learn this solo?"

"Yes. God, yes."

"Okay," Charles agreed. "You can start by helping me bank out of this. We're caught in an updraft, which is why we're so high. Lean with me."

Ash followed his directions, trying to figure out what he was doing. Some of it made sense—in his mechanical training, the principles of hot and cold were important to understand, for example.

It took them a few minutes to get to the ground, and even though his heart pounded at the final part of the descent, he was still grinning as the glider hit the ground, rolled, and stopped.

By the time he was unhooked from the harness, everyone had made their way along the field to greet them with cheers and applause. Charles detached the camera from the wing of the glider while Chris handed Ash his cane and waited for him to steady himself.

Then, Chris went down on one knee. Everyone was already grinning.

"Oh, my God," Ash whispered. There was no way this was happening.

"I know it's early, but I also know you're the one. I knew it was you from the second we met. I'm so damn proud of how far you've come, baby. And you still have so much to do. I want to be by your side every step of the way."

Ash didn't even try to stop the hot tears running down his cheeks as he nodded before Chris could even finish speaking.

Chris laughed, taking his free left hand. "Will you marry me?"

It was all Ash could do to whisper, "Yes." He nodded as hard as he could, hoping to convey some sense of the awe and wonder that still flooded through his body. Chris had been the one for him since the moment he looked up from the sidewalk into his deep, calming gaze.

"There's only one condition. Sophie wants to be our flower girl."

Ash hiccuped a laugh and nodded hard. "Of course."

Chris slid the cool metal band around his finger, then rose to his feet as Ash wiped his eyes so he could look at the gleaming silver band. It was plain, but beautiful. Just how he felt. No flashy diamonds, but hard-wearing and tough.

"I love you, babe," Ash whispered. He dropped his cane and leaned into Chris to hug him as hard as he possibly could, and those strong arms crushed him against his body in response.

"Fuck, Ash. I love you too."

Chris kissed him underneath the wide blue sky, and Ash was flying again.

AFTERWORD

Dear reader,

Thank you for reading *Afterglow*. It's an honor to get to share this story with you. There are so many under-recognized but important societal issues that showed up as themes in this book. I hope I could shine a little light at the end of the tunnel.

Chief Jace Williams's story is up next in *Aftermath*, which also addresses difficult subjects. Take care of yourself, and please seek support if you need to.

Thank you to my Facebook group, Ed's Petals, for embracing and uplifting this series, along with all my other books. This was such a hard series to write! If it touches you, please consider leaving a review so others can find it, too.

Make sure you sign up for my newsletter to hear about: exclusive free short stories and sales; new releases in ebook, audio, and print; preorder alerts; sneak peeks at upcoming books; event appearances; and other exciting news as it happens!

I also have a reader group on Facebook if you want to chat about your favorite parts of *Afterglow*, see cute bee photos and good news stories, and keep on top of my upcoming releases with a whole bunch of lovely readers: https://www.facebook.com/groups/edavies

Last but not least: always be you!

~Ed

NEXT IN AFTER

AFTERMATH

I'm not supposed to like him.

Santa Barbara fire chief Jace Williams' perfectly organized life fell apart: he's newly-divorced, suspended from work, and haunted by memories. Where did he go so wrong? And why on earth would anyone trust him to put together their wedding?

Hang-gliding instructor Charlie Bryan hides it with a smile, but he's haunted by his past, too. His dad's memory is failing him, and he hasn't had the heart to tell him he dumped the abusive jerk years ago. He's never let a guy tie him down since.

The hot clash between messy Charlie and neat Jace gives way to growing affection, but neither of them know what to do about it. They didn't expect to find the one at the best, yet worst, possible time. Is this what real love feels like?

Aftermath is the third book in the After series, which explores mental health challenges with gentle humor and heart while hunky firefighters turn up the heat. It can be enjoyed on its own, and promises a happily-ever-after.

ABOUT THE AUTHOR

E. Davies grew up moving constantly, which taught him what people have in common, the ways relationships are formed, and the dangers of "miscellaneous" boxes. As a young gay author, Ed prefers to tell feel-good stories that are brimming with hope.

He writes full-time, goes on long nature walks, tries to fill his passport, drinks piña coladas on the beach, flees from cute guys, coos over fuzzy animals (especially bees), and is liable to tilt his head and click his tongue if you don't use your turn signal.

f facebook.com/edaviesbooks

🐦 twitter.com/edaviesauthor

📷 instagram.com/thisboyisstrange

BB bookbub.com/authors/e-davies

ALSO BY E. DAVIES

Hart's Bay:

Hard Hart

Changed Hart

Wild Hart

Stolen Hart

Significant Brothers:

Splinter

Grasp

Slick

Trace

Clutch

Tremble

Riley Brothers:

Buzz

Clang

Swish

Crunch

Slam

Grind

Brooklyn Boys:

Electric Sunshine

Live Wire

Boiling Point

F-Word:

Flaunt

Freak

Faux

Forever

After:

Afterburn

Afterglow

Aftermath

Men of Hidden Creek:

Shelter

Adore

Miracle

Redemption

Coauthored with Zach Jenkins:

Sugar Topped

Just a Summer Deal

Audiobooks:

The list is growing rapidly! You can see all my books available in audio here: www.edaviesbooks.com/audiobooks

Lightning Source UK Ltd.
Milton Keynes UK
UKHW010633030920
369287UK00001B/128

9 781912 245079